BETWEEN THE LIES

BEAR & MANDY LOGAN
BOOK 5

L.T. RYAN

with

K.M. ROUGHT

LIQUID MIND MEDIA

For information contact:
Contact@ltryan.com
https://LTRyan.com
https://www.facebook.com/JackNobleBooks

THE BEAR & MANDY LOGAN SERIES

Close to Home

Under the Surface

The Last Stop

Over the Edge

Between the Lies

Caught in the Web (Coming Soon)

Love Bear? Mandy? Noble? Hatch? Get your very own L.T. Ryan merchandise today! Click the link below to find coffee mugs, t-shirts, and even signed copies of your favorite thrillers! https://ltryan.ink/EvG_

1

THE TEXTURED GRIP OF HIS PISTOL FELT TOO COMFORTING AGAINST HIS palm, tucked inside his pocket.

Bear trudged down the crowded sidewalk with his hands deep in his jacket pockets. The morning chill had given way to a milder temperature as the sun crested the steel and glass canyons rising from either side of the street. Although he didn't look out of place wearing a coat, he wouldn't have risked a stroll without it.

Two months had passed since he'd joined Iris in her mission to discover Mr. Reagan's identity. Iris had told him how the elusive criminal overlord had been involved in the HealTek conspiracy in Upstate New York and the drug ring in North Carolina, in addition to the mess Bear had walked into when he'd arrived in Boonesville, Illinois. Stumbling into those situations had been nothing more than coincidence and had led Bear to question how far and wide Reagan had cast his net across the country. Coincidence or not, Bear had become a thorn in the man's side, and it was only a matter of time until Mr. Reagan sent his minions to remove it.

Bear suspected that Iris' motivations were more personal. Her cousin Lily had died in Illinois, though that hadn't been a direct result of Reagan's orders. No, whatever drove Iris to take down Reagan was bigger than that, but Bear had no intention of prying. He wasn't trying to add her burdens to his own. There were more important things to concentrate on.

Since leaving Oregon, not a single person had approached Bear and Iris. No warnings. No attempts on their lives. And yet, Bear felt like the target on his back grew bigger and brighter every day. Bear had his concealed carry license for New York City, though there was no guarantee the police would ask questions before taking matters into their own hands if he was caught with it.

But if he was caught without? Reagan's men would ensure he was dead. And Mandy would be on her own.

Bear kept his eyes moving as he followed the flow of the crowd. Most people gave him a wide berth if they were paying enough attention, not only because of his size but because of the scowl on his face. It helped that most New Yorkers didn't look you in the eye as they passed by, but his irritable expression ensured that anyone who did glance up would turn away just as quickly. He was not the kind of man to go unnoticed.

He turned down West 29th Street and kept up his relentless pace. With his long legs, anyone who wanted to tail him would have to stay close for fear of losing him. Just because he hadn't spotted anyone yet didn't mean they weren't out there.

His old friend Paranoia lingered nearby. Like a blade whose handle fit perfectly in the palm of his hand, its edge was still sharp despite the time he and Mandy had spent crossing the country over the last year. The thought rankled him. This was meant to be his retirement, spending time with his daughter and watching her grow up before she inevitably struck out on her own. Instead, they'd come up against corrupt pharmaceutical companies, South American drug runners, Midwestern distributors, and one Oregonian farmer who sold literal manure to a terrorist organization for profit. It hadn't exactly been the vacation he'd hoped for.

Then again, he was grateful his skills were still honed. If they weren't, something could've happened to Mandy, and Bear would've followed her right over the edge and into oblivion. There was no point existing in a world where his daughter wasn't living, breathing, and driving him crazy.

Another thought pierced his mind like a steel rod. What if he wasn't as sharp as he'd once been? Mandy shouldn't have had to kill a man in order to defend an innocent woman's life.

A familiar pang of heartbreak gripped Bear's chest. He resisted removing his hand from his pocket to rub at the spot, as though that would make it fade. For the millionth time over the last two months, he reminded himself Mandy was safe and sound at a boarding school in Virginia that Iris had vetted with all the resources at her disposal. No one but she and Bear knew where Mandy was, and the school even had its own security. Not only that, but she attended therapy on a weekly basis to help with the transition into the private school life. Mandy had cried and screamed and given him the cold shoulder for days, hoping she could guilt Bear into letting her come with them while they tracked down Mr. Reagan. He'd been immovable. In the end, she had relented, and he hoped her time at Eastern Blue Ridge Academy would provide her with the social skills she hadn't gotten while attached to his hip.

This wasn't the first time he'd had to leave her behind to take care of business. After spending so much time together and watching her grow up these last few years, hugging her goodbye had been harder than he could've imagined, but it had been the right move. Mr. Reagan had proved a dangerous adversary already. The closer they got to him, the more unpredictable he'd become. Bear refused to have Mandy at his side in case that target on his back became fatal.

Despite his wandering thoughts, Bear never let himself become distracted enough to forget his surroundings and every person who passed him by. Cataloging details had become second nature. He kept up a constant stream of awareness as he pinpointed who might be a threat and who was more likely to be a regular person on their way to work or lunch or back home to their family.

Taking a circuitous route, Bear snaked his way west, toward the river. The crowd thinned here, which was both a blessing and a curse. He stood out more. But he'd be able to spot a tail that much easier. Either Reagan had no idea where they were, or he had some of the top people in the business if Bear couldn't spot them. The former option was more likely, but the latter wasn't out of the realm of possibility.

Bear looked both ways at an intersection and used the opportunity to check behind him out of his periphery. He jogged across the road when the coast was clear, ignoring the red light that told him not to use the crosswalk. He hooked right and strode down the sidewalk with his shoulder brushing up against the large tan building that took up most of this block. When he made his way to the opening of the alley at the other end, he stopped and leaned his back against the building, one foot propped up, as though waiting for a friend. He spent two minutes scouting the area, making sure he was alone before he slid into the shadows and made his way to the other end of the narrow passage toward an inconspicuous door.

After one last look over his shoulder, Bear raised his large fist and knocked twice, paused, then three times, paused, and finally knocked one last time. Ten seconds later, a bolt slid, and the door cracked open wide enough for him to slip through. It nearly caught his sleeve as he shut it behind him.

"Were you followed?" Iris asked.

"No."

"Are you sure?"

"No."

The woman huffed out a breath. It was the same exchange they'd had every day over the last two months, yet the annoyance radiating out of her every pore told him she didn't appreciate his honesty. There was no way to be certain he hadn't been followed, but he was reasonably sure no one had been watching him as he entered the alley.

This was the sixth or seventh meeting space they'd found over the past couple of months. It was essentially a traveling workstation consisting of a pair of laptops, a couple collapsible chairs, and some other tech they'd picked up along the way as the need arose. Most could be discarded if it came down to it, and the essentials would fit in a backpack either one of them could carry for miles without breaking a sweat. They'd gotten their setup down to a science—up and working in under fifteen minutes, dismantled in under five. It wasn't pretty, but it was operable.

"Get some sleep last night?" Iris asked.

"A few hours. You?"

"Same."

Bear held Iris' gaze for a moment, the lie clear in her eyes. She hadn't slept much over the last couple of months, and it showed. She was thinner and though her muscles were just as taut, the hollows of her cheeks were deeper. If Bear didn't value his life, he would've told her that her sky-blue eyes looked cloudy and her corn-yellow hair was dull and disheveled. But what would've been the point?

Her obsession with finding Mr. Reagan would catch up sooner or later. Bear just hoped it wouldn't cost one of them their life.

Pounding machinery from the other side of the wall drew Iris' attention, breaking their locked gaze. Their office space was no more than a glorified janitor's closet for the packing facility housing them. Like all their other traveling workstations, Bear had found someone willing to turn a blind eye to their presence for the right amount of money. The constant noise caused more than its fair share of headaches, but it was worth it to keep their conversations private.

"Good news." Iris crossed the room and slid into one of the chairs in front of her laptop. "Farro agreed to meet."

Bear scoffed. "He's said that before."

"Can you blame him for being squirrely?"

Bear couldn't, not after all the trouble they'd gone through to stay off the radar these last few months. He'd been the boots on the ground since Iris still worked for the FBI. She had been relegated to desk duty, but that had worked out in their favor. A few of the rumors she'd heard around the office had been worth following up on. Farro had been one of them.

"When?" he asked.

Iris checked her watch. "An hour. Uptown. Little Japanese place called Rayoka."

Bear kept his groan to himself. He hadn't even had time to sit for a minute. Hell, he hadn't even had time for a damn cup of coffee. It was a travesty, but he wasn't about to waste an opportunity like this.

"Then I guess we better leave now if we want to make it on time." Bear took a step toward the door, then looked over his shoulder at her. "You think he'll show?"

There was a fervor in Iris' eyes that he'd seen one too many times in the past few months to take for anything other than a fanatic's delirium. "He'll be there."

Unconvinced, Bear turned his back to the door. "Only one way to find out," he muttered.

2

Even with a five-minute head-start on Iris, Bear knew she'd end up at the restaurant before him. She was careful but despite her experience, she didn't carry the same paranoia he did. Though he didn't know specifics about Mr. Reagan, he'd come up against plenty of men like him. Caution had kept Bear alive.

After circling the block and heading in the direction of the nearest subway station, Bear pulled out his phone and told Iris the coast was clear. She'd leave in a minute or two and walk opposite him, jumping on a different train that would take her uptown. Bear would go down before heading back up again. He'd be cutting the time close, but it'd be worth it if someone was tracking him.

It was warm downstairs in the tunnel despite the crisp air filtering through from the outside. A bead of sweat snaked down his spine. He ignored it and kept his jacket on. He could survive twenty or so minutes of discomfort for the sake of keeping his gun close.

A myriad of people filed onto and off of the train during his ride. Parents with their children, teenagers who reminded him of Mandy and her fierce independence, construction workers in bright vests, and even a few elderly women who looked like they might float away with the next gust of wind. Most people had in headphones, and the few who talked kept it amongst themselves. Bear stared straight ahead but used his peripherals to track any movement within the confines of the car. The lack of caffeine in his body made his eyelids heavy. Only the sheer force of his will kept him from nodding off.

When the train pulled into a station two stops down, Bear got off, crossed the platform to the other side, and got on the next one, taking it one stop past where he needed to go. He crested the stairs to street level and rolled his head back and forth, letting the breeze cool him down before heading toward the restaurant. A buzz in his pocket told him Iris had made it and was wondering where he was. He didn't bother taking out his phone to look at the message. He'd get there when he got there.

Making his way through the crowd, Bear reviewed everything Iris had told him about Farro. The guy was a criminal investigator for the FBI. A contact's contact. Iris had reached out through back channels and set up two previous meetings that the man had flaked on. But he hadn't cut off contact yet, which either meant he'd been too paranoid to show—something Bear could understand and even appreciate—or he was just screwing with them.

Iris was convinced Farro was the real deal and had information they needed, and they didn't have much else to go on. Months of searching had turned up little. Bear was antsy. All he wanted was to finish this and get back to Mandy. His hope for a somewhat normal life with her dwindled by the day. If Reagan's power and influence extended as far and wide as they believed, then taking him out would have consequences.

Another buzz from his pocket. Iris was getting impatient. After spending so much time with the woman, he could anticipate her text messages. Good when you had to go into battle together. Bad when all you did was wait for the other shoe to drop. That kind of intimacy with no outlet, violence or otherwise, bred bitterness and resentment.

Bear spotted the restaurant ahead. He crossed the street and took in his surroundings. The crowd flowed with ease. No one lingered, watching the entrance. At least not on street level.

Turning his back to the street, Bear pulled open the door as his phone buzzed a third time. He ignored it like he had before. Bear strode across the small dining area and straight through to the kitchen in the back. No one stopped him, though a few of the workers looked up and away again. Had they been warned of a meeting, or was this a common occurrence?

Bear walked the length of the kitchen, the overwhelming scent of ponzu and chili oil making his nose tingle. The heat was oppressive in here. He considered swinging off his jacket for some relief. Ignoring the thought, he pushed through a door into the back office. It was dimly lit and stuffy, with papers scattered all over a small desk. But it was private enough for the conversation they were about to have. Shutting the door behind him drowned out the sizzling stovetops, clatter of plates, and banging of pots.

Iris sat on the edge of the disorderly desk, a look of disapproval and anticipation on her face. Farro was there, standing off to one side, hands on his hips like a disappointed father. He wore a baseball cap low over his eyes, and there was something off about his face, like someone who'd always worn a beard but recently shaved it off just for the hell of it. His eyes were dark like his hair, and he had a small scar at the corner of the right one that dragged the skin down a little. He was on the shorter side. There was no mistaking the bulge of muscles under his tight windbreaker.

"You're late." Farro's voice was deep but quiet. Restrained.

"You sweep the place?" Bear asked Iris, ignoring the newcomer.

"It's clean," Farro replied.

Iris rolled her eyes, knowing that wouldn't be good enough for Bear. "I swept it. It's clean."

Bear nodded. Farro never took his eyes off him.

"You're late," he repeated.

"Better late than dead," Bear said. "Wanted to make sure I wasn't followed."

Farro lifted his arm to check his watch, and the movement caused his jacket to slip enough for Bear to see he was carrying a firearm in a chest holster. Bear's hand tightened around his own gun in his pocket. If this was a setup, he wanted to be ready to fire off a couple shots before he hit the floor.

"Relax," Iris said. "He's here to help us."

"I've got ten minutes." Farro lowered his arm and looked at Iris. "Any more than that and they'll start asking questions."

"Who?" Bear asked.

"Don't worry about it."

"I think I will."

Farro sighed. "Look, man. I'm here to help you. You don't want it, I'll leave."

"He wants it." Iris shot Bear a look. "Don't you?"

"Of course." Bear leaned against the wall like they were having a casual chat about sports or the weather. "Just making conversation."

"I'm risking more than my career talking to you." Farro glanced between the two of them. "The only reason I'm here is because I want to see Reagan go down as badly as you do. But I'm not about to risk my neck for it."

"How very noble of you," Bear said.

Farro shrugged. "I don't really care what you think of me. I've got a family. I'm not letting them pay the consequences for my actions."

Bear wanted to argue that he had a family too. A little girl who depended on him. But it wasn't worth wasting time trying to get this guy more on their side than he already was. Farro had made up his mind. If he was telling the truth, it was a good enough reason not to get more involved.

If he was lying and this all went sideways? Bear had his face memorized. He'd make sure the man paid for his lies.

"All right," Bear said. "Let's hear it."

Farro checked his watch again before answering. "Reagan's network is getting more brash. I think something's happening—soon."

"We need better than that."

"Then go get your information elsewhere," Farro said, sounding more exhausted than angry. "No one talks about Reagan by name. It's all just whispers and rumors. His network is big. Agencies, politicians, cartels, gangs, you name it. Sounds like he's been putting this together for years, which means he's patient. Methodical. Anything that slips isn't going to lead back to him. It's guesswork, at best."

"And a death sentence at worst."

"You're not wrong. But pieces are definitely moving around the board. If Reagan isn't too worried about staying quiet, he's about to kick off his grand finale."

"You have any idea what that is?" Iris asked.

"No." For a second, Farro looked disappointed in himself. "We've tried picking up some of Reagan's known contacts before. None of them have talked, no matter what kind of pressure we put on them. And the moment it looks like they might crack, they wind up dead. We haven't been able to make any connections to Reagan's identity or what he's planning outside the small-scale stuff."

"Drug rings and weapon trafficking," Bear said. That's all they'd been able to find, too. But Bear had a feeling Reagan had his sights set on something much bigger. "Hard to believe no one is willing to talk."

Farro shot him a look. "You calling me a liar?"

"Just stating a fact, man. Take it easy."

Farro glowered. "Reagan chooses his associates carefully. All kinds of people, all walks of life. But they all have something in common: Reagan has ensured their compliance. Whether that's through money, favors, or intimidation, it doesn't matter. None of them are willing to risk their families or their lives by crossing him."

Bear crossed his arms over this chest. "Then why are we here?"

"About a week ago, one of our informants went dark."

"Dead?" Iris asked.

"Cut off communication. And the sensitive information we had on him disappeared. I think it's Reagan's doing."

Bear scoffed. "You *think*? I'm not risking my life for a hunch."

"Up to you. I'm not here to persuade you one way or the other. I'm just here to relay information." Farro looked to Iris, knowing she'd be the one to listen to what he had to say. "This guy has been working with us for years in exchange for staying out of a jail cell. Never went dark before. He's a computer geek. Not someone willing to put up a fight. If he cut off communication, he did it because he was scared. Then evidence against him went missing right under our noses? This has Reagan's fingerprints all over it. This is what he does."

"What could Reagan want from him?" Iris asked.

Farro checked his watch and then rubbed a hand over his mouth and along his jaw, as though still getting used to the smooth skin there. He looked at war with himself. "I'm not sure. He was following up on a lead for us, something tied to Reagan. It was thin at best, but enough to chase down. Reagan's been looking for something. Sensitive information. And he's left plenty of bodies in his wake trying to get it."

"Who's your informant?" Bear asked.

"Silas Marino. Wicked smart, above anything I've seen before. But not known for having a steel spine. For a long time, he got away with some hacktivist garbage before upgrading to serious felonies. Confidential government information. We decided to recruit him rather than throw him in a jail cell. He's always been cooperative."

"You think he went back to dealing in government info?" Iris asked. "Something Reagan would be interested in?"

Farro shrugged. "At this point, your guess is as good as mine. But if I had to lay money down, that's what I would bet on."

Turning to Iris, Bear tried to ignore the itch of his mounting frustration. "There's not a lot to go on here. No real connection to Reagan. We could be wasting our time."

She lifted an eyebrow. "You got another lead we can follow up on?"

Bear didn't bother answering.

Farro looked at his watch again before turning to the desk behind him and scribbling something down on a piece of paper. When he turned back to Iris, his gaze was sharp. "This is Marino's address. Do me a favor and be discreet. If you find something, I don't want to know what it is. In fact, don't contact me again. If I learn anything else, I'll send a message."

Iris looked disappointed, but she nodded her head and took the paper. Without so much as a glance at Bear, Farro pulled open the door. The sizzling and clanging of pots and pans swelled again for a moment before he shut it behind him with a *click*.

Bear looked over at Iris, who studied the paper in her hand. "Where does this Marino guy live?"

"Queens."

"Good."

When Iris looked up, her mouth was pulled down in a frown. "Why's that good?"

"There's bound to be one good coffee shop between here and there."

3

MANDY SAT ON HER HANDS TO KEEP FROM DRUMMING HER FINGERS ON the armrest of her plush chair, but she couldn't do the same for her jiggling leg. Boredom and anxiety were a lethal mixture, not to mention being placed under a proverbial magnifying glass.

She hated therapy, but it wasn't Ms. Antoinette's fault. The woman had done everything in her power to help Mandy feel as comfortable as possible—and that was sort of the problem. How could Bear make her see a therapist knowing full well that she couldn't talk about any of her real issues?

After all, how many other kids' fathers were former contract killers? How many had moved around their entire life because they stumbled upon trouble in every town they visited? How many had killed a full-grown man in self-defense by the age of fifteen?

Ms. Antoinette was in her mid-thirties, which made her one of the youngest faculty members at the Academy. Her long, straight hair was thick and always tied back in a loose ponytail.

"Mandy? Did you hear what I said?"

Mandy looked up and tried to reground herself. Ms. Antoinette's office was like something out of a fancy magazine. The wood, from the desk to the bookshelves, was rich and dark, like mahogany or maybe cherry. All the plush elements were made of velvet and were in colors like *sage* and *ochre* and *mauve*. A beautiful stained-glass lamp glowed from the corner of the woman's desk, and it took every ounce of Mandy's willpower not to get lost in its swirling beauty.

"Mandy?" Ms. Antoinette repeated.

"Sorry." Mandy shook her head to clear it, bringing her gaze back to the woman's hazel eyes. "What did you say?"

Ms. Antoinette repeated her question. "I asked about the new friends you made. The ones you talked about last week? Henrietta and Charles."

"Etta and Charlie," Mandy replied. She didn't understand the question. "What about them?"

"What can you tell me about them?"

Mandy sighed. The question seemed pointless, but she was smart enough to see this for what it was. Ms. Antoinette and the rest of the staff at Eastern Blue Ridge Academy were told that Mandy had mostly been homeschooled by her father since she was little, and that this was the first time she'd attended a private institution. She'd been required to take an entrance exam, which she passed, though maybe not with flying colors. She was permitted to attend classes with the other sophomores —on one condition. She had to attend mandatory weekly counseling with Ms. Antoinette. Mandy had begged and pleaded with Bear to get them to reconsider, but he'd thought it was a good idea.

The traitor.

Ms. Antoinette was only doing her job and Mandy could hardly hold that against her, especially since she was the nicest adult at the academy and the only one who didn't treat her like she was a delinquent. The woman listened to what Mandy had to say and was thoughtful about her answers. She wanted to help Mandy adjust to this new lifestyle. But Mandy was adaptable, and she'd gotten the hang of the school's etiquette in just a couple of days. The more Mandy appeared to be unlike anyone else at the school, the more attention it drew to her. Not that she'd been able to convince her counselor of that fact. Besides, Bear had been very clear about what was expected of her while she attended Eastern Blue Ridge.

Keep your head down and stay out of trouble.

There was a part of Mandy—a large part—that wanted to do the exact opposite of what Bear had told her. This whole thing felt like a punishment. Mandy knew going after Mr. Reagan was dangerous, but she'd been in perilous situations before. Why was this any different?

"Etta has two sisters and one brother, all older. Her mom is an accountant, and her father is a banker. They're still together. At home, she eats a peanut butter and jelly sandwich every day for lunch and always has her mom cut off the crust. She's allergic to pineapples and is obsessed with volleyball." Mandy took a deep breath, readying herself to continue her best impression of an auctioneer. "Charlie has one younger brother. His one father is a real estate agent, and his other father is a publicist for some big actor. He has a bee sting allergy, and he doesn't like when his food touches."

Ms. Antoinette let silence hang in the air for a moment, and Mandy wondered if she expected her to say more. Finally, Ms. Antoinette said, "You seem to know some intimate details about your friends and their family life."

"They mention things off-hand. I remember them."

"Cataloging them for later," Ms. Antoinette said, as though to herself. "And you met them both through the A.V. Club."

"Yes."

"How's that going? Are you having fun?"

She was, actually. The A.V. Club occupied her mind. She was learning a lot about sound and video recording and editing it all together. She was excited to apply her newfound knowledge in practical ways once Bear freed her from this prison.

"It's all right," she said.

"And you still talk to Marcus pretty regularly?"

Mandy's heart picked up in speed, but she ignored it. Marcus was her best friend, the only one who had stood by her side over the last couple of years. They talked now more than ever since she was stuck at school and had a regular Wi-Fi connection. She hadn't wanted to mention him at first and was still getting used to the idea that someone other than Bear knew he existed. It wasn't hard to convince herself that she wanted to keep him a secret for his own protection, but even she knew that wasn't the whole truth. It was nice having someone all to herself, especially now that Bear had left her behind for who knew how long.

"Yeah, when I can."

"I'm glad to hear that. You seem to be adjusting well."

"Thanks."

It was like everyone had expected her to be some wild animal who didn't know how to communicate with kids her own age, and while there had been a learning curve—considering most kids were more interested in the latest movie than the best way to incapacitate an opponent in under thirty seconds—she'd gotten the hang of it.

Bear had taught her to observe people. She could pick up on the subtle messages conveyed by their body language. It wasn't difficult to figure out who wanted to be her friend, who wanted to steer clear, and who saw her as a target. The hardest part was schooling her reactions so she didn't draw more attention to herself than necessary. It meant avoiding situations that could cause those problems. She'd found that to be the toughest problem so far.

"Let's switch gears a little bit," Ms. Antoinette said, "and talk about your favorite subject."

Mandy groaned. "Do we have to?"

"You know we do."

Mandy huffed and pulled her hands out from under her legs, crossing her arms over her chest. She'd tried lying in the beginning, but Ms. Antoinette had seen right through that. It was better to be honest. Or, *mostly* honest. "Fine."

"In the last week, how often have you performed rituals or repetitive behaviors?"

"A few times," Mandy replied. "This week wasn't too difficult."

"Good. That's really good. Do you mind sharing what you did?"

"The lock on my door. I was worried someone might be able to get in. I went back a couple times to check that it was still working." She ground her teeth together, forcing the next words out through a locked jaw. "I was late to class one day because of it."

"What else?"

"Counting. Counting steps."

"When you're anxious?" When Mandy nodded, Ms. Antoinette continued. "There's no shame in that, Mandy. Remember what we talked about? It's a coping mechanism to help you feel more in control. There's no judgment here."

"I know." She hated how small her voice sounded. She hated talking about this.

"And repositioning your items in a particular order before you leave for class?"

"Yes. I tried not to do it yesterday, but"—she fought the urge to hang her head in shame, swallowing a few times before she continued—"I ended up going back and doing it anyway."

"That's okay. You tried, and that's a huge first step. Remember, working on your compulsions is not going to be a straightforward journey. Sometimes, you'll take a step forward or a step back or a step to the side. Any movement is good movement because it means you're trying, okay?"

Mandy nodded.

"We're looking to build an arsenal of corrective experiences. I'd like you to try hard this week to not give into these compulsions at least twice. Only when you realize that nothing bad happens if you don't double-check your door or situate your book *just so* on your nightstand will you be able to resist those temptations more in the future. Does that make sense?"

"Yes," Mandy said, but the answer was rote. What Ms. Antoinette didn't know was that an unlocked door could mean death. A book slightly off-center from where she'd placed it could mean someone had searched her room. Bear and Iris had assured her she'd be safe here but being this far from Bear scared her. And she understood that if someone —like Reagan—wanted to hurt Bear, they'd go through her to do it. She was Bear's weak point.

"Wonderful." Ms. Antoinette looked at her watch. "That's all the time we have today. Same time and place next week?"

"Yeah," Mandy said, like she had a choice.

She launched to her feet and grabbed her backpack off the floor, swinging it over her shoulder. The doorhandle was in her grasp as she stopped and turned to the guidance counselor. It wasn't lost on her that these tactics were good to learn, even if she hated to admit her struggles with OCD. "Thank you, Ms. Antoinette. For all your help."

"You're welcome. Where are you off to now?"

"Meeting Etta for a volleyball game."

"Have fun!"

Mandy made her way to the gymnasium as fast as her legs would carry her without drawing any undue attention. She wanted to make sure she got a seat next to Etta, but her bladder was about to explode. The discomfort made her forget about her awkward therapy session with Ms. Antoinette. But later, when she was trying to fall asleep and had nothing better to think about, it would come back to haunt her.

Leaving the bathroom feeling a thousand times better, Mandy nearly collided with another student whipping around the corner of the hallway just down from the gym entrance. The boy didn't look her in the eyes as he mumbled a quick apology and scurried off in the opposite direction, as though he were being chased by a pack of wolves.

Mandy pressed a palm to her chest, heart pounding with adrenaline. It had taken all her control not to flip the kid onto his back and pin him to the ground when he'd surprised her like that. She had to get herself back to normal before walking into the game or else Etta would pepper her with a million questions.

She closed her eyes and took several deep breaths. She catalogued the sounds around her. The roaring crowd drowned out the squeak of sneakers, and she guessed their team had scored a point. When the noise died down, she could hear a pair of voices heading in her direction. But they didn't sound like they belonged to students.

"Did you tell him what would happen if he didn't do as he was asked?" one man said. His voice was deep and commanding, like he was used to his orders being followed.

"Obviously," the other said. His voice had a lazy kind of swagger to it. "He didn't believe me."

"Then I guess we have to make a believer out of him."

"And how do you suggest we do that?"

"My son knows his son—"

The first man broke off as he turned the corner and almost ran over Mandy. Their lowered voices had echoed strangely in the hallway, and she hadn't realized they'd been so close. Goosebumps erupted across her arms as she looked up into the steady gazes of the men standing in front of her. The first one looked like a model with sharp cheekbones, a square jaw, and blond hair gelled to perfection. Green eyes that should've been mesmerizing were dark with suspicion, while the second man's lids were lowered in sleepy amusement. He was the other man's opposite with dark hair, a heart-shaped face, and deep brown eyes.

"What are you doing?" the first one barked at her.

"Bathroom," she said, clutching her stomach. She didn't have to fake feeling woozy. "Stomach ache. It was real bad—"

"All right, all right," the first one said, and the second one laughed at the discomfort on his friend's face. "Go home before you get everyone sick."

"Yes, sir." Mandy skirted around them and rushed down the hall. They didn't move again until she turned the corner toward the exit. She could've doubled back to join Etta in the stands, but all of a sudden, her fake stomachache felt very real.

They were definitely up to something.

4

BEAR MANAGED TO DOWN TWO CUPS OF BITTER BLACK COFFEE ON HIS WAY
to Queens. He'd had better, but also much, much worse. As the caffeine
coursed through his system, his brain fog lifted and his senses sharpened. Years of training and experience meant he was always ready to
take action, but the jet fuel in his veins shortened his reaction time.
More than ever, he was ready to uncover Reagan's plan and end it once
and for all.

Iris stood on the platform, waiting for him as he exited the train.
Without exchanging words, they headed up the stairs and out onto the
street. It was nearing noon, and the sidewalks were crowded with the
lunch rush. Bear tossed his empty coffee cup in the nearest trashcan and
stuck his hands deep inside his pockets, reassured by the heft of his
weapon in his right hand. Taking a deep breath, he inhaled the scent of
grilled meat in the air and his stomach rumbled in response.

"Lunch?" Bear asked.

Iris shook her head. "Let's do this first. Find out what we're up
against."

Bear thought they'd both be sharper with some food in their stom-
achs, but he didn't argue. For the first time in months, it felt like they
were close to something. What that something was, Bear had no idea.

Farro's confidence that this had to do with Mr. Reagan was shaky at best. Hopefully they'd be able to follow that back to him one way or another.

Iris led the way as they turned onto 41st Avenue, cutting a line through the crowd without much difficulty. Keeping up with her wasn't an issue, and Bear let his strides turn leisurely as he studied the crowd around him. The ebb and flow of students, businessmen, and shop owners made him feel more at home than he had in years. With a sharp pang, he wished Mandy were here to see the city with him. If she'd grown up here like a normal kid, what would her life be like now?

A few minutes later, Iris stopped in front of a wrought iron fence outside a six-story apartment complex that took up half the block. Bear guessed it contained at least a hundred or more apartments. The landscaping left little to be desired, as did the crumbling façade.

"We know which one is his?" Bear asked.

"Apartment five-sixteen." Iris leaned her back against the fence and took out her phone as though she were going to scroll through it, but her eyes never settled on the screen.

"Plan?" Bear asked.

"Knock on the door. Ask politely."

"And when that doesn't work?"

"Isn't that what you're for, Big Man?"

Bear's face cracked into a smile. The nickname reminded of Jack Noble. Not for the first time, he wondered what his old friend was up to and how he was faring on his own. Bear wanted nothing more than to tell Jack about how quickly Mandy was maturing. How terrified he was about her becoming a young woman and striking out on her own someday. If anyone would know how exciting and frightening a prospect that was, it would be Jack. He wondered when the man had last seen his own daughter, Mia.

Iris' voice broke through the memories. "We're up."

A young couple had turned down the walkway to head toward the building. Without wasting a second, Iris and Bear fell into step a few paces behind them. Far enough away that the pair wouldn't feel crowded, but close enough that they'd be obligated to hold the door open for them. Iris reached out and took Bear's hand, all but sealing the deal. On his own, Bear would be a threat. But holding hands with someone like Iris? No one would question why they were in the building.

Sure enough, when the couple opened the door in front of them, the man kept a hand on it until Bear was close enough to grab the handle. The two of them stepped inside the drab entranceway. They were greeted by faded linoleum and a thinning rug. The couple made their way over to their mailbox, while Bear and Iris eyed the elevator and the entrance to the staircase.

They headed toward the stairwell in unison. Neither expected trouble once they got to the fifth floor, but the energy they'd save using the elevator wasn't worth risking a surprise when the doors opened. Besides, Bear thought, if he couldn't handle five flights, then he might as well be dead.

The stairs didn't show as much wear as the entrance. Their footsteps echoed through the stairwell as they ascended. Bear's lungs had just started to burn when they made it to level five, and he joined Iris in taking a moment to catch their breath before cracking open the door and checking the hallway for activity.

"Clear," she whispered.

Bear nodded, and they strode through the door, keeping eyes and ears peeled for anything out of the ordinary. The carpet up here was a dizzying pattern of red and gold, something that looked like it could've been out of the 1950s. Faded in the center, it was bright along the edges, a relic of its former glory.

Muffled chatter slipped through closed doors, though Bear couldn't tell which came from the apartment's inhabitants and which came from their television screens. The scent of marijuana lingered in the hallway. As they passed apartment 510, someone let out a laugh that had both Iris and Bear tensing, though neither of their steps faltered.

Reaching Silas Marino's apartment, Iris and Bear stood on either side of the door, both drawing their weapons. They could cause a panic if they were spotted by any nosey neighbors, but Iris' badge might be enough to negate any problems before they got out of hand.

Their eyes met. Bear gave her a sharp nod of his head. Iris leaned forward to rap her knuckles on the door. It was a polite knock, like a neighbor asking to borrow some sugar. The sound itself wouldn't be cause for alarm, but if Silas was the paranoid type, he'd panic when he wasn't able to spot anyone outside his door through the peephole.

Silence ensued. No shuffling feet or creaking floorboards. No panicked breathing or the cocking of a gun. Laughter erupted down the hall again, though quieter now that they'd put some distance between them and that apartment. A door slammed on the floor above them, but Silas' apartment remained quiet.

Instead of knocking again, Iris pulled her hand inside the sleeve of her jacket and wrapped it around the doorhandle. When it twisted beneath her touch, Iris' wide eyes met Bear's, and he straightened in preparation for whatever came next.

She swung the door open. They both paused to see if anyone rushed them. When they were met with more silence, Bear took the lead and stepped inside, raising his gun until he could guarantee a shot at center mass. He cursed the fact that he didn't have a silencer. Pulling the trigger in a crowded apartment building was the last thing they needed.

The apartment was small and stuffy. The short hallway led to a tiny kitchen on the left, opposite the bathroom and next to the bedroom. At the end was the living room. Everything was decorated in muted grays and blues, but Bear's attention was stolen by the items strewn across the floor. The place had been ransacked.

Iris swore under her breath before stepping into the bathroom to clear it while Bear cleared the kitchen, then the bedroom. Together, they stepped into the living room, both zeroing in on the crimson stain smeared across the charcoal rug. A moan sounded from the corner of the room. They twisted to find the source of it and pointed their guns at the figure slumped against the wall, a puddle of blood spreading across his abdomen.

He was a frail man in his forties with pale blond hair and large wire-rim glasses. Sweat beaded on his forehead and upper lip. His eyes were fighting to stay open as he looked up into their faces. The man had his hands wrapped around the handle of a butcher knife sticking out of his gut, as though he intended to pull it free to use against them.

"Don't." Iris tucked her gun away and knelt beside him. "You'll just make it worse."

Silas attempted to scoot away from her, but all it did was cause a flash of pain to crease his forehead. Another groan escaped his lips.

"Silas Marino?" Bear lowered his gun but kept it out.

The man's eyes sharpened as he looked up at Bear. His voice was nothing more than a raspy whisper as he said, "Who are you?"

"We came here to talk to you," Iris said. If the fists clenched by her side were any indication, it was taking all her willpower not to touch the man, to find out the extent of his injuries. "Who did this to you? Was it Mr. Reagan?"

Silas flinched at the mention of Reagan's name, and that was all the answer they needed.

Bear stepped forward. "What happened?"

"Hired me for a job." Silas was panting now, his hands shaking. "Handed what they wanted over. This was my payment."

"What kind of job?" Iris asked.

Silas shook his head, squeezing his eyes shut. A tear dripped out of the corner of his eye and melted into his thin hair.

"Don't let Reagan win," Bear said. "Tell us what you were after, and we'll take him down. He'll pay for what he did."

Silas opened his eyes, but he kept blinking like he was trying to bring Bear into focus. After a minute, his hands dropped to his side. A single finger stretched out to point at his foot. "Shoe."

Iris looked up at Bear, then pulled off the man's right shoe. Inside was a keycard. She held it up. "What's this for?"

"Eleven. Forty-eight," Silas said, his voice quieter now than it had been. "Twenty-seven. Thirty-two. Nineteen. Twelve." He took a shuddering breath. "Eighty—" A cough interrupted him. "Eighty-nine."

Bear committed the numbers to memory. "What can we expect when we get there?"

But his question fell on deaf ears. Silas took one more shuddering breath, and then stilled.

5

BEAR WATCHED AS IRIS REPLACED SILAS' SHOE AND POCKETED THE keycard. Searching the apartment yielded nothing else, and Bear wondered where they would've been if they'd arrived just a few minutes later. Another dead end on the journey to discovering Mr. Reagan's identity.

Then again, they could've arrived a few minutes earlier and been witness to the attack. Would that have led them back to Reagan, or just landed them in more trouble? Had Farro known what was waiting for them?

Bear shook the thought free. No point in playing what-if games. Silas was dead now, and they had their next bearing.

Iris used Silas' cellphone to dial 911, wiping it down before leaving it ringing next to him. Bear could hear the operator's voice calling out on the other end as they moved across the room, down the hall, and out the front door. This time, they didn't bother taking the stairs, and in under two minutes, they returned to the cool November air.

They walked several blocks west before coming to a halt. Iris slipped the keycard out of her pocket. "Prime Mini Self Storage," she read.

Bear took the keycard from her and inspected it. The off-white plastic was worn and dirty, with bold red words written across the front that had faded along the edges. It contained no other information.

"It's only a couple blocks away." Iris had her phone out and enlarged the map with her thumbs. She spun on the spot, orienting herself. "That way."

Sirens sounded from the opposite direction. A small blessing.

"Let's go."

The building was as innocuous as the card, made of pale bricks and with a heavy door at the front. There was no guard. They had to insert the key into a slot and wait for the bolt to slide across. Bear pulled the door open, itching to bring out his gun in case they were met with a surprise on the other side.

Someone sat at the front desk off to the right, but the young man paid them no mind as he scrolled through his phone and popped his gum. Across from them were hundreds of storage units, ranging from the size of a microwave to a single-car garage. Along the aisles hung signs with a series of numbers.

"He gave us the pin," Iris said, "but not the lockbox number."

"Fourteen digits is high for a passcode." Bear pointed to the box units in the eleven-hundred range. "The first two were for the unit."

Only a few people milled about, most not paying attention to the two of them. Bear threw looks over his shoulder, but no one had followed them inside, and no one waited for someone to show up at Silas' unit with the code. The aisle containing the lockbox was empty.

Bear followed the numbers until he got to 1148. It was one of the smaller units, nondescript and utterly ordinary. The same as every single one around it. Yet, whatever Silas had hidden inside was important enough that he'd died without giving it up to his attackers.

Iris leaned forward and read the directions on the front of the unit. "Insert keycard, then enter your ten-digit passcode."

Without a word, Bear did as he was told, using the miniscule keypad to punch in the numbers Silas had relayed. But when he pressed the enter key, nothing happened. Bear pulled on the handle to the unit, but it stayed shut.

Iris used her hip to shove Bear out of the way. "You probably hit a wrong number with those sausages you call fingers." She entered each number with the delicate touch of her thumb. When she hit the enter key, the door swung open with a click. She looked up at him.

Bear chuckled, but his attention was stolen by their first success in two months. "What's inside?"

Iris reached in, pulled out a sleek black device and flipped it over, scanning its specifications. "A hard drive. A pretty nice one, from what I can tell. Farro said Silas was one of the best tech guys he'd worked with. This is gonna be a pain to get into."

"One problem at a time. Let's just focus on making it back in one piece now." Bear glanced around inside the unit to make sure it didn't house anything else before swinging the door shut and locking it again.

Now that they had something in their hands that could lead them back to Reagan, Bear felt like he held a nuclear warhead in his pocket. At any moment, it could go off.

THIS TIME, Bear didn't bother traveling separately from Iris as they headed back to their secret office. They stopped only long enough to grab a couple slices of greasy, cheesy pizza to eat on the train.

Once back at their makeshift headquarters, they locked the door behind them. Bear removed the hard drive from his pocket and set it on the edge of their shared desk as though it were a hot coal. The machinery on the other side of the wall pumped in rhythm with Bear's beating heart.

They stared at the device for a moment, as though it would transform into a neon blinking sign containing all the information they were looking for.

Bear broke the silence first. "Could have a tracker inside."

"Something tells me the only person who would be able to track it is dead."

"We should pick up and move soon anyway. Just in case."

Iris nodded, but she looked distracted while she stared down at the device. "What do you think is on it?"

"Silas said he handed over whatever they hired him for. This must be his insurance policy."

"Could have a virus. Could shut us down if we're not careful."

"Silas seemed pretty pissed he was on the wrong end of that knife. Don't think he's setting us up from beyond the grave."

"He barely got those numbers out. Might not have had the energy to warn us about anything else."

Bear agreed, but this felt like the point of no return. The closest they'd come to Reagan so far. Whatever was on the hard drive was something worth killing for. They already had targets on their backs, but whatever information they uncovered could put a bullet in their brain. Both of them had already prepared for that eventuality. But sometimes preparation mattered little when staring down the barrel of a gun.

Iris slid into her chair and plugged the hard drive into her laptop. Bear moved to stand behind her, hands on his hips, heart steady but threatening to beat faster as every second ticked by. A dialog box opened asking for a password.

"The same combination for the unit?" Bear asked.

"Doubtful," Iris said, but she tried it anyway. Red text popped up telling her she'd used one of three attempts. She twisted in her chair to look up at Bear. "This was the kind of thing Silas did. Whatever he's got protecting this is going to be better than anything I can get into. Even if I had the right tech, I wouldn't want to risk it."

"What about Farro?" Bear asked. "He sent us after this."

"He sent us after Silas. He probably didn't know about the drive."

"Or he was using us to get to the drive."

Iris smirked, but there was a hard edge to it. "Anyone ever tell you you're paranoid?"

"No." Bear scowled at her. "Why? You hear something?"

She rolled her eyes. "Farro wanted us to check up on Silas. He couldn't have known about the drive. If he did, he wouldn't have needed us to get it for him."

The pounding of the machinery on the other side of the wall escalated, and Bear waited until it quieted down again before speaking. "You should send him a message. Let him know his informant is dead. See how he reacts."

"He told me not to message him again."

"I think he'd want to know."

Iris hesitated for only a minute before switching windows. Her fingers flew across the keyboard as she typed out an initial message, letting Farro know she had sensitive information. But as soon as her pinky finger hit the enter key, an error popped up.

Iris sat back and cocked her head to the side as though she couldn't comprehend what she was reading. "He blocked me."

Bear swore. "Think he sent us there hoping we'd be on the other end of that knife too?"

"No," Iris said, but she didn't sound as confident about Farro as she had that morning. "He could've set us up at that restaurant, and he didn't. He's on our side. He couldn't have known about the attack. And if he knew about the drive, if he wanted it from us, he wouldn't have cut me off. He's just being careful."

The logic was sound, but Bear felt like someone had placed blinders on both of them.

What weren't they seeing?

6

MONARCH SAT AT HIS DESK, COUNTING DOWN THE SECONDS UNTIL THE phone rang. He stared at the ticking hands in his vintage onyx-faced Omega Speedmaster. Not the most expensive one he owned, but a favorite: it had been a gift from his wife. He took comfort in the soft and sturdy feel of the material around his wrist.

The second hand hit the twelve, indicating it was precisely nine o'clock in the evening. The phone on his desk rang once, sharp and clear. Despite expecting Reagan's call, his heart jumped in his chest and thundered so loud it nearly drowned out the second ring. There would be consequences if he waited for a third. Monarch lifted the phone and raised it to his ear, watching the curly cord stretch across his mahogany desk as he did so.

"Are you alone?"

Monarch's eyes darted around his office, as though he couldn't be sure despite having sent the last of his staff home hours ago and locking his office door prior to the call. "Yes."

"Update me."

"Ortiz is being difficult."

"We knew he would be."

"More difficult than expected."

"Money isn't an obstacle."

"Money isn't the issue."

"Oh?" Reagan's voice was lazy, even pleasant. "And what is?"

"Integrity." Monarch saw his own spittle fly across the room. "He thinks what we're doing is wrong."

"Have you tried to persuade him otherwise?"

Monarch forced himself not to sigh in agitation. He'd spent the last several weeks doing nothing *but* trying to persuade Ortiz of their cause. It was lies, of course, but he hadn't gotten to where he was today by being an honest man. Charismatic, charming, and ruthless, yes, but not honest. Yet none of his usual tactics had worked on Ortiz.

Monarch brought a hand to his hair to run his fingers through it and stopped short, not wanting to displace a single strand on his head. He had to keep it together. Just for a little while longer. Through gritted teeth he said, "Yes. He is unmoving."

"What are our options?"

"He has a wife."

Reagan made a contented sound. "And a son."

Monarch had thought as much, even said so out loud to one of his cohorts. But he didn't want to bring kids into this. Perhaps only the threat of violence would be enough. "My son knows his son. We can force his hand."

"See that you do." Reagan's voice had an edge to it now. Monarch could hear the hidden command loud and clear. *Don't fail me again.* "Is there anything else?"

"Silas Marino is dead."

"Excellent. Did your men find the backup?"

"No. The apartment was clean." The men he'd sent to kill Marino weren't *his*, technically. But splitting those hairs would only aggravate Reagan.

"He has it stashed somewhere else, then. Keep your men on it. No loose ends."

"Understood."

"Is that all?"

Monarch hesitated. Biting out his next words felt like failure, and Reagan wouldn't tolerate that. Not even for him, the most loyal servant. "Duvall is still sticking her nose where it doesn't belong."

"We expected as much. Iris doesn't give up easily."

"She won't stop until she finds something."

"Let her keep looking. She has no idea what's coming, and by the time she figures it out? Well, it'll be too late for her. For all of them."

"We can't get close to her. Not with Logan around."

"I told you before, you won't be able to get the jump on him. Steer clear of Riley Logan. Of both of them. You have no idea what he's capable of." Reagan's voice had such a snap to it that Monarch reeled back as though he'd been slapped.

"He's one man—"

"He's not," Regan replied. "He's not just one man. I have witnessed firsthand what he is capable of. Your men cannot handle him. And if I hear you've sent anyone after him, I will not hesitate to cut the throats of your loved ones and force you to watch the light drain from their eyes. Do I make myself clear?"

Monarch gulped down the terror that had risen in his throat, hoping Reagan wouldn't be able to hear it on the other end of the line. "Yes. Of course. My apologies."

"Excellent." Just like that, Reagan's voice turned lazy once more. "The end is in sight. We just need to be patient. And smart. Deal with Ortiz by whatever means necessary. Get him on our side. If he refuses to cooperate, do what's necessary. Your part is almost over. And then you can live the life you've always dreamed."

Monarch did not believe Reagan's words for a second. Still he said, "Consider it done."

The other line went dead without any last words from Reagan.

Monarch replaced the phone on the hook with a soft *click*, then leaned back in his chair and glanced down at his watch. The conversation had lasted less than ten minutes, yet it felt as though his entire world had been turned upside down. He had no idea how Reagan knew

Duvall and Logan. And no idea why they were off limits. But that wasn't his concern. All he cared about was getting out of this with his family intact. If he could manage that, he'd get everything he'd been working for and so much more.

"It'll all be worth it," he reminded himself.

The words tasted sour in his mouth.

7

MANDY HURRIED DOWN THE EMPTY HALLWAY TO HER FIRST CLASS OF THE day, a string of curses leaving her mouth in ragged breaths. She'd tried so hard to do what Ms. Antoinette had suggested. How hard was it to lock her bedroom door and walk away without checking it three extra times? Impossible, apparently, because she'd been unable to make it more than a couple dozen steps down the hall before turning around and sprinting back to her door. And now she was going to be late.

Again.

A sharp cry of pain had her skidding to a stop before she rounded the next corner, her ugly tartan skirt swinging around her knees and her stupid fancy shoes squeaking on the floor in response. There was a beat of silence, then a dull thud and a winded gasp. Marching forward, Mandy turned down the next hall, blood draining from her face at the scene before her.

Charlie Archambault lay on the floor, curled up in the fetal position with his hands protecting his face. Even from the other end of the hallway, Mandy could hear his sobs and his quiet protests. His whole body was shaking, and her heart broke at the sight of him. He was small for his age, both in frame and height, and he often got picked on by the older kids. Having glasses and freckles and a gap-toothed smile didn't help either.

Standing above him was Roy King, the self-appointed ruler of their grade at Eastern Blue Ridge Academy. Unlike Charlie, he was taller and bulkier than most their age. He'd turned sixteen earlier in the year and if they didn't all live at the school, Mandy was sure he'd be the guy to show up driving a different fancy car every day.

As Mandy approached, she could see a wild gleam in Roy's eyes. That look wasn't unfamiliar to her. She'd seen bloodlust before. She'd seen it on the man she'd killed earlier that year. And though Roy was younger and weaker and far less dangerous, Mandy's muscles still tensed in anticipation.

The boy looming over her friend noticed Mandy when she was a few feet away. His head whipped in her direction. His eyes glared with alarm, likely over the prospect of getting caught before his expression settled into one of familiar arrogance. This was not the first time Mandy and Roy had gone head-to-head, but it had never been because he'd laid a hand on her friend.

Charlie looked up at her approach, clearly hopeful that someone had come to his rescue. When he saw it was Mandy, he let out a shuddering breath and sat up. A trickle of blood seeped out of the corner of his mouth where his tooth must've cut his lip. There weren't any bruises blossoming on his face just yet, but in a few hours, that might be a different story.

"Ah, Davis," Roy said, spreading his hands out like he was greeting an old friend. "Excellent timing. I was just getting started."

Mandy stopped about five feet away, her hands balled into fists. At some point her jaw had clenched, and it was already starting to ache. She tried to loosen it, to relax and not give Roy the satisfaction of knowing how badly he got under her skin, but it was an uphill battle. She hated the fake last name she had to use at the school. It made her miss Bear even more. Reminded her how he'd left her behind.

"Get away from him," Mandy said.

Roy tipped his head back and laughed. It echoed around the empty hallway. "Or what? What could you possibly do to stop me? Go tattle? Do that, and I'll make sure Charlie here breaks something important."

Mandy had no interest in *tattling* on Roy. Not only would that leave Charlie to the other boy's mercy, but it wasn't in her nature. Bear had taught her to assess her situation and face her problems head on. Roy had no idea what she was capable of. While she was itching to show him, Bear's voice boomed in her head.

Keep your head down and stay out of trouble.

Stalking forward, Mandy purposefully put herself between Charlie and Roy, bending down to her friend and taking a closer inspection of his face. He avoided her gaze but let her check him for injuries. She wished she could tell him that he'd done nothing wrong. That Roy was just a bully and deserved to be put in his place. But she was so angry, the words wouldn't come out of her mouth.

She pulled Charlie to his feet, hooked his arm over her shoulder, and turned them in the direction she'd come from. The nurse would ask too many questions, but the lunch ladies would only click their tongues before making him an ice pack to hold against his face. They knew how cruel children could be, and they knew the people who ran this school wouldn't do anything to punish Roy King. His father's donations were what kept the school afloat, after all.

"Where do you think you're going?" Roy asked.

Before Mandy could answer, Roy grabbed her arm and pulled. The movement made her lose her grip on Charlie, who stumbled and fell into a nearby wooden door, causing it to rattle on its hinges. His cry sounded more like it came from surprise than pain, but the sound broke the last of Mandy's restraint.

As Roy spun her around to face him, she curled her loose hand into a fist and allowed the momentum to guide her arm into a vicious right hook. It caught Roy in the cheek. Mandy's knuckles erupted in pain. He stumbled back several steps, bringing a hand up to where she'd hit him. His eyes went wide with shock before they narrowed into anger.

He brought his hands into a fighter's stance. "You're going to regret that. I have no problem hitting girls."

If Mandy were anyone else, she'd worry about facing off against Roy.

He was the best fighter on the school's boxing team and everyone knew it. Most kids who had politicians for fathers wouldn't join such a brutal sport, but rumor had it his dad had told him he couldn't play football because it was too dangerous, and boxing was the only other way for Roy to let off some steam. Unfortunately, he didn't always keep the punching within the confines of the ring.

Lucky for Mandy, Bear had taught her how to take a punch. Even better, he'd taught her how to dodge one. Roy, apparently, hadn't gotten that lesson.

Attempting to surprise her with a quick jab, Roy stepped forward and launched his fist at her face. There was a lot of power behind the telegraphed blow, but Mandy ducked to the side with ease. Roy swung again with more force, anger burning behind his eyes, and Mandy repeated the move. She couldn't help but let out a little laugh.

"I thought you were supposed to be good at this?" she taunted.

Charlie gasped behind her, and she realized she'd forgotten he was there. Her entire focus had narrowed in on Roy and the fight in front of her. She wouldn't lose. And she'd make him regret ever laying a finger on her friend.

When Roy aimed lower, hoping to land a hit on a bigger target, Mandy brought up her left arm and blocked the punch, moving it away from her with such force that it knocked him off balance. She gripped his wrist and, using his current forward momentum, pulled him toward her and pulsed her knee in his gut. The air whooshed out of his lungs with a wheeze. He fought to stand back up straight and regain his breathing.

The reasonable part of her mind was telling her to stop, to end the confrontation here and now. She'd already bested him, and if he knew what was good for him, he wouldn't try to hit her again.

But Roy King was more ego than intelligence. Straightening, he lurched forward, intent on wrapping his hands around her neck. She blocked him again, having brought both fists to cover her face, following up with a pair of jabs to his eye socket that rocked his head backwards. She would've gone for a third hit, but a large hand wrapped around her arm and pulled her away from the fight. She cried out in surprise and when she tried to twist out of the other person's grip, she caught sight of Mr. Foley's face.

He was the P.E. teacher.

And Roy's boxing coach.

"You idiot," Mr. Foley said, but he wasn't looking at Mandy. "What the hell were you thinking?"

"She attacked me!" Roy replied, his voice higher and whinier than she'd ever heard it. "Did you see what she did to me?"

"No less than you deserve," Mr. Foley said. "Go to the infirmary now. Get some ice on your face. Then meet me in my office. We're going to have a little chat about your extracurricular activities."

Roy didn't say anything as he slipped away down the hall. It was only then that Mandy noticed the small crowd of kids who had gathered around them. Charlie seemed shocked by the encounter. He leaned up against the wall to the left of the door he'd fallen into earlier.

"Ms. Lang," Mr. Foley said, and a girl in a grade above Mandy stepped forward. "Take Mr. Archambault to the infirmary. Make sure Mr. King doesn't cause any more trouble."

"Yes, sir." The girl took Charlie gently by the arm and led him away.

"The rest of you. Get out of here."

The kids scrambled and in under thirty seconds, Mandy was left alone in the hallway with Mr. Foley. Her muscles tensed in anticipation of what would happen next. Would he yell at her, or would his voice be deadly quiet as he told her she'd have detention for the rest of her life? Or would it be worse, and she'd be suspended? Her throat closed as she thought of Bear receiving that news and having to drop whatever he was doing to come take her away.

But she also couldn't stop the hope that swelled in her chest, even as it fought against the dread building.

Mr. Foley dropped her arm and Mandy took a step back, looking up at him, waiting to be convicted for her crimes.

The man looked down at her, assessing. Then he crossed his arms over his chest and chuckled in a way that reminded her of Bear.

"I'm impressed," he said. "You want to join the boxing team?"

8

THE PREVIOUS NIGHT, BEAR HAD WATCHED AS IRIS USED A SET OF DELICATE tools to open the drive and peer inside at the hardware, searching for a tracking device or any other information. She found neither. He exhaled and felt light. They wouldn't have to fear some unknown adversary stalking them to their next location. It wasn't a guarantee, but it was as close as they would get.

Iris found their new makeshift office inside an apartment that was a single subway stop from their last place. Bear would've preferred somewhere farther away, but they were desperate. Their contacts were running thin, and not everyone was willing to look the other way while they did God knew what.

They only had a few days before the crew would return to finish renovating the place. Dust had settled onto the plastic-lined floor. As long as they didn't kick up too much, their equipment would be safe.

Bear dropped his duffle on the floor as soon as they walked through the door. It sent up a cloud of fine white dust. "Comfy."

"We can rent a room at the Ritz if your delicate sensitivities are offended." Iris toed the door closed behind her. "But you're paying."

Bear let her have that one. The tension between them grew the longer Reagan was out of reach. Getting the hard drive yesterday had repaired a portion of their strained relationship. He liked Iris, but she knew Bear's true identity. She knew about Mandy. About where'd they'd been and what they'd done. That information could be invaluable to certain people. Bear had no doubt that he and Iris were a team in the present. But situations like this could change with the right incentive.

"I'll set up here in the corner, away from the windows. Did you bring the desk lamp?"

Bear unzipped his duffel and pulled out the small light and handed it over. They'd been assured that while the apartment wasn't furnished, it did have working electricity and water.

Bear stepped around a paint tray and peered out the window at the street below. Nothing looked out of place. In the background, Iris unfolded the small card table she'd hauled up the stairs along with their vital pieces of equipment. A laptop and the hard drive were the two most crucial pieces, but she'd also brought along a few other devices to speed up some of their more illegal operations. Too bad none of them could crack the drive.

Iris plugged in the lamp, clicking it on. "What's our plan?"

"Lay low. Gather information. Same as usual."

Iris huffed. "About the hard drive."

"I've got a guy, but I'm hesitant to involve him in this." Bear turned from the window and stepped to the side, out of view from anyone across the street.

Iris didn't know who Brandon was, but she nodded her head like she understood. Bear and Brandon had been through a lot over the years, and he trusted the guy with his life. That trust had worked in his favor dozens of times in the past. He was a great team asset when you needed someone to watch over you from afar, but he'd been through his fair share of trauma. Brandon was Bear's friend, and he wouldn't risk putting him on Reagan's radar unless he had no other choice.

"I might know someone," Iris said.

Bear raised an eyebrow. He didn't like her tone of voice. "Oh?"

"She's good. One of the best in the world. Has access to tech I can only dream of. I know she'll be able to crack this open."

"But?"

"She works for the NSA."

Bear didn't react outwardly, but the gears in his head spun at top speed. Someone like that was good to have on your side, and terrible as an enemy. Bear's slate had been wiped clean, but there was always a chance that one of his files had been tucked in a drawer somewhere. He was careful about not leaving a digital footprint for a reason. And that reason was the NSA.

"Can she be trusted?"

"I wouldn't be bringing her up otherwise."

Bear bit his tongue to keep from saying what was on his mind. The last two months hadn't been easy on him either, but he could feel the desperation emanating off Iris. Her reasons for wanting to bring down Reagan were noble, but there was a personal element to this. Something that made her more reckless than he'd ever seen her. That headspace could be an asset in the right situation. And a death sentence in the wrong one.

Looking at her sharp cheekbones and the dark circles under her eyes, Bear chose his next words carefully. "Does she have any connection to Farro?"

"No. Why?"

"Just wondering."

"Say what's on your mind, Logan."

Bear ran a hand over his jaw, barely containing his flare of annoyance at her tone. "Farro ghosted us."

"He told us not to message him. You can't be surprised."

"I'm not surprised. Just stating a fact." Bear dropped his hands to his hips. "But the point still stands. He sent us after Silas, then he disappeared. Maybe he's just laying low. Maybe he's been compromised. Maybe he's building up to something else. The fact that we don't know for sure is cause for concern."

"I trust Farro."

"And I don't. We don't have enough information for a guarantee."

"There are no guarantees in our line of work. At some point, you have to trust someone."

"And most of the people I trust are dead." Bitterness tinged Bear's words, and he hated the way his chest squeezed in anger and frustration at the thought. "The ones who are still alive have earned my respect. Farro hasn't. We need to be careful."

"And what about me? Where am I on your list of people you trust?"

"I'm here, aren't I?"

Iris' gaze remained hard. "It's up to you. Either you call your guy, or I call mine. She'll be discreet. She *knows* what Reagan is capable of."

Bear didn't like involving another new person in their operation. Especially someone who worked for the NSA. There was no telling what they knew or what their true motivations were. It felt like kicking a hornet's nest. But what other choice did they have? He didn't want to involve Brandon. Not unless it was absolutely necessary.

Bear turned back to the window, his mind made up.

"Make the call."

9

MARCUS SAT UP IN BED. HE LEANED BACK AGAINST THE WALL AND dragged a pillow onto his lap as a makeshift table for his computer. His heart pounded like it always did before Mandy called. Once they were on the line together, both of them slipped into their respective roles and the feeling that his whole body was on fire went away. He wished Mandy led the kind of life he could be a part of without a computer screen between them, but he was grateful she hadn't forgotten about him when she moved away.

It was almost lunch time when Mandy had messaged him to see if he could talk. Normally he'd be in school, but his mom had let him skip today so she could drop him off at his uncle's for the weekend. He always loved visiting his uncle.

When Mandy called, Marcus answered.

It had always been like that between them, from the moment they'd met in school to well after she'd moved on from his little Upstate New York town, traveling across the country with her father. Marcus shuddered at the thought of Mandy's dad. The guy was like a real-life superhero and also one of the most terrifying men he'd ever met. Sometimes he couldn't believe Bear was Mandy's dad, and other times, he couldn't imagine anyone else fitting the role.

A notification popped up on his laptop screen—Mandy was calling. He didn't hesitate before answering. He heard other boys talk about how they'd ignore texts from girls they liked, play hard to get. But Marcus didn't see the logic in that. If Mandy needed him, the least he could do was be there.

Clicking the answer button, Marcus' heart reached a fever pitch as he took in Mandy's face, always somber with a hint of mischief in her eyes. She hated being at that school, and while he wouldn't tell her, he couldn't help but feel the opposite. Not that he'd ever admit that to her out loud. This was the most they'd talked since she'd moved away. While she may have felt confined to the four walls of Eastern Blue Ridge Academy, he liked knowing she was stationary and safe. There had been too many days where he'd been left to wonder what she was doing and if she was okay.

Mandy came into focus. "Hey."

"Hey," he said, glad that his voice remained steady. "What's up?"

"Is your uncle around?"

"He's in the kitchen." Marcus had made sure he had at least a few minutes alone with Mandy in case she had to share sensitive information. His uncle was pretty cool and had always encouraged his interest in computers, but he was still an adult. Marcus could get away with some things, but Mandy had this uncanny ability to push him over certain lines they both probably shouldn't cross. "I've got about ten minutes until lunch."

"That should be long enough."

Marcus furrowed his brows. "Everything okay? What's going on?"

Mandy chewed at the inside of her cheek, and he could hear her fingers drumming on the desk in front of her. He couldn't tell where she was. It didn't look like her room. Was she hiding out in the bathroom?

"Yesterday, I left therapy to go to the volleyball game. I was supposed to meet Etta there, but I really had to pee." Mandy scowled at the way Marcus chuckled at her bluntness, but she didn't slow down her story. "When I got out of the bathroom, I ran into these two guys. Parents who were at the match, I think. They were talking about getting this other guy to fall in line, that they had to make a believer out of him. The one guy said his son knows the other guy's son, and I'm worried something is going on. That someone is going to get hurt."

Marcus sat up a little straighter, adjusting the computer on his lap so he had a better angle of Mandy's face. He didn't know how she always got herself into these situations, but sometimes he envied her for it. Marcus would never describe himself as brave. Not like Mandy. But he wanted to be.

Some people are meant to be superheroes, and some are meant to be sidekicks.

He'd repeated that thought often since meeting Mandy. It gave him an odd sort of comfort. He might not be able to fight like her or think on his feet like she did, but he had skills that had helped her. He'd even helped Bear once or twice, and *that* made him feel like someone special. Someone who could help save the world someday.

"Do you know who the guys are? Or their sons?"

Mandy shook her head, and he could read her frustration in the movement. "All those rich assholes look alike. Probably politicians or lawyers or judges. I've seen them around at other games. It always looked like they were up to something. I need to find out who they are."

"Do you trust anyone else enough to ask?"

"I can probably talk to Etta. And Charlie will probably help me. I laid the smackdown on his bully today."

Marcus' jaw clenched. He wasn't sure what he thought of Charlie, but he was also afraid she'd get herself in trouble. "Your dad said—"

"I know what he said." She took a deep breath, then blew it out. "I'm sorry." Her eyes implored him to believe her. "I really tried to walk away. But I didn't have much of a choice. Besides, I didn't end up getting into trouble for it."

"Really? Why?"

"The boxing coach saw the whole thing. No one disciplines Roy King without pissing off his father, but Roy isn't going to say anything because then he'll have to admit he got beat by a girl. The coach asked me to join the team."

"Are you going to?"

Mandy shrugged, but he could tell she was excited by the prospect.

"I'll check it out. I know those two guys I ran into go to all the biggest games and matches at our school, and our boxing team is pretty good. They'll be there."

"If you get some pictures, I'll be able to find more about them." He'd gotten very good at scouring the internet for any nugget of information that might prove useful to their cause. "Then maybe we can figure out what they're up to."

"Sounds like a plan."

Mandy opened her mouth to say something else, but there was a soft knock on the door before Marcus' uncle pushed it opened and entered the room.

"Hey, man. Lunch is ready." He saw the computer on Marcus' lap with Mandy's face front and center. Waggling his eyebrows, he said, "Did I interrupt?"

Marcus flushed, hoping for once that the quality of his camera was bad enough that Mandy didn't notice. "No, we were just finishing up."

"Is this the Mandy I've been hearing so much about?"

"Yes, sir."

His uncle came closer to the bed, peering at Mandy with a strange look on his face. Leaning forward, Marcus watched as something clicked into place, and then his uncle's eyes went wider than he'd ever seen them before.

"Mandy?" he repeated. "Mandy Logan?"

Mandy went stock-still, and Marcus could see her fighting the impulse to slam her computer shut. How in the hell did his uncle know who she was? Did he look her up or something? But he'd purposefully never told him Mandy's last name, just in case he got curious.

"How did you know that?" Mandy finally asked.

"Your dad and I are practically best friends."

"My dad has only one best friend."

"Jack doesn't count. They're like brothers. Besides, I've probably saved his life more than Jack has."

Mandy was so close to her camera now, her face took up the entire screen. "You really know my dad?"

His uncle's face fell. "Didn't Bear ever talk about me? Brandon

Cunningham?" Mandy's mouth went slack with recognition, but Brandon didn't appear to notice. "I'll call him up right now and give him a piece of my mind—"

"No, you can't!" Mandy said reeling back in her chair.

Brandon had been pulling his phone from his pocket, but he froze. Then his eyes narrowed and he looked between the two of them. "Why not?"

Marcus and Mandy exchanged a look, and he could see the gears turning in her head. This was someone her father trusted with his life, and apparently, they'd worked together before. Marcus couldn't help but wonder who his uncle really was. He hadn't realized Brandon knew Bear at all.

"He's on a mission," Mandy said. "He wouldn't let me come along. It's dangerous."

Brandon sobered. "I understand. Bear can take care of himself. I've seen him get out of some pretty interesting scrapes. If you do end up talking to him, tell him I'm here if he needs me."

Mandy nodded, her eyes glossy. "Thank you."

"That goes for you too, kid." Brandon's face softened. "If you're anything like your dad, then trouble probably finds you as often as it finds him."

Mandy's lips twisted into a mischievous smile. "You could say that."

10

Knowing he'd want to be behind the wheel if anything went wrong, Iris let Bear drive her car from their makeshift office in downtown Manhattan to a parking garage in the heart of the metro D.C. area. The five-hour trip was uneventful. Bear had kept his eyes peeled for any suspicious cars but hadn't spotted a single one. He'd still spent an extra forty-five minutes backtracking and taking circuitous routes just in case.

Iris had spent the entire time glued to her phone, tapping out messages and scrolling through emails and various webpages. Bear had assumed she was solidifying plans with her NSA contact. Despite his doubts the day before, he trusted her determination to find Reagan. It was everyone else he worried about.

Bear pulled into the parking garage and followed Iris' instructions to the top level. He parked in a spot cloaked in shadow. The car was a rental under a fake name. The plan was to return for it after they made contact and got the information they needed, but on the off chance they had to abandon it, the company wouldn't be able to find the woman who'd rented it in order to collect any fees.

The five-hour drive left Bear feeling kinked and knotted. He stepped out, stretched his back and legs. Iris followed suit, twisting once to the left and then the right. Bear heard her back popping and envied her flexibility. It'd been decades since his back had whispered, much less audibly popped. With the number of injuries he'd endured, he knew he should be grateful he was still standing at all, let alone breathing, but it was hard not to think back on everything he'd been capable of twenty years ago.

There was movement from the shadows surrounding the pillar next to their car. Bear pulled his gun and pointed it at the newcomer. The pupils in the center of her hazel irises dilated, and her raven hair swung around her shoulders as she took a step back. Her all-black outfit made her look more like a ghost than she was. Spotting the gun, she let out a little gasp and raised her hands, each finger stacked with silver rings. The satchel she'd been clutching fell to her hip, secured by a strap across her chest. She looked no older than twenty-five, but Bear figured her to be early- to mid-thirties.

Iris stepped forward and placed a hand on Bear's arm. "Relax. It's her."

Bear lowered his weapon, but he didn't put it away. "The hell you doing skulking in the shadows like that?"

"Got here early," the woman's said in a smoky, alluring voice. "Wanted to see when you arrived. Make sure no one was watching this spot."

"Were they?"

The woman shook her head, her hands still in the air. "All clear."

"Logan, this is Raine, my contact at the NSA." With a pointed look at his gun, Iris said, "She's here to help us."

"And how does she plan on doing that?"

"Not here." Raine hooked a thumb over her shoulder and then lowered her arms. "My car."

Raine turned her back on them and paced down the ramp. Bear and Iris were forced to follow in her wake. The young woman kept her head on a swivel, peering into the dark corners of places that might've held a threat. She was young and looked fit enough, but Bear wondered how extensive her training had been. The satchel she clutched to her chest was the right size to hold a laptop, but how about a weapon?

Two levels down, Raine stopped next to a silver Nissan Altima. She drew her keys from her pocket to unlock it and then turned to Bear. She tossed the keys. He caught them with one hand, then raised a single eyebrow in question.

"Iris said you have a hard drive you need to open. I can't look at it and drive at the same time. And you look like someone who needs to be in charge."

Iris laughed. Bear stowed his gun. He could recognize an olive branch when it slapped him in his face. He turned to Iris. "Sit in the back with her in case she needs help."

Iris rolled her eyes at the less than subtle directive to keep an eye on the woman, but she did as she was told. When they were all in place, Bear turned on the car but twisted in his seat to look at the young woman. "What's your stake in all this?"

Raine looked to Iris, who nodded, before turning back to Bear. "I've heard whispers of Mr. Reagan for years. My superiors have done everything they can to find him, but he's always ten steps ahead. He seems to enjoy leading us on wild goose chases. Every time we think we're close to finding out who he is and what his plans are, he slips away. No amount of physical or digital evidence has led us to his doorstep. He's a ghost."

"Ghosts aren't real," Bear said. "But Reagan is. Flesh and blood."

Raine nodded, her eyes wide. Not in terror, Bear realized, but in wonder. This was a giant puzzle she wanted to solve.

"Reagan has a lot of people on his side, across all government bodies and agencies. I've heard rumors about a corrupt ring of officials and of dissension in the ranks, both in the NSA and elsewhere."

This was the first he was hearing about that. Everything they'd found so far had led him to believe that Reagan's people would rather kill themselves than risk ending up on the other side of the equation. So far, Reagan had presented a united front.

Bear looked at Iris. "Did you know about this?"

"If I had, I would've chased that lead down a long time ago." Iris had an edge to her voice. She looked at Raine. "Do you have any information about the dissenters? That could be our way in."

"I don't know much. From what I gather, Reagan is everywhere. The NSA, the FBI, the CIA. His plans are airtight. Reagan is patient and methodical. He doesn't make mistakes."

"Trust me," Bear said, "you're not telling us anything we don't already know."

Raine's hands shook a little as she rested them on the computer bag in her lap. "Vincent Ortiz. He's a Chief Technology Officer for the Pentagon, and I know for a fact he's traveling to a meeting in Chicago today."

"A meeting for what?"

"I'm not sure. There was a discrepancy in his travel calendar. This meeting wasn't on the official one. It stood out to me. I told my boss. He looked into it, but said it was just a simple mistake. I think he was lying to me. I—" She looked at Iris with wide eyes. "I think he might be compromised."

Iris laid a comforting hand on Raine's arm. "You did the right thing telling us about it."

Bear pointed to the woman's laptop. "Is that enough to get into the drive?"

"Can I see it?" Raine replied, and when Iris handed the drive over, Raine's eyebrows shot up. "Who did this belong to?"

"Silas Marino."

Raine looked up at the pair of them and laughed. "Then no, my computer is not enough to get into it. Silas is one of the best."

"Was," Bear said. "He's dead."

Raine's face paled. "How?"

"Reagan," Iris replied. "It wasn't pretty. But he led us to this. It must be important."

Raine nodded, a little bit of color coming back into her cheeks. "I have a space across the river in Crystal City. Secure. It'll have the tools I'll need."

"I'll stay with her while you go to Chicago," Iris said. Bear opened his mouth to argue—he didn't like the idea of splitting up—but Iris didn't let him interrupt. "I could be spotted. I have no idea how many eyes are on me. I'm having enough trouble keeping my boss out of my hair. You have a better chance. Besides, I want to know the second we get into the drive."

"And you don't trust me." Raine eased away. "At least not enough to be alone with it."

"It's the smart thing to do."

"I don't blame you."

"Fine," Bear said. "I'll head to the airport, then you can take the car back to Crystal City. But we stay in contact the entire time." Bear twisted around in his seat but looked at Raine in the rearview mirror. "And I want to know everything you have on Vincent Ortiz."

11

MANDY, ETTA, AND CHARLIE GATHERED AROUND THE COMPUTER IN THE dimly lit classroom that doubled as headquarters for the A.V. Club. The other students and their teacher had left ten minutes ago. Mandy had wasted no time telling Charlie about her run-in with the two men on her way to the volleyball game. Etta noticed Charlie's swollen lip. Mandy told her about the fight with Roy King.

"He invited you to join the boxing team?" Etta's brown curls bounced with every shake of her head. She was still a little upset with Mandy for ditching her at the game, but now her chocolate eyes were wide as saucers. "Just like that?"

Mandy shrugged like it was no big deal, but she had trouble keeping the excitement off her face. "Better than getting in trouble."

"You're going to be seeing a lot more of Roy now," Charlie said. "You need to be careful."

"I can handle him." Mandy believed it down to her bones. She'd faced off against worse. "I'm more worried about those two guys. They really sounded like they were blackmailing someone."

"Why are we trying to figure out what they're up to?" Etta asked. "I mean, what can we do about it?"

A chuckle sounded from the computer's speakers, and all three of them turned to look at Marcus, who sat in his bedroom at his uncle's house, ready to help them with their extracurricular research project.

It had been a tough decision to introduce Marcus to Charlie and Etta, but Mandy had deemed it necessary if she wanted to get to the bottom of this. Etta knew more about the kids at school and their parents than anyone else, and Charlie was obsessed with building his own technology. Both of those skills could be invaluable to her. But Marcus was the real asset.

Her guy in the chair.

As long as they could keep the activity hidden from his uncle.

Mandy still couldn't believe Marcus' uncle was *the* Brandon Cunningham. She'd heard dozens if not hundreds of stories about the man over the years. Bear had no idea Marcus was related to his friend, and she couldn't wait to tell him. Then again, that could cause more trouble than it was worth. She had to walk a fine line here, getting Marcus to use Brandon for her own means without tipping off her dad that she was definitely sticking her nose where it didn't belong.

"What's so funny?" Charlie asked, frowning at Marcus.

"This is what Mandy does." Marcus shrugged and wore an unfamiliar haughty expression on his face. "You'll figure that out soon enough."

Mandy watched as a strange look passed between Charlie and Marcus, but she didn't bother analyzing it too closely. She had more important things to deal with. "It sounded like they were going to hurt someone," Mandy said, turning to Etta. "And I can't stand by and let that happen."

"Yeah," Etta replied, skepticism drenched her voice. "But what can *we* do about it? No one will believe us."

"If we have evidence they will," Mandy said. "Which is where you three come into play." Mandy described in detail the two men she'd run into in the hallway yesterday. "Do you have any idea who they are?"

Etta laughed a little, then looked at Mandy like she was surprised she wasn't in on the joke. "You're kidding, right? The blond one is Raymond King. Roy's father."

Mandy groaned. "Of course he is."

"And the other one sounds like it could be Lochlan Reid, Jory's dad."

"What does he do?"

"I think he's a lawyer or something," Etta said. Keyboard clicks came from Marcus' earpiece as he took notes. "They're always at all the games and matches together."

Mandy knew the chance of Etta knowing the answer to her next question was slim, but she had to ask. "Do you have any idea who they might be blackmailing?"

Etta frowned. "All the parents are friendly with each other, at least in public. I've seen those two talking to half the crowd at the volleyball matches. It could be anyone."

"They said they were going to make a believer out of him," Mandy said. "*And* they were talking about the person's son."

"Who must be another student," Charlie said. "That narrows it down, but it still leaves us with a lot of options."

"If they're trying to get this other person to do something for them, maybe he shows up at the games too," Mandy said. "We need a way to monitor them."

Charlie sat up straighter. "We can film them!"

Etta rolled her eyes, her curls shimmering against the bright blue computer screen light. "Yeah, that won't be obvious."

Charlie waved his hands excitedly. "No, I mean the matches. We can do it under the guise of a project for the A.V. Club. Film the boxing matches and try to catch them on tape. If nothing else, it'll help us see who they're talking to most."

"What's the point in videotaping them if we can't hear what they're saying?" Marcus asked. "Do you know how to read lips?"

"No, but I can rig up some recording devices and tape them to their seats. With the right software, I can separate their voices from the background noise. I can do it right here on the school computers."

Etta leaned in. "Won't that be obvious?"

"Not if the devices are small enough." Mandy scrunched her face, knowing Etta wouldn't like what she had to say next. "Since I'm on the team and Charlie will be filming them, you'll have to keep an eye on the mics and make sure no one tampers with them."

"Okay." Etta tried not to look scared, but Mandy heard the way she gulped. "I think I can do it."

Mandy turned to Charlie. "If we're caught, we're all going to be in big trouble."

It was Charlie's turn to gulp. "Then we better not get caught. I'll just need a couple of days."

"The sooner the better." Mandy glanced at the clock on the wall. "My first match is tonight, and we have no idea how soon these guys are going to make their move."

12

Flying to Chicago solo was strange. Bear felt like he'd forgotten something back in D.C.

Bear and Iris had been in each other's space during every free moment they had over the last two months. Whenever Iris could get away from the office, she would meet up with Bear and they would pour over their options for tracking down Reagan. Even when they traveled by themselves, they'd meet back up to tackle their next problem together.

After all these years, Bear still took issue with flying. Short distances or long, he clutched at his armrests upon takeoff and landing. Sweat gathered on his brow. His hands and feet tingled. His lungs tightened. His abs knotted. He'd faced the worst adversaries, been witness to horrific crimes, and flying in an airplane was the one thing that made him panic.

Go figure.

The plane landed at O'Hare in under two hours, pulling into the gate a few minutes ahead of schedule after the longest taxi known to man. The first thing he did was message Iris to check up on the drive. She replied immediately. Raine had managed to crack the encryption and open the drive, but each folder was secured with its own password. She was working through them all first so they could peruse the information without having to stop and start.

Relief flooded through Bear, not just from being on solid ground again, but from gaining traction in their investigation. He just hoped that whatever Silas had on that drive would be useful to them. If not, then they'd have to hang all their hopes on tracking down Vincent Ortiz.

Raine had given him the basics about Ortiz. As a Chief Technology Officer at the Pentagon, he was responsible for the research and development of prototypes that would eventually make their way to the United States military. He was exactly the kind of person Reagan would want on his team—someone connected and influential enough to get done what Reagan needed.

He had been in the Pentagon for six years and had a wife and son at home. He didn't often travel long distances for work, but his personal calendar said he was meeting with a supplier to negotiate prices. Raine had been smart to flag it as suspicious, not only because of the discrepancy in schedules, but also because that didn't seem like a job suitable for a CTO.

Ortiz was staying at the Waldorf on Walton. The meeting would take place at DuSable Harbor, of all places. Either the supplier was selling boat parts, or they wanted a private place to meet. One was a hell of a lot more likely than the other. He'd find out soon enough. First, he needed lodging.

Bear found a motel that took cash and rented a room there. He stuck around long enough to dump his belongings on his bed and splash some water on his face. Since he'd flown commercial, he had left his pistol with Iris back in D.C. and didn't have enough time prior to the meeting to procure one from any of his contacts. It wasn't ideal, but he'd seen a picture of Ortiz. Overpowering him wouldn't be an issue.

He didn't spend more than five minutes in his rustic motel room before making his way to the Waldorf and waiting across the street with a fresh cup of coffee in one hand, and a rolled-up newspaper in the other. It took about ten minutes for him to spot Ortiz leaving the hotel. The man hopped into a taxi that drove off to the harbor. Bear followed.

Traffic was light enough that he could keep Ortiz in sight along the way.

When they arrived at the Harbor, Bear made the driver pass Ortiz's stop before handing the man a couple bills and stepping out of the car. He shoved his hands in his jacket pockets and walked back toward Ortiz's drop off location. The breeze from the lake was much colder than anything in New York City, and he regretted not bringing a heavier jacket.

From a distance, Bear watched Ortiz hurry down one of the docks. Even from his vantage point, dozens of yards away, Bear could sense the terror emanating from the man. He kept looking over his shoulder, and when he finally got to the ship, he stood there for a solid minute before squaring up and climbing aboard a small yacht. If Bear didn't already believe this wasn't a simple supplier's meeting, Ortiz's behavior confirmed it. But if he was working for Reagan, why was he so terrified to meet whoever was on that boat? The only possible answer was that Ortiz was being coerced. And if that were true, then Bear had a golden opportunity in front of him.

Twenty minutes later, Ortiz emerged from the ship looking as terrified as he had before the meeting. Bear wasted no time before stalking toward the man, meeting him just as he stepped off the docks and back on solid ground.

Bear plastered a smile on his face, swinging his arms open. "Vincent!"

Ortiz looked up sharply, his eyes narrowing in suspicion and then growing wide as he took in Bear's large frame. His voice was shaky and low as he asked, "D-Do I know you?"

"Vinny." Bear forced his lips into a cartoonish pout. "You don't remember me?"

"No, I'm sorry. I don't." He tried to sidestep Bear. "If you'll excuse me, I have to go—"

"You're gonna want to hear what I have to say, Vinny."

Ortiz stopped and looked up at Bear, his eyes swimming with concern. "Who the hell are you?"

"A friend." Bear threw an arm around the smaller man's shoulders. It nearly knocked Ortiz off his feet. "And I'd love to catch up."

"Are you w-with *him*?"

"With who?"

"Mr. Reagan," Ortiz whispered. Bear could feel him shudder and his gaze darted around like saying the name would summon the devil himself.

Bear looked down at the man, calculating his options. Everything they'd read had suggested Ortiz was working with Reagan. But it appeared he had taken this meeting under duress.

"I'm not with Reagan," Bear said. "I'm against him."

Ortiz sagged a little, but his eyes were still wild. "It's not safe. If I'm seen with you, the consequences will—"

The sound of a bullet was nearly deafening as it passed Ortiz's head so closely that his hair ruffled from its trajectory. It embedded itself in the stone of the building behind them, making no more noise than that of a large rock hitting cement. Ortiz turned to look at the sound, but Bear grabbed him by the collar and tugged.

"Move!"

Another bullet made its way towards them before they made it two steps, this time almost grazing Bear's thigh before it embedded itself in the concrete underfoot. The lack of a crowd made it easier to target them, but at least the bullets wouldn't hit any innocent bystanders. A small consolation as far as Bear was concerned.

Another bullet raced past, but Bear and Ortiz were running at full speed now, zigzagging toward the street to put a building between them and the shooter. Bear wished he had his gun with him, but it wouldn't have done any good anyway. His little pistol didn't have the same range as the rifle spitting bullets at them.

"I told you!" Ortiz yelled. "I told you it was too dangerous!"

Bear said nothing. He led the other man at a full sprint toward the road and the taxi waiting there for him. He was glad to see the man hadn't just driven off with the wad of cash he'd given him to secure his services for the next two hours.

Bear yanked the door open and shoved Ortiz inside before climbing in.

"Go, go, go!" Bear yelled at the driver, who looked at them in stunned silence, confusion and fear written plainly across his face. The back window shattered as a bullet hit it, and the two other men yelled in surprise. Bear pointed straight ahead. "Drive!"

The driver slammed his foot on the gas, the force of the momentum pinning Bear and Ortiz against their seatbacks. Vincent had been smart enough to keep his head down, though it was harder for Bear given his size. The driver swore profusely as he drove as fast as traffic would allow.

After a few blocks, Ortiz sat up and straightened his suit. When he looked at Bear, the fear in his eyes was mixed with bitterness. "I hope you know what you just got us into."

13

Mandy had to leave A.V. Club shortly after her chat with Etta, Charlie, and Marcus to meet Mr. Foley in the training room. It smelled like ten-day old gym shorts in there. He'd gone over the basics of the sport with her. Knowing how to fight was different than knowing how to participate in a boxing match, but Mandy had picked up on the rules quickly enough. As a last-minute addition to the roster that night, there was only one opponent she could fight, and Mr. Foley had told Mandy point-blank that she probably wouldn't win. Her opponent was in the same weight class as Mandy, but she'd been training for years.

It wasn't worth telling Mr. Foley that she'd faced bigger and stronger opponents before. That would raise too many questions. She didn't want Bear to get in trouble for child endangerment or something stupid like that. Besides, as fun as boxing sounded, she was mostly doing this so she could keep an eye on Raymond King and the other parents.

The gloves she had to wear were cumbersome. After a half hour with the punching bag, she had gotten used to them. It certainly beat using her bare knuckles. She'd get far fewer bruises this way. And not as many looks from other people when she showed up somewhere looking like she'd gotten into a brawl with someone much bigger than her.

The number one rule Mandy had to remember was that she could only use her fists. Every instinct told her to use her legs to take Mr. Foley down when she did some light sparring with him. They were far stronger than her arms. It would take him by surprise. But using the legs was more than a little illegal in the boxing arena. If she kicked out at her opponent, she'd be disqualified.

There were two other girls on the boxing team, Amy and Lelani, but they as well as the boys ignored Mandy. Roy King shot her a look that could've melted the skin from her bones. She had to work hard not to antagonize him. She was nervous enough about the match ahead of her. It did give her some sense of satisfaction to see the bruise blossoming under his left eye. Under the watchful gaze of Mr. Foley, Roy turned his back on her. Was he focused, like the rest of the team?

As the other kids went up for their fights one at a time, Mandy split her focus between the ring and the stands on the other side. They were full, but it wasn't hard to pick out Raymond King and Lochlan Reid. They looked just as they had the other night. A thin woman sat next to Mr. Reid, her red hair pinned back, away from her angled face. She looked hawkish, and Mandy could feel her gaze on the team even from across the room. This woman would miss very little. Was she part of the inner circle?

Cheers sounded around the gymnasium as the first kid on their team won his match. Mandy was still trying to work out how to keep track of the points, but she figured it didn't much matter at the moment. All she had to do was block her opponent's hits and make sure the other girl was unable to do the same to her.

Hit her more than she hits you, Mr. Foley had said.

Yeah, Mandy could do that.

Her eyes found Etta in the crowd, sitting by herself near the top of the stands. Her objective had been to get as close as she could to the group of parents. It appeared she'd been beaten out by a large group of students from the grade above them. There was no way she'd be able to overhear anything Raymond and Lochlan were saying. When Etta gave her a sad little wave in apology, Mandy nodded her head in understanding.

Without the mics, they had to rely on the camera to do most of the heavy lifting. It might not be able to capture the conversation happening in the stands, but analyzing the footage for body language could help point them in the right direction. Especially if they could figure out which other parents might be in on the plan.

Mr. Foley had been happy to have Charlie record the matches and had even requested copies of the footage so the team could analyze each other's forms. Luckily, Charlie had the perfect setup to capture the ring and the group of parents beyond. No one would know he was pulling double duty and recording both, especially if he edited out the moments where he zoomed in on the audience.

Before Mandy knew it, Mr. Foley stood in front of her, hands on his hips and an excited gleam in his eyes. "You're up, Davis. Ready for this?"

Mandy swallowed her fear. She wouldn't let Roy or anyone else see that she was afraid. "Born ready."

"I like your attitude, kid. Let's roll."

Her coach led her to the ring and lifted the heavy blue ropes so she could step inside. Her opponent was already there, jumping up and down to loosen her limbs and rolling her head from side to side. She was a stocky girl with her hair pulled back into cornrows. Her arms were a lot bigger than Mandy's, but Mr. Foley had showed her some of the other girl's tapes. She was good, but Mandy had agility and real-world experience on her side.

Unable to help herself, Mandy's eyes drifted from the girl in front of her to the group of parents in the bleachers. Raymond King had his eyes locked on her. Was she imagining the malice there? Did he have any idea what she was up to? Did he know she was the one who had given his son that bruise on his face?

The referee caught Mandy's attention and gestured her to the center of the ring, where he made the two girls tap gloves before walking back to their corners. "Davis versus Okoro," he shouted to the crowd.

A few seconds later, the bell rang. The fight was on.

Mandy put up her hands and bounced on the balls of her feet, assessing the other girl. Okoro did the same, sending out an exploratory jab that Mandy dodged with ease. They circled each other for a moment, each throwing a punch just to warm up and get a feel for their opponent.

But as confident as Mandy was in her ability, she'd never been on a stage like this. It was hard to concentrate with the bright lights and murmuring crowd. People talked and laughed and shouted encouragement. She could see Okoro's teammates on the other side, watching the two of them circle each other. Mandy knew her teammates were probably doing the same. Even if none of them were interested in being friendly, she knew they were all curious as to why Mr. Foley had brought her onto the team in the middle of the season.

Against her will, Mandy's eyes traveled to Roy's father, who sat with his arms crossed and his gaze locked on her. There was now no doubt in her mind that Raymond knew she'd been the one to hit his son, and his gaze made the lights feel all the hotter. Her vision narrowed to just the two of them, and Okoro took advantage of the distraction.

A blinding pain against her left cheek drew tears from Mandy's eyes, and she stumbled back a step at the force of the blow. Instinct had her raising her arm to block Okoro's next jab, and for the next minute, she was on the defensive. She had no issue blocking Okoro's hits, but she couldn't find an opening to land any of her own.

Anger swelled in Mandy's chest. What would Bear think of her distraction? He'd taught her better than this. Sure, Raymond King was the bigger threat, but he wasn't the one trying to knock her out at the moment.

Channeling her fear and anger, Mandy stepped into the next blow, forcing the other girl to move backwards. Throwing Okoro off her momentum, Mandy blocked another jab and then threw a right hook into the side of the other girl's helmet. It was so fast, Okoro didn't have a chance to block it. And that was all the opportunity Mandy needed.

Throwing a combination of jabs at Okoro's torso, Mandy surprised the other girl with a left hook and a right uppercut. As Okoro stumbled backward in surprise, Mandy took another step forward and put every ounce of her strength into her next hit. Her fist connected with the side of the girl's face hard enough that it knocked Okoro to the canvas. The crowd was deadly silent as Mandy stood over her opponent, waiting for the girl to get back up. But Okoro just lay there, dazed, until the referee declared the round over.

When Mandy stepped back into her corner, her eyes locked with Raymond King. She'd figure out what he was up to. Just like she knew she'd win the next round against her opponent. First, she'd beat Okoro. Then she'd come for him.

A grin spread across Mandy's face as the bell rang a second time and she raised her fists against the inevitable.

14

MONARCH LEANED BACK IN HIS CHAIR, STARING INTO THE DARKNESS OF the room, recalling how his ambitions had led him down this path. He had one rule in life: *Handle yourself.*

That mantra had served him well for decades, and it was why he'd landed a seat in the Virginia State Senate. Sure, he was charismatic and good looking and intelligent—some would even say cunning—but at the end of the day, he wasn't afraid to get his hands dirty. If a problem needed solving, he preferred to do it himself. That way, he had no one else to blame.

It was one of the reasons Mr. Reagan had sought him out. One of the reasons he was one of the few people—perhaps the *only* person—who knew Reagan's true identity. Monarch handled himself, and he did it well. He'd never needed to call up Mr. Reagan and say that he'd failed. Never needed to—until today.

Knowing he was only delaying the inevitable, Monarch picked up the phone from the middle of his smooth, solid desk and dialed the familiar number. He'd been in contact with Reagan for years, and yet this was the first time he'd had to call his boss with bad news. He didn't know the protocol, and that terrified him. He wasn't afraid to admit it, at least to himself, in the quiet of his own office.

The line rang twice before Reagan answered. "This is unexpected."

"Apologies for the unscheduled call." Monarch did everything in his power to keep from stuttering. What was it about Mr. Reagan that set his nerves on edge? He'd never been afraid of another person in his entire life. Then again, he'd never met someone like Reagan. Someone that he knew, deep down, he'd never be able to beat. Not with charm or money or physical strength. That was a losing battle on every front. "There's been a problem."

"Oh?"

The one-word question was full of languid surprise. Even Reagan knew this was out of the ordinary. Monarch gritted his teeth in frustration, then relaxed his jaw and leaned back in his chair. The only way out was through. "Ortiz attended the meeting this afternoon, but there was a problem upon his departure." Monarch paused long enough to see if Reagan would say anything. He didn't. "Logan was there. One of our guys tried to take him out and failed. He got away. Ortiz went with him."

"Willingly?"

"It seems like it."

"How did Logan know about Ortiz?"

"Raine Bauer. It appears she didn't trust her superior's judgement when she noticed the discrepancy in Ortiz's travel calendar. She's with Duvall and Logan now."

Monarch tried not to fidget as the silence stretched on.

Finally, Reagan said, "They found something at Silas' apartment."

"I can send some men—"

"They'll all be killed." Reagan sounded flippant, even bored. "No matter how many you send, how good they are, Logan will kill them all."

Monarch gritted his teeth against the accusation. He'd hired the best men in the industry as his personal security team, and their connections to other more ruthless soldiers were unparalleled. He could have the best in the world descend upon Logan and Duvall, wiping their existence from the face of the earth without leaving a trace.

"They're the best—"

"They're not the best!" Reagan's voice went from bored to furious in the span of a single breath. "Logan is the best. He always has been. I've seen it firsthand. Do you doubt me?"

"Of course not—"

"Then don't question me again." Just like that, Reagan's tone was neutral again. "No, Logan is only a distraction at this juncture. We need to move up our timeline. Give them something else to worry about while we finish what we started."

Monarch gulped, hoping Reagan couldn't hear it on the other end of the line. "What would you have me do?"

"The kid. Ortiz's son. Take him."

Monarch's stomach twisted at the thought. His son knew little Vinny. They weren't friends, exactly, but they'd been going to the same school for years. He'd originally planned on sending Vinny home with a message, making it clear to Ortiz that they would go through his kid if they had to. But that's all he'd planned on doing.

The silence must've gone on for too long because Reagan said, "Is there a problem?"

"No. There's no problem." What other answer could he provide? Monarch licked his lips, which were suddenly dry. "What do you want us to do to him?"

"Nothing for now," Reagan said. "Just make sure Ortiz knows you have him. Logan will feel responsible, and it'll give us enough time to finish the next step."

The words tasted like ash in his mouth, but he voiced them anyway. "Consider it done."

"Ortiz's dissension will not go unnoticed. Once he's back in our grasp, kill them both." Reagan paused for a moment, as though pondering what to have for lunch. "And kill his wife too. No loose ends."

"No loose ends," Monarch replied, but he didn't relish the task at all.

15

As soon as the taxi pulled up to Bear's motel room, he tossed a wad of bills into the passenger seat and climbed out. Ortiz had barely finished shutting the door before the driver peeled out, glass falling from the broken window onto the street behind him.

"Is this where you're staying?" Ortiz looked the dilapidated building over with a mixture of apprehension and relief.

"Not anymore," Bear said. "You have your phone on you?"

Ortiz nodded, bringing it out of his pocket. "The only thing—hey!"

Bear took the phone and dropped it to the ground, slamming his heel down on it twice before it came apart. "It's for your own safety. Come on. We don't have much time."

Ortiz looked up at him in disbelief and bristled behind as Bear walked away from the scene.

He returned to his room and gathered his belongings, then called for another cab. He told the man to drive them to the other end of the city, toward a second motel even more run-down than the first. The entire way, Bear glanced over his shoulder, searching for any vehicles that looked like they might be tailing them. Ortiz flinched each time Bear turned around. The driver kept peering at them in the rearview mirror with questions in his eyes.

When they pulled up to their destination, Bear paid the man and led Ortiz to the front counter where they secured a single room with two double beds. The bored man behind the desk didn't even look up at them while he handed over their room keys and Bear dropped a wad of cash on the counter.

Once Bear found their room, he did a preliminary search while Ortiz sat on the edge of his bed, wringing his fingers until they turned white. When Bear returned, he gestured to the front door. "I need to make a phone call. Stay here."

Ortiz acknowledged the order with a single nod of his head, not meeting Bear's eyes. There was a chance the man would try to sneak out the bathroom window, but Bear didn't think so. He knew what he was involved in. Knew that Bear had saved his life back there on the pier. Even if he was upset about his phone, the man was smart enough to surmise why it had to be destroyed.

As terrified as Ortiz was, Bear was his only lifeline.

Bear slipped out the door and stepped to the side, not wanting to stray more than a few feet in case Ortiz decided to surprise him by making a run for it. He surveyed the parking lot, taking in the scene for a moment, cataloguing the cars and the people coming and going. When he was sure he wasn't being watched, he pulled out his phone and dialed the familiar number.

Mandy answered on the second ring. "Bear!"

"Hey, sweetie." Bear's entire body flooded with relief. He knew she was safe at school, but it didn't stop him from worrying. "How are you?"

"I'm great." Her words came out breathy and excited. "Guess what?"

"Chicken butt?"

He could practically hear her eyes roll over the phone. "No, seriously."

"What?"

"I won my first boxing match!"

"That's great!" Confusion and pride warred with each other inside Bear's mind. "When the hell did you join the boxing team?"

Mandy laughed. "Today. *Kind* of a funny story, but I'll tell you later. How's everything going on your end?"

Mandy was dodging his question, but he didn't have time to pull the answer from her. "Complicated. But we're making progress. Just needed to hear your voice."

"I'm glad you called." Mandy's breathless excitement turned into something more subdued and wistful. "I wish you could visit. To see me fight."

"Hey, I'll try, okay? But right now, things are—"

"Complicated." Mandy laughed, and even though it was tinged with sadness, she understood what he couldn't say over the line. "I know. Are you safe?"

"Yeah." The half-truth lodged in Bear's throat. It had been close today. Not that he hadn't had been close before. But it wasn't like when he was younger. He'd only been fighting for himself. And he could bounce back much faster. "I'm safe. I'll call again soon, okay?"

"Okay. Love you, Bear."

"Love you too, kiddo."

He hung up, blinking back the emotions that had gathered in his eyes. He had the best kid in the world, and it killed him to be so far away from her, fighting someone else's battle. But he owed Iris for saving Mandy's life on that bridge two months ago, a debt he could never truly repay.

Looking back down at his phone, Bear dialed Iris' number. She picked up on the first ring.

"What happened?"

If he'd had any humor left in his body, he would've chuckled at her knowing question. "I made contact."

"You were just supposed to observe."

"Situation changed." All the patience and happiness at hearing Mandy's voice had drained away, leaving the cold, calculating soldier who would get him through this situation unscathed so he could go back home to his daughter. "Ortiz is terrified. I could see it from a mile away. Whatever he's doing, he wants no part of it. I approached him, and someone shot at us."

Iris' tone turned gentle. "Are you hurt?"

"No, we both got away fine. Physically, at least. Ortiz is shaken up."

"Have you talked to him yet?"

"No. I needed to talk to Mandy first." He choked on the rising emotion. "Had to hear her voice. Then I called you."

"She's doing okay?" Iris asked.

"She joined the boxing team. Won her first match."

"Not surprised. She's one tough kid."

"The toughest." Sometimes he hated that life had forced Mandy to be so strong. Other days it felt like the greatest accomplishment of his life that she could handle whatever anyone threw at her. "Any progress with the drive?"

"Actually yeah." There was a ruffling noise and the sounds of fingers flying over a keyboard grew louder. Bear pictured her moving closer to Raine as the other woman hunched over her computer, furiously hacking away at whatever encryptions Silas had set up on the device. "There's a lot of information to go through here," Iris said. "I think we found something big."

"Something useful?"

"Something dangerous. Silas has a list of about a dozen current undercover CIA operatives stationed around the world. Real names, addresses, background information, missions, you name it."

"If Silas had that information, we have to assume Reagan does, too."

"This is a big step up from pharmaceutical companies and drug rings, Bear. What is he planning?"

"I have no idea."

Silence crawled across the line and sat between them as Bear thought through what Reagan would do with that list of operatives. The information was invaluable. Would he sell it to the highest bidder? Use it as blackmail against the United States government? Release it to the public? The drug operations had netted Reagan a lot of money, but this, more than anything, felt like his endgame.

But why the CIA? Were they involved in something related to Reagan, or had he chosen them at random? Was the CIA just one part of the puzzle, or is this what he'd been after the whole time? Was it about gaining influence, or was it about revenge?

With that singular thought, lightning struck, and Bear knew what he had to do next.

"We need to visit an old associate of mine." It was the last thing he wanted to do, but his gut told him it was the right move.

"Who?" she asked.

"Daniel Thorne."

16

It was just before dawn when Vincent Ortiz tried to escape the motel room.

Bear had always been a light sleeper. It had been drilled into him since the day he'd enlisted at eighteen. Years of practice meant he could fall asleep and wake up at the drop of a hat. It also meant he could survive on just a couple of hours each night. Out of the myriad of skills he had honed, this one had proved the most useful.

"I wouldn't do that," Bear said, not even rolling over as Vincent crept past the end of his bed.

The man froze. "I-I was just going to the bathroom."

"Bathroom's in the opposite direction." Bear sat up where he'd fallen asleep on top of the covers. "Look, I'm not going to hold you against your will. But you should know that you're a lot safer with me than on your own."

"And what about my family?" For the first time, Vincent sounded more angry than scared. "Who's going to protect them?"

Bear stood and stretched. The pop in his shoulders sent relief through the rest of his body. "If Reagan sent someone to kill you and your family, do you think you'd be able to protect them?"

Vincent's silence was answer enough.

"I need you to tell me what you know about Mr. Reagan and what he's planning. Then I can help you and your family get out of town and lay low for a while. Until all this blows over."

Vincent looked at Bear, studying his face as though trying to read his life story in the wrinkles and scars written across his skin. "Who are you?"

"Long story." Bear sighed as he sat down on the edge of the bed. "Suffice it to say that I've run into a few of Mr. Reagan's operations over the last year. Caused some trouble for him. Now I'm on his radar. I plan on taking him out before he has the chance to do the same to me."

An unhinged laugh bubbled out of Vincent's mouth. "Do you have any idea who Mr. Reagan is? What he's capable of? You're insane."

"It's what I do."

Vincent stared at him, but Bear couldn't tell if it was in awe or trepidation. "Those men shooting at us. That was for you?"

"Could've been either of us. I know what *I* did to piss them off, but what about you?"

Vincent sat on the edge of the opposite bed. He stared down at his palms, as though pondering what they'd done to get him to this point. He'd been too shocked to talk last night, but it looked like reality had sunk in during the witching hours. "Mr. Reagan wanted me to use a specific supplier for weapons development for the military. When I did a background check, I found ties to several international crime organizations. I had to deny the application."

"Have you spoken to Reagan directly?" Bear found himself leaning forward in anticipation. "Do you know who he is? Where to find him?"

Vincent shook his head. "I was approached by someone I thought was a friend of mine. Or at least a friendly associate. Raymond King. I looked into the company they wanted me to use, and then told them why I had to reject them. Ray wasn't happy. He asked me to reconsider. Told me my family would benefit from the windfall this would net me. The threat was implied."

"Is that why you took the meeting today?"

"Yes." Vincent finally looked up from his hands. "I was to meet with a representative of the company. I didn't know what else to do. If I agreed to the deal, I'd be compromising my integrity, not to mention risking my job and my reputation. But if I didn't agree to it, I'd risk my family's life."

"Considering you were shot at a couple minutes after leaving that meeting, I'm guessing you refused?"

Vincent stood and took a step toward the door. "I just couldn't do it. You see why I have to leave? I have to get to my family. Before something happens."

Bear mirrored Vincent's movement toward the door and put his hands up to placate the other man. "Whoa. Hold on. Let's think this through. You're in the same predicament you were a couple minutes ago. If you return to your family, you won't be able to stop Reagan's men. I know people who can. But I need you to tell me everything you know about his operation."

"I don't know anything." Vincent was shaking now, but whether it was from fear or restraining himself from bolting out the door, Bear didn't know.

"You know more than you think," Bear said. "What's the prototype you're working on?"

"I-I can't tell you that." Vincent looked at the door and back again. "It's classified."

"The only way I can stop Reagan is if I know what he's up to. Right now, you're the biggest lead I have."

"And if I refuse to tell you? What will you do to me?"

"Nothing." Bear shrugged, dropping his hands to his side. "I'm not going to keep you here against your will. I'll still help you protect your family. But the best way to keep them safe is to stop whatever Reagan is planning. If we can distract him long enough to hide your family, you all can lay low while this blows over."

"Reagan's network is huge. Raymond King is a state senator. I know he's got the FBI and the CIA in his pocket. And there's plenty I don't know about. You're one man. What makes you think you can stop him?"

"It's what I do," Bear said again. "I hate to put you in this position, but you've got to make the call. I can't do it without you."

Vincent chewed on his lip, looking to the door again. When his shoulders sagged a little, Bear knew he had him. "You look like the kind of guy who knows what LAWS are."

"Lethal autonomous weapons systems."

"We've been developing them for years to varying degrees of success. In almost all cases, they're not exactly autonomous. A human being must give the final command to attack. The newest versions are smaller, faster, more durable, longer lasting—and one-hundred percent self-governing."

Bear's eyebrows rose into his hairline. "Are they in use?"

"Not yet. We're still developing the software. It's good, but not perfect. I thought Ray had handed me the solution on a silver platter. A software company named Victoria Industries that appeared to be a cut above the rest. Their demo was spectacular. But when I ran a background check on the owner and delved into the company's history, I found a sea of red flags."

"What kind of red flags?"

"The kind that told me they weren't a trustworthy company. Fines and citations, rumors, that sort of thing. The trail didn't lead back to a neon sign, but I'm not an idiot. I think Victoria Industries sells their products to the highest bidder. I saw enough to decide not to hand over a considerable amount of money for their software and tie the Pentagon to a company like them. Ray was not pleased. He asked me to reconsider, saying his associate wouldn't be happy, that my actions would have consequences."

"You mean Mr. Reagan."

Vincent nodded. "Not the first time I've heard the name, but the first time I've been contacted by one of his people. I knew what could happen if I said no, but I figured if I died for the right reason, I'd go out on my own terms. And my wife and son would be set for life."

"Who did you meet yesterday?"

"He said his name was Bishop." Vincent looked up at the ceiling, his gaze distant. "Big guy with short brown hair. Wore a suit. Seemed expensive. More soldier than CEO."

"You think he was there to convince you to take the deal."

"Yeah, and they weren't being subtle. But I listened to what he said, told him no and to never contact me again, and walked out of there without an issue."

"Until someone tried to put a bullet in your head."

"They only did that once you showed up."

Bear rubbed his jaw. The man had a point. If the negotiator hadn't killed Vincent on the spot, that meant they still needed him. Those bullets could've been warning shots. Or maybe they had been for Bear after all.

Bear switched his train of thought. There was one more lead to follow. "Do you know the name Daniel Thorne?"

"No. Should I? Who is he?"

"Dangerous. And our next lead." Bear pulled out his phone and dialed Iris' number again. "But first, let's get your family somewhere safe."

17

IT WAS BRIGHT AND EARLY WHEN MARCUS GOT A NOTIFICATION FROM Mandy, asking if he could video chat with her. He was exhausted from staying up way too late the night before, and his eyes still hurt from staring at his computer for hours on end. Curiosity got the better of him. He'd only exchanged a quick message or two with Mandy since their meeting with Etta and Charlie. He wanted to hear firsthand about her match.

He sat up in bed, returned his glasses to his face, and pulled his computer onto his lap, squinting against the bright light emanating from the screen and using one eye and two fingers to tap in his password. As soon as he was online, Mandy called. Trying to calm his flyaway hair, he ran a hand down his face and slapped his cheeks a couple times to wake himself up.

Marcus clicked the answer button. Mandy's face filled the screen. Her hair was tied back into a messy ponytail, but her eyes were wide with excitement. Her day yesterday had been as long and tiring as his, if not more so, and yet she looked like she'd just downed an entire energy drink.

"I won!" she said, not bothering to even say hello. "I won my match!"

"Congratulations!" Marcus had already known the outcome. He

allowed the buzz of her excitement to wake him up even more. In the back of his mind, an anxious voice asked him how much time she would have for him now that she had to train for boxing, but he ignored it. "Was she a tough opponent?"

"Not really. She caught me off-guard at first. But once I got into the rhythm of it, I beat her pretty easily. My coach says I'm really good. He says I might even be able to win some awards this year."

"That's really cool. Do anything else last night?"

"I talked to my dad!"

Marcus pictured the hulking mountain of a man and tried not to shudder. "How is he? Everything okay with his mission?"

"I think so." Mandy's face fell a little, and she turned contemplative. "He sounded like he really missed me, and he said he'd try visiting soon. I wish you could come too. You'd like it here. And I know you'd like Etta and Charlie!"

Marcus knew he would too, even if Charlie gave him the stink-eye whenever they were on a call together. They were the kinds of kids he wished he had in his school. Kids who were interested in technology and movies and video games the way he was. "Or maybe you can come here and meet my uncle. I bet your dad would like to see him again."

"Oh my gosh." Mandy tipped her head back in laughter. "I totally forgot to tell him."

Marcus ignored the pang of fear erupting in his chest. Mandy hadn't forgotten about him. She was sitting right here in front of him. Virtually, anyway. "You had a pretty eventful day. You can tell him when he visits. That way you can see the look on his face."

"He's going to be so shocked. Hey, did you get Charlie's email? The recording of the match?"

"Yeah." Marcus moved the video call over to one side of his screen, large enough that he could still read her expressions, and clicked into the recording of the match. "I've gone through it and picked out a couple people Raymond King and Lochlan Reid talked to. I know there are ways to use facial recognition software to figure out their identities, but I'm not sure how to do that without getting in trouble."

"Etta might know who they are. I didn't get a chance to talk to her last night. But if she doesn't, then maybe you can ask your uncle. Just don't tell him what we're up to."

Marcus didn't need Mandy to tell him that. He wouldn't have told his uncle even before he found out Brandon knew Bear. And now? This time, he couldn't stop the shiver from passing through his body and making him shake. If Bear found out what they were doing, he'd skin them both alive.

Refusing to think about that more than he already had, Marcus said, "Raymond took a couple of phone calls while he was there. And he left early. He looked pissed."

Mandy twisted her lips in frustration. "We really need Charlie to get those mics set up. We'll gather everything we can, and then decide whether or not we can handle it on our own. If we can't, we'll tell your uncle and my dad. They do this sort of thing all the time."

Marcus nodded, but his attention had drifted. He'd told his Uncle Brandon about how he'd met Mandy and Bear, even about how he'd been helping them whenever he could. It was one thing to provide tech support if Bear was involved, knowing that Mandy's father was looking out for both of them. It was another thing entirely to have Mandy leading an investigation with her team of teen detectives.

For now he would keep the truth from his uncle and do what he could to help. If they figured out what Raymond King and the others were up to, then he'd tell Brandon and face the consequences of not saying anything sooner. Not that Marcus was too worried about it. His uncle was cool, and more of a rule breaker than his mom. Brandon hadn't told him everything about what he'd done to help Bear over the years, but between that conversation and what he'd heard from Mandy, Marcus felt like he understood his uncle more than ever before. He doubted Brandon wanted him to follow in his footsteps—it seemed like a dangerous life, even if they stayed behind the computer screen—but Brandon loved that Marcus had taken after him.

A knock at Mandy's door made both of them jump. Mandy stood, blocking Marcus from view. It was early for visitors, and Marcus had the sudden fear that one of the teachers had overheard what they were talking about and were there to confront Mandy.

Seeming not to have the same fear, Marcus watched as Mandy crossed to the door and looked through the peephole. Jumping a little, she opened it up far enough to let the person on the other side slip through, then closed and latched it behind her.

"What are you doing here?" Mandy said.

"Did you hear?" Etta asked, out of breath.

"Hear what?" Mandy brought Etta closer to the computer so Marcus could be part of the conversation.

"Did you hear about Vinny Ortiz?"

Mandy rolled her eyes and crossed her arms over her chest. Marcus could practically hear her thoughts: *No, and why do I care?* "What about him?"

"He's gone," Etta said, and Marcus now realized how scared she looked. "No one can find him."

18

BEAR DIDN'T LIKE THE IDEA OF LEAVING VINCENT ORTIZ BY HIMSELF IN Chicago, but he didn't have much choice in the matter. He didn't want to alert Reagan.

For the briefest of moments on his flight to meet with Thorne, Bear had wondered if the man could be Mr. Reagan. There would've been a time when the former CIA operative would've topped Bear's list of suspects. But after everything that had happened, the man was rotting away in USP McCreary just outside of Pine Knot, Kentucky. And had been for the last fifteen years.

As Bear drove through the dense forest toward his destination, he allowed the rhythm of the windshield wipers and low-level radio noise to regulate his heartbeat. The dark clouds above threatened to open up a nastier rainfall than the current sprinkling. He could relate.

Bear hadn't thought about Daniel Thorne in years. He never thought he'd have to make this trip out here and found himself wondering what Jack Noble would say about his current predicament.

Probably that he couldn't possibly be desperate enough to contact someone like Thorne.

He and Jack had first met the man ahead of a job they were doing for

Frank Skinner in Costa Rica. That had gone to hell in a number of creative ways, and so had every other interaction with Thorne since then. The man couldn't be trusted. Every move he made was solely for his benefit.

Bear had spent some time in a prison down in St. Lucia before heading to North Korea and eventually London, chasing leads and trying to outmaneuver Thorne, a man who was as cunning as he was deadly. Sometimes they were allies. Mostly they were adversaries.

At the end of the day, Daniel Thorne was just a patsy for the then Vice President of the United States, who had aspirations to kick off World War III and make a profit. Despite the fact that Thorne had tried to stop it in the end, the CIA had cut all ties with the man, labeled him a traitor, and thrown him in prison. They could've killed him, but he was still useful to them alive. He knew too much.

For the first time, Bear was glad they'd spared his life.

McCreary was a high-security federal prison about ninety miles north of Knoxville. Someone like Thorne should've been in ADX Florence out in Colorado, but he apparently still had some friends. It worked out all the better for Bear, anyway. Raine was able to get him in to visit Thorne at McCreary without raising any eyebrows.

Bear pulled into the visitor's parking lot, noting the lack of cars. Before he could talk himself out of the visit, he pushed open his door and stepped out into the rain, pulling up the collar of his jacket and ducking his head against the precipitation. Thanks to the weather, his face would be even harder to distinguish on any video footage outside the prison. If his image was flagged in some system somewhere back East, it wouldn't save him a lot of time, but every second counted.

Without Raine, getting into the prison on such short notice would've been an impossible task. She wasn't against playing dirty to take down Reagan and had assured both Bear and Iris that she could get him in and out without anyone being the wiser. Bear was more worried about someone catching on to what she was doing than being spotted. If someone found out Raine was helping them, her career would be over. And so would her life. Her taking that risk was why he trusted her to do what needed to be done.

Bear kept his heart steady and his eyes distant as he went through the check-in process, handing over his ID, emptying his pockets, and going through the customary pat-down. A young, sharp-eyed officer led him through the prison to a meeting room hardly bigger than a jail cell. The officer stopped outside the door and leveled a look at Bear.

"This is a dangerous man, Mr. Fahrenholz. We typically don't let visitors meet with him alone."

Bear kept his gaze trained on the officer. "I appreciate you making an exception for me. What I have to discuss with the prisoner is highly classified."

The man looked Bear up and down, equal parts curious and wary. Bear could practically hear his next question on the tip of his tongue: *What makes you so special?*

Instead, the man nodded and placed his hand on the door to the room. "There's a panic button on the inside. Do not hesitate to hit it if needed. I will be just outside the door. You have fifteen minutes."

With one last look at Bear, the man swiped his keycard and pulled open the door. He stepped aside, allowing Bear to walk into the room before shutting the door behind him. The sliding of the bolt was like a gunshot in the silence as Bear took in Thorne's appearance for the first time in a decade and a half.

Many of the men in this prison were the worst of the worst—violent offenders. Thorne was, without a doubt, the most dangerous of the lot, though you wouldn't have known by looking at him. His dark hair had been kept closely cropped and had wisps of gray. His face was clean-shaven. He hadn't aged much in the last fifteen years aside from a single line on his forehead and the initial etchings of crow's feet at the corners of his eyes. In fact, Bear thought he might've put on some muscle.

When Thorne's gaze met Bear's, there was a small flicker of surprise and uncertainty. His gaze flicked down to the visitor's badge pinned to Bear's chest.

"Mr. Fahrenholz," Thorne said. "To what do I owe the pleasure?"

On his flight to Kentucky and the subsequent drive to the prison, Bear had thought of a thousand ways to play this, but in the end, he had one choice.

Bear sat down across from Thorne, noting the thick chains that kept his hands and feet in place. The gray shirt and pants should've made Thorne look sloppy, but he managed to pull them off. "I need information. Name your price."

"My freedom."

"Next option?"

Thorne eyed Bear. "That is the only option, Mr. Logan. If you're desperate enough to want information from me, you'll find a way to make it happen."

Bear sat back in his chair and crossed his arms over his chest. He couldn't afford to walk away emptyhanded, and they both knew it. "I'll see what I can do."

It was Thorne's turn to sit back in his chair and assess Bear, though his restraints meant he couldn't mirror the way Bear had crossed his arms. Bear would never help Thorne get out of prison, and yet an impasse wouldn't serve either of them in the moment.

After what felt like an eternity, Thorne leaned forward again, though Bear could still see the gears turning in his mind. He would find an angle for this. "What kind of information you after?"

"Have you ever heard of a man by the name of Mr. Reagan?"

Thorne's eyebrows shot up. "Of course. He's been making quite a name for himself. A man after my own heart, in fact. His network is quite impressive."

"You know his real identity?"

Thorne chuckled. "Few people do. He's done well to keep himself out of the spotlight."

"You didn't answer my question."

"I have my suspicions. Nothing I'm willing to share with the class. Not without more certainty."

Bear ground his teeth together. "I need a name."

"I can't give you one." The chains on his cuffs jingled as he settled further back into his seat. "If the stipulation for my freedom is that I give you information that leads somewhere, I'm only providing you with the type of information that will ensure I leave this hell behind."

Bear wished he could revel in the other man's discomfort, but he didn't have time for that. "What do you know that can help me?"

"Come now, Mr. Logan. You have to ask the *right* questions."

A growl escaped Bear's mouth, and he hated how that honed Thorne's smirk further. "Reagan has a list of undercover CIA operatives from around the world. Why?"

"Beats me."

Bear placed his hands flat on the table to keep from fisting them at his side. "He's trying to secure Victoria Industries as the software supplier for advanced LAWS currently in development. Why?"

"Ah. Now you're getting closer. I've heard through the grapevine he's planning something big. Something that will *shock the nation.*"

"I need a solid lead, Thorne. Otherwise you're never getting out of here."

"Oh, I'll get out of here one way or another. It's only a matter of time."

"This was a mistake." Bear rose from his chair. "I should've known that after fifteen years you'd hardly be the man you once were. You know, I almost feel bad. Your name used to mean something. But they won't remember you when Reagan finally steps into the spotlight. He's doing everything you wished you could've all those years ago."

The chains clanked as Thorne jerked on them, a sneer on his face. "Reagan only exists because of me. What I was able to accomplish. You think he deserves credit for stepping on the backs of his forefathers?"

It wasn't easy to bait someone like Thorne, and that made this all the more satisfying.

"Reagan has a weak link he hasn't cut from the chain yet," Thorne said.

"Who?"

"Oscar Bergin. Mr. Ortiz should know where to find him."

Thorne was much more connected than he had been letting on if he knew Bear had already picked up Vincent. Revealing this information hadn't been a mistake. Oh no. It was just another tactic to get Bear to do what he wanted. To prove that he knew something of value.

Bear wouldn't give him the satisfaction. Turning away, he banged on the door for the officer to open up, knowing that in another thirty seconds, the man would've come in anyway.

"It was a pleasure meeting you, Mr. Fahrenholz. I look forward to seeing you again soon."

Bear's spine tingled as Thorne's laugh echoed down the hallway after him.

19

SHE WOULD NEVER ADMIT IT TO ANYONE ELSE, BUT MANDY'S FAVORITE place at Eastern Blue Ridge Academy was the library. The building was ancient by her standards, made of dark bricks in serious need of a power wash. Inside, the floors were warped and creaky, the carpets well-worn, and the air stuffy with the scent of furniture polish and old books.

All of that was great, but Mandy really loved it because there was a table on the third floor, all the way in the back, that no one else ever seemed to sit at. Rumors told of a young student back in the seventies who had fallen to her death from the balcony on the other side of the now permanently locked doors. Strange noises and falling books meant most students wouldn't venture within fifty feet of that back corner, which suited Mandy just fine.

"I hate it back here." Charlie pulled up the hood of his sweatshirt and looked around like they could be attacked at any moment.

Next to him, Etta rolled her eyes. She was as practical as Mandy, but even she tossed a couple looks over her shoulder every once in a while. Sitting across from them, Mandy did her best to look unmoved by Charlie's concern. There was a chill in the air, and the floors creaked even worse up here, but she didn't believe in ghosts.

Most of the time.

"No one will bother us back here," Mandy said. "And we can't be overheard. There could be spies everywhere."

Etta rolled her eyes again, looking more dubious about spies than ghosts. "Seriously?"

"Yes, seriously." Mandy leaned forward. "We know Raymond King is blackmailing someone, and his son knows that other person's son. Then Vinny Ortiz goes missing? It's not a coincidence. And you know better than I do that the Kings run this school."

Charlie shivered again, tugging on the strings of his hoodie. "But what can we do about it?"

Mandy pointed to the computer sitting at the fourth spot at the table. If she squinted her eyes, she could almost believe Marcus was there with them. "He's going to help us get to the bottom of this. Let's review what we know."

Etta sat up a little straighter. Mandy had noticed she liked being the person who kept her ears open for information, though she was a lot more skeptical about getting involved in their machinations. "I overheard Amy Stonewall and Lonnie McGregor talking about how Vinny Ortiz snuck out of his room the night before and never came back. His mom had been checking his phone location and saw that it was outside school grounds. When she called, he didn't pick up. The school retrieved his phone from the side of the road, but there was no sign of Vinny."

"Either he ran away," Mandy said, "or he was kidnapped."

"He left his room voluntarily," Charlie said.

"Doesn't mean he wasn't kidnapped. He could've been tricked into leaving. Do we know where his phone is?"

"The police have it," Etta said. "They're trying to keep it quiet, but Lonnie said they searched Vinny's room this morning."

Mandy nodded. "Alright. What do we know about Vinny?"

It was Charlie's time to shine. "He's in a few of my classes. Quiet, but not really shy, you know? More just keeps to himself. Likes to read comic books and play video games. Really into computers. I think I heard him mention once that his dad is some kind of tech guy. I think that's where he gets it from."

Mandy tapped her chin with a finger. "Have you ever seen Raymond King talking to Vinny's father at one of the games?"

Etta twisted her mouth to the side while she thought. "Vinny doesn't play any sports, but I think I've seen his dad at a volleyball match or two in the past. They look a lot alike."

"Do you remember anything about their interactions?" Mandy asked. "Was Raymond angry or Mr. Ortiz scared? Did he leave early?"

Etta shrugged. "I wasn't really paying attention."

"It's okay. You said—"

A creak in the floorboards cut Mandy off mid-sentence. The whole table froze except for Marcus, who must've thought his connection had gone out.

"Guys? Are you—"

"Shh." Mandy placed a finger to her lips. "Hold on."

Rising from her seat, Mandy crept around the table and into the stacks next to them. Moving as stealthy as the floor would allow her to, she made her way up one row of books and down another until she cleared the whole section. When the floor creaked again behind her, she whirled around to find no one there. A shiver ran down her spine despite the fact that she still definitely didn't believe in ghosts.

Mandy returned to the table and forced herself to look annoyed rather than scared. "It was nothing. Just the old building creaking." Taking a deep breath to center herself, she asked her next question. "You said Raymond King took a phone call and left early that night."

"A couple phone calls," Marcus said. "But he looked particularly angry after one of them. Then he left."

"Can you pull up the footage from that night? I want to see if we can catch anything useful."

"Sure thing." Marcus clicked around until his screen switched over from his face to the video from that night. His voice could still be heard over it. "Where do you want me to start?"

"The beginning." Mandy said.

When he pressed play, Raymond King was already sitting in the top corner of the bleachers on the lefthand side.

"He gets there early and is always on his phone," Mandy said. "He usually sits in the same area, doesn't he?"

"I've seen him on both sides of the bleachers, but it's usually the back corner," Etta said.

"Offers him a little more privacy." Mandy nodded at the computer. "Okay, Marcus. Speed it up. I want to see who joins him." After a minute of fast-forwarding, two people arrived. "Stop! There. That man is Lochlan Reid. I recognize him from the other day. But who's the red-haired woman?"

Etta leaned forward. "That's Mrs. Stonewall. Amy's mother."

Mandy leaned in close too, and sure enough, she could see the resemblance to her teammate. "Amy knew about Vinny going missing, and her mother is talking to Raymond King? That's not a coincidence." Mandy nodded toward the computer once again. "Keep playing. I want to see when he takes his phone calls."

The four of them studied the footage for another couple minutes. Every time Raymond King held his phone up to his ear, Marcus would stop the video, rewind, and play it at regular speed until the phone call was over. The entire time, King's facial expressions remained neutral, sometimes even bored. It wasn't until the last phone call that his surprise morphed into anger. Less than a minute later, he got up, stalked down the bleachers with no regard for the other audience members, and stormed out of the gymnasium.

"Really wish we knew what he was talking about on that phone call," Charlie said.

Marcus' face replaced the video on the screen. "I might be able to get into some emails and phone records. I can't make any promises, but my uncle may be able to give me some pointers."

"Be careful," Mandy said. "If he finds out—"

"Don't worry, he's pretty chill. I think I can convince him it's just for fun and nothing serious. He's already offered his help if I decide I want to learn more from him. I doubt he'll show me anything too illegal, but he can point me in the right direction. I can figure out the rest on my own."

Mandy wondered if her smile looked as devious as it felt. By the worried expression on her friends' faces, it probably did. "Charlie, how are those mics coming along?"

"I've got all the components I need. I'm just fixing them so they'll wirelessly transfer the audio to my computer as they record. That way if someone steals the recorder, we'll still have what we need."

"Good thinking." Mandy noted the way Charlie puffed out his chest a little bit. "Etta, do you think you can talk to Lonnie and get more information on Vinny's disappearance?"

"Sure. He usually hangs out by the pool on weekends. I'll see what I can dig up." Etta looked from Marcus to Charlie and then back to Mandy. "What are you going to do?"

"I'm going to become Amy's new best friend."

20

MONARCH WELCOMED THE COOL AIR PIPING OUT OF THE OVERHEAD VENT. Waiting always induced anxiety, which in turn increased his blood pressure. He felt like a furnace. He drummed his fingers on his desk, awaiting Mr. Reagan's call. He would have much preferred to place the call himself, but he had a feeling this was Reagan's way of maintaining control. Reminding him who ran the show.

Not like Monarch could ever forget.

He'd done a lot of terrible things over the course of his life, but kidnapping a child was probably the worst. He'd never murdered anyone with his own two hands. That's just about the only act that would've topped this one. There was no love lost between Monarch and Vincent Ortiz, but his kid had nothing to do with this. Not to mention the boy's mother was probably going out of her mind, wondering why she couldn't get ahold of her son or her husband.

When the phone rang, he didn't bother waiting to pick up. He also didn't bother waiting for the person on the other line to speak first.

"It's done."

"Good. I'm glad this didn't prove too difficult for you."

Monarch gritted his teeth and squeezed the phone in his hand until he heard it crack beneath his fingers. It wasn't his fault he hadn't been able to find the backup drive in Silas Marino's apartment. Or that Vincent Ortiz was now with Logan, both of whom were in the wind. But he got blamed for it anyway.

Monarch forced himself to relax and switched the phone to his other hand. Its warmth filled his palm from how tightly he'd been gripping it. He took a moment to cool down. He was a leader. He took responsibility for the actions of his subordinates. He could live with that, but he refused to take their punishments, too. Right now, he was too valuable to warrant getting benched, but he had his own wife and son to think about. What happened when the plan came together? Reagan had promised Monarch more power than he could've ever dreamed of, but he wasn't blind to the dangers of working with him. The man who was obsessed with cutting off loose ends.

Monarch hadn't wanted to admit as much to Reagan, but it was better to be up front about their shortcomings. "We can't get in touch with Ortiz. My men found his phone outside a motel, smashed to pieces."

"I'll worry about getting into contact with Ortiz," Reagan said. "You worry about staying on task."

Monarch refused to let Reagan's subtle reprimand get to him. Through gritted teeth he said, "Of course. The meeting has been scheduled, and a location has been chosen. The deal will go down as planned."

"Best not to count your chickens before they've hatched. We cannot afford any distractions. Not when we're this close." For the first time, Monarch thought he detected a hint of desperation in Reagan's voice.

"Logan feels less like a distraction than a problem that needs to be solved. Duvall and the computer chick have been poking their noses where they don't belong. Sooner or later, they'll turn up something."

"Perhaps you're right. But Logan isn't going away any time soon. It's not in his nature to walk away from something like this. What do you suggest?"

Monarch hesitated. Reagan wasn't in the habit of asking him for advice. It felt like a trap. Or possibly, an opportunity to prove himself. "Why don't we let slip some details that lead Logan exactly to where we want him? He won't expect us to be ready, and then we can take him out."

Reagan tsked, and Monarch knew it had been the wrong choice. "You've already forgotten what I said about him. Logan can take down anyone you throw at him—ten at once if he had to. Even if we managed to get the drop on him, it wouldn't do us any good. Besides, I don't want to remove him from the board just yet. He may prove useful to this little game we're playing."

"Oh?"

Reagan's voice turned hard. "Our target will be where we want him soon enough. Ignore Logan for now. The child will be enough of a distraction. Logan's bleeding heart will keep him out of our way. When the dust settles, we'll make sure he's no longer standing. And we'll both get everything we've been working for. Is that understood?"

Monarch knew there was no room for dissension. "Understood."

"And Monarch?"

"Yes?"

"Ensure your men do not disappoint. Or it'll be your head that'll roll."

Monarch didn't have time to answer before the line went dead.

21

BEAR WAS ITCHING TO GET BACK TO THE MOTEL ROOM TO CHECK ON Ortiz and make sure he had stayed put, but he had one more stop to make before he could do that. He'd called Iris as soon as he'd left the prison holding Thorne and asked Raine to give him as much information as she could on Oscar Bergin . She already knew who he was. He was on the NSA's radar, though they hadn't done anything about him. He was a small-time criminal with connections to a larger network. They'd been monitoring him simply because there was a chance he would eventually lead them to someone worth their time.

Raine had given Bear an address back in Chicago. He reversed his trip out to the Kentucky prison, hopping back on a plane, then picking up his rental in the Chicago airport parking lot. Bear's anxiety on the flights to and from McCreary had been high. Higher than usual, in fact. But if Bergin was the weak link Thorne had purported he was, it would all be worth it in the end.

Back in the city, the skies were overcast, but the rain he'd experienced during his few hours in Kentucky was nowhere to be found. Inside the car, stale cigarette smoke fought with the orange air freshener, and he couldn't tell which one made his lip curl more. His gaze shifted forward. Traffic was heavy at this time of day. All these observations were background noise to the orchestra playing in his mind.

And the show's number one star was Daniel Thorne.

It would be naïve to think Thorne didn't still maintain some of his contacts from when he was in the CIA, though his network would be much smaller. Perhaps more concentrated.

The real concern was how much more Thorne knew beyond what he'd already told Bear.

Blinking away the thoughts, Bear realized he'd arrived at Bergin's rundown apartment building in a seedy part of the city. When he stepped out of his car, most of the people lingering on the sidewalk looked the other way. Nothing to worry about here, as long as he didn't leave his car unattended for too long.

And as long as Bergin cooperated, that wouldn't be a problem.

Bear circled the block twice to check for any outlying civilians before heading inside. The back entrance had been propped open with a splintered piece of wood. He slipped inside using the cuff of his jacket to pull open the door wide enough. The hallway was dark, and it took his eyes a moment to adjust despite the overcast skies.

The inside was no better than the outside. Dirt gathered in the corners, scuff marks littered the stairs, and the light hanging from the ceiling was so dim, Bear hadn't even realized it was on until it flickered twice and died. But all of that took a backseat to the smell of piss and marijuana lingering in the air so thickly he could taste it on his tongue.

Forcing down the bile that rose in his throat, Bear trudged up the stairs until he hit the fourth floor. He paused for only a few seconds before pulling open the door and stepping into the hallway in search of Bergin's apartment. The smell was marginally better here, and he allowed himself a few gulps of somewhat clean air before turning left and heading toward number 412.

Like most of the doors on the floor, Bergin's was scuffed and dirty, and the shiny gold doorhandle suggested it'd been replaced in the last six months or so. Bear had used his time ascending the stairs and ignoring the stench of bodily functions to debate how he should approach Bergin. Knock and risk him escaping out a window? Bang the door down and bring more attention to himself?

Bear stood outside the door for a moment and couldn't hear a single noise from inside the apartment. Bear's next move was decided.

He pulled a lockpicking kit from his inside jacket pocket and checked left and right before kneeling and inserting his tools into the small opening on the door handle. With a little finesse and a sharp twist to one side, the mechanism gave way with a soft *click.*

He tucked his tools back into his jacket and checked the hallway again. Empty. Bear rose to his feet, turned the handle, and slipped inside the dark apartment. The door closed quietly behind him. Jack had always said how shocking it was that Bear could move so quickly and silently given his big frame. Bear's joints creaked more than they used to, but he was glad to be as light-footed as ever.

The apartment was even darker than the hallway downstairs. His eyes adjusted much quicker. A single glance told him the drawn curtains weren't the only reason for the darkness. Even the microwave clock didn't emit its usual glow.

The creak of a floorboard made Bear freeze, and he watched the hallway until he was sure no one approached. That same creak came again, and he pinpointed it to the last room on the left. The door was ajar, a dim flickering light the only indication that anyone was home.

Instead of clearing any other rooms first, Bear waited and listened for more noise. Hearing nothing, he moved forward on light feet until he could press his eye to the door's opening. Inside, a man paced and muttered to himself, running his hands over his chest like his skin crawled with bugs.

Bear pushed the door open with one hand and leaned against the frame as though he'd been invited over for a drink. It took the man a few seconds to notice, and in that time, Bear took in the scene before him. Blackout curtains and a single flickering candle. Lines of coke next to a half-consumed brick. Soiled clothes and moldy pizza boxes.

Then there was the man. He was nearly as tall as Bear, but half his weight. He was shirtless. Bear could count every rib, and the clear points of his shoulders and sweep of his collarbone caused a pit to form in Bear's stomach. He could break the other man in half as easily as he could a toothpick.

On his next circuit around the room, the man froze and looked up at Bear. He had dark hair that fell to his ears in greasy strings. Wild eyes with the pupils so blown out, Bear couldn't even tell what color they were. A scruff of a beard rimmed his chin, patchy and course. Dried blood caked one nostril and the back of one hand.

"Oscar Bergin?"

"W-who are you?"

"The more important question is who sent me."

If Bergin's eyes grew any wider, they'd pop out of his skull. "R-Reagan?"

Bear pointed a finger gun at him, and the man flinched as though it were real. "You have any idea why I'm here?"

The man resumed his pacing, patting his chest and running his fingers through his hair. "The location is good. No one will know. It's secure."

Bear resisted the urge to chuckle. Thorne hadn't been wrong about this guy being a weak link. It was shocking they'd let him live this long. "Would you bet your life on it?"

"Already have. Already have." Bergin stopped and stared at the coke by his feet. "I'm good for it. I promise."

Before the man could kneel down and snort another line, Bear crossed the room and wrapped his hand around Bergin's bicep, nearly lifting him off the floor in the process. Bergin squealed like a pig, but Bear ignored it, waiting for the man to meet his eyes.

"Tell me exactly what you told them."

For the first time, clarity seemed to dawn on Bergin, and he blinked away the blur of his eyes to study Bear's face. When he spoke, his voice shook a little less than it had. "Who are you?"

"Told you that already."

"With Reagan." The man nodded, letting his head loll back and forth until Bear shook him. "The meeting is solid. I'm good for it."

"Where? Tell me."

"Jonesy's hangar just outside the city. Private. Jonesy owes me a favor. No one will bother you there. I'm good for it."

Bear let the man go. "What's the address? The *exact* address?"

Bergin collapsed to the floor now that Bear was no longer holding him up. He scrambled around the debris, and just as Bear was about to haul him to his feet again, he held up a piece of paper with an address scrawled on it. "Exact address. Just like I said."

Bear took it and slipped it into his pocket. "When?"

"Next week. Friday. One in the morning."

"What's the meeting for?"

Bergin looked up at Bear for a long moment, and finally the hint of clarity Bear had seen before took over the man's eyes. "You're not with him, are you?" He started crying and clawing at Bear's leg to get the paper back. "Please. They'll kill me."

"Not if I do first." Bear used minimal force to shove the man back with his foot. "Tell me."

"Some kind of meeting. An exchange."

"Drugs?" Bear asked. "Weapons? People?"

"They don't tell me. I'm just the location guy. Please. They'll kill me."

Bear leaned in close, ignoring the man's rancid breath. "Only if they find out. I'm not going to tell them. Are you?"

Bergin shook his head so hard a drop of drool splattered his cheek.

Bear patted the man's other cheek hard enough that Bergin flinched. "Then we're good here. Yeah?"

"Yeah." He nodded vigorously, but no drool came out this time. "We're good."

Bear turned his back to the man and headed for the door. "Tell anyone, and Reagan will be the least of your worries."

Bear waited until he was back out on the street before he dialed Iris' number. Without giving her a chance to speak, he said, "I need you in Chicago. Now."

22

MARCUS TRIED TO HIDE HIS EXCITEMENT AS HE WATCHED HIS UNCLE OUT of the corner of his eye. Brandon sat on the plush couch, his knuckles turning white from the way he gripped his armrest. He was doing everything he could to enjoy the moment with his nephew and failing miserably.

"Oh, come on! Really?" Brandon shook his head, not taking his eyes off the screen. "You can't be serious."

Marcus shook with silent laughter. Forcing his brows up and his mouth to turn down, he turned to his uncle with innocent eyes. "What?"

"This whole movie is ridiculous. None of it makes sense. None of it is real. It's barely even plausible."

Marcus smothered another laugh. "You don't watch *The Fast and the Furious* for its plausibility, Uncle Brandon."

"Then why *do* you watch these movies?"

"For the fast cars and the awesome fight scenes." Marcus gestured toward the television. "This isn't even the worst one. In the next one, they drive a car into space."

Brandon whipped his head around so fast Marcus was afraid it'd fall right off his neck and bounce to the floor at his feet. "You're joking."

"Nope." Marcus sat up a little straighter. Now was the time to make his move. "Okay, I'll give you that some of it is a little outside of reality. But not all of it, right? It's gotta be a little real. I mean, the government probably has loads of technology we don't know about."

"There's plenty the government keeps under wraps, but nothing like the God's Eye exists." Brandon shook his head. "A device that hacks into any type of technology as long as they're close enough? You've got to be kidding me. How does that even work?"

This was exactly why Marcus wanted to watch *Fate of the Furious*. His uncle was reacting exactly how he hoped he would. Marcus shrugged. "Like any other hacking, I guess."

Brandon scoffed. "You know the easiest way to hack into someone's device?"

Marcus tried not to let his excitement show on his face. This was exactly the information he needed to know. "How?"

"Trick them into giving you their password."

Marcus deflated. "Really? But that's not going to work on most people, right?"

"You'd be surprised. Most people aren't that creative. Or smart."

"Okay, but what about the smart ones?" *Like, I don't know, the State Senator from Virginia.* "How would you hack into their stuff?"

"Phishing mostly."

"That's, like, sending emails pretending to be someone you're not, right? How does that work?"

"When they click on a link, it downloads malware onto their computer, and you can use that to access their information."

"But that won't work on most people, right? Especially, like, people in big businesses or the government?"

"It works on everyone. You just have to be clever about who you pretend to be." Brandon's gaze slid to Marcus. "Why? You planning on hacking the Pentagon or something?"

Marcus' laugh was a little too high to be believable. "No way. That would get me in so much trouble. Mom would ground me for the rest of my life."

"You'd never see the light of day again, I'm afraid."

It was silent for a few minutes while the movie continued to play, though Marcus barely paid attention. Not that it mattered. He'd seen this one at least five times already. The movies might be ridiculous, but they were still entertaining. "What about facial recognition software?"

"What about it?"

"I see that in movies a lot. Is that as easy as it looks?"

Brandon leaned over and grabbed his drink, taking a sip before setting it back down. "Depends. There are a bunch of free websites you can use for that sort of thing, but they're not all that accurate. The government not only has access to better technology, but also have a better database to search. Hell, even gaining access to the DMV will get you better results." Brandon twisted his face up like he was fighting a sneeze. "Not that I've ever done anything like that."

"Of course not," Marcus said, and the pair of them grinned at each other, sharing a little secret.

"Your mom really would ground you forever if she found out you were hacking into things. And then she'd blame me. Probably bury me alive for my crimes."

"Definitely." He wasn't about to tell his uncle the truth, but maybe they could still have an honest conversation. "But you do those things to help people, don't you? Like Mandy's dad?"

A pained look crossed Brandon's face, and for the first time, Marcus saw him as more than his cool uncle, more than a guy who was good at computers. He was someone who had been through all of it, who had probably gained friends and allies, and lost them to the inevitable. Marcus knew only a fraction of what Mandy had been through, and that was more than most people could handle. Bear had experienced so much more, and Brandon had been by his side more than once.

"Yes," Brandon said, drawing the word out. "I help people. But it's not always easy. Or that straightforward. Sometimes you have to do the wrong thing for the right reason. And sometimes, you think you're doing the right thing, but it ends up being for the wrong reason or the wrong people. And that's not to mention all the other people out there who don't have a conscience. Being the computer guy in movies usually means you're safe, sitting at your desk and watching things from afar. But it can be just as dangerous."

Marcus nodded, not sure of what to say. This was the most his uncle had ever talked about his other life, the one Marcus knew little about.

"Will you promise me something?" Brandon asked.

Marcus turned to him. "What?"

"If you feel like you're ever in over your head,"—Brandon met Marcus' gaze and held it a moment—"you'll tell me? Even if you're scared of getting in trouble with your mom or someone else, you can always come to me, okay? And we can figure it out together."

The truth of what was going on gathered into a lump in his throat, but Marcus swallowed it down before he could speak it into existence. He wasn't in over his head, he convinced himself. Not yet anyway. But still, he told his uncle what he wanted to hear.

"I promise."

Brandon reached over and ruffled Marcus' hair. "Now I have another important question for you."

"Yeah?"

"Do they really go to space in the next movie?"

"Oh yeah. They definitely do. We're *so* watching that one next."

Brandon groaned theatrically, but he didn't argue as they settled back into their marathon.

23

BEAR LOOKED THROUGH THE PEEPHOLE IN THE DOOR OF THE MOTEL ROOM to find Iris and Raine on the other side. In the time it had taken them to arrive, the temperature had dropped and a few flakes of snow still clung to the tops of their heads. It wouldn't stick but seeing the first fall of the year made Bear want to wrap his coat tighter around him. He didn't hate winter like most people, but the way it stiffened up his limbs made him long for spring and summer.

"Get a room okay?" Bear asked.

"Couple doors down from you." Iris shook the snow out of her hair. "Last one."

Bear turned to the man sitting on the edge of the bed. He gripped his knees until his fingertips turned white. "Vincent, this is Iris, the FBI agent. And Raine. She works for the NSA."

"The one who figured out where I was going," Vincent responded, not bothering to stand and shake anyone's hand.

Raine looked sheepish as she gave a little wave, dressed in an outfit so similar to the last one Bear saw her in, he wasn't entirely sure it wasn't the same. "Sorry?"

"Don't be," Bear said. "He's lucky we found him before Reagan had a chance to punish him for having the audacity to say no."

A shudder ran through Ortiz, but he pushed to his feet and looked directly at Raine. "You really couldn't find my wife and my son?"

Raine shook her head, and Bear saw the tears gathering in her eyes. "Like we told Bear, Vinny had been removed from school. Your wife had packed up her clothes and taken the car. The best we can assume is that she felt something was wrong, and the pair of them got out of there. She didn't answer my messages. I'm not surprised. She's probably waiting for you."

"Can we reach her now? Tell her I'm okay?"

Raine nodded and move to sit on the man's bed. She flopped her ever-present satchel down on the covers and pulled out her laptop. Her fingers danced over the keyboard until they were nothing more than a blur.

"Remember," Bear said. "Do not tell her anything about where you are, what you're doing, or who you're with."

"I know." Vincent sounded half-terrified and half-exasperated. "I just need her to know I'm safe."

Bear locked eyes with Raine, who gave him a subtle nod before returning to her computer. Convinced that Ortiz wouldn't give them away, he stepped to the other side of the room and motioned for Iris to join him.

Iris asked the question Bear had been pondering for the last several hours. "Can Bergin be trusted?"

"I think so. Thorne said he was a weak link. He definitely works for Reagan. Whether the meeting is legitimate is a whole other ballgame. Considering how coked out he was, I would venture to say it is. Don't think he was in his right mind to lie."

"The location is a hangar," Iris said. "Could be that they're transporting something."

"Or someone's coming in on a private plane to meet them and does not want to be seen coming or going. Either way, no point in guessing games. We'll find out when we get there."

"How do you want to play this?"

"Quietly. We need the information."

"And if we're caught?"

"I've already talked to a couple contacts. I'm getting weapons lined up as we speak. Won't be much, but it'll be enough to cover our backs. We'll leave Raine here with Ortiz. She'll keep an eye on him."

"Surprised he didn't run already."

Bear shrugged. "He knows what we're dealing with. Realized he's safer with me than on his own."

"Looks like he's itching to get back home, though."

"And he knows it's a death sentence for them all if he does. Smartest thing to do right now is stay in the wind." Bear watched for a moment while Raine handed over her computer to Ortiz and let him type out a short message. "What about her? Think she's compromised?"

"No doubt," Iris said. "Didn't take much convincing to get her to come to Chicago with me. She knew what she was getting herself into when she agreed to help me."

"And what about you?" Bear asked. "How's the field office taking your absence?"

"I've got someone covering for me. Richard Peake. He doesn't know what's going on, but he'll watch my back."

"That's the same guy who told you that you were off the Reagan case."

Iris nodded. "The order didn't come from him. As far as he knows, I'm doing what I'm told. Working on something else. He'll let me know if people start asking questions."

Bear opened his mouth to argue, but a strangled cry put their conversation to a halt. Ortiz jumped to his feet, sending the laptop careening toward the floor. Raine lurched forward and grabbed it just in time, casting an angry glance at Ortiz before checking for any scratches or dents.

Ortiz didn't notice. He was halfway to the door before Bear put out a large hand and stopped him in his tracks.

"What's going on? What's wrong?"

"Get out of my way," Ortiz said through gritted teeth, trying and failing to move past Bear.

"It's his son," Raine said, her eyes wide. "He's been taken."

Iris planted herself in front of the door. "Reagan?"

"Who else?" Ortiz said. "Now, move. I need to get my son. I need to—"

"You can't help him," Bear said. When Ortiz reeled back as though he'd been punched, Bear modified his voice. "Not right now, at least. Come on, man. You're smart. Think this through."

"He took my son," Vincent said, unable to hide the emotion in his voice.

"He took your son to draw you out. The second you go to him, they kill you both. Your best bet is to wait here with us."

Disbelief distorted Ortiz's face. "How can you say that? How can you tell me just to sit by and do nothing?"

"I'm not telling you to do nothing," Bear said. "I'm just telling you to play this smart. Reagan wants you out of the picture, which means your son is safe for now. The only way to get him back without getting yourself killed is by trusting us."

"I don't even know you. What can you do?"

"I'll find out where your son is, and I'll get him back. Then we'll send you and your family somewhere safe. I promise."

Ortiz looked up into Bear's eyes, pupils blown out with fear and desperation. The man's voice was weak. "He's just a kid."

"I've got a daughter," Bear said. "I know how you're feeling right now."

Ortiz clutched his stomach. He didn't bother saying anything as he turned on his heel and sprinted for the bathroom. The door slammed shut behind him, but they could all hear him retching into the toilet. Once, twice, three times, until it was nothing but dry heaves. The toilet flushed, and then the shower turned on.

"Think he'll be okay?" Iris was still leaning against the front door.

"Not for a while," Bear said. "But he'll get through this."

"It's a distraction."

"I know. But what choice do we have?"

Iris nodded, though he caught the way she clenched her jaw, as though stopping herself from saying what she really thought. Bear turned his back to her.

"Any idea where they're holding the kid?" he asked Raine.

She shook her head. "Not a clue. I'll do my best, but he could be anywhere."

"Until we know more, we focus on this meeting. Might be able to hit two birds with one stone. Find the kid and figure out what Reagan is plotting."

Iris pushed off the door and sat down on the edge of the other bed. "You're being awfully optimistic."

"Only way out is through," Bear said. "I'm ready to make something happen."

The three of them were silent for a moment, listening to the sound of the shower running. It took Bear a moment to realize there weren't any other sounds, like bottles being picked up or elbows hitting walls. He walked over to the door and knocked.

"Vincent, you okay in there?"

A chill squeezed out from under the gap at the bottom of the door, encircling Bear's ankles in its icy grip. He swore and shouldered the door open. The water was running, but the shower curtain was open. The bathtub empty.

A cold breeze wafted through the open window.

24

MANDY MANAGED TO MAKE FRIENDS WITH AMY STONEWALL. TURNS OUT, winning matches and being a general badass helped a lot with your popularity in high school. Mandy didn't really care what her classmates thought of her, but she had to admit that it came with perks. For one, no one picked on Charlie anymore, even if Roy King stared daggers at them whenever they passed each other in the hall.

Mandy wasn't untouchable, of course. Roy was still the most popular kid in school, and everyone was as afraid of him as they'd always been, but news of Mandy's fight and her newfound friendship with Amy had turned her into a novelty. Now everyone said hi to her in the hallway and ask if she wanted to sit with them at lunch.

She always declined, instead preferring to sit with Charlie and Etta.

Normally she met up with them after school and headed back to their usual corner in the library to sometimes do homework but usually to do more research. Not that they'd made much headway. Etta had talked to Lonnie about Vinny's disappearance. He didn't know anything new. Now everyone was acting like he'd been simply pulled out of school. Something was definitely off.

Today Mandy was meeting with Amy to grab dessert in the cafeteria and work on a project for one of their classes. Not that Mandy had any intention of doing homework. And neither did Amy.

"Oh my god, this lemon pound cake is *so* good." She closed her eyes and swallowed with such pleasure, Mandy had to look away. "My mom would kill me if she saw me eating this."

"Is your mom pretty strict then?" Mandy couldn't believe that she'd gotten an opening to talk about Mrs. Stonewall this early into their conversation.

"Have you ever heard the phrase *almond mom?*" she asked. When Mandy shook her head, Amy scoffed. "Lucky you."

"What is it?"

"Well, I don't know about anyone else, but my mom is always on some diet or another."

"But she's so skinny."

Amy rolled her eyes. "Tell me about it. She's crazy about that kind of stuff." Amy affected a grating voice. *"A moment on the lips is a lifetime on the hips, Aims."*

Mandy scrunched up her nose. "Gross."

"Tell me about it. At least when I'm here, I can eat whatever I want." She took another huge bite of the poundcake. "And I work out enough that she'll never notice."

"I'm surprised your mom lets you box."

"My dad has always been into martial arts and self-defense. I've been in classes since I was little. The boxing team was the closest I could get to it here. But she said the second I got a black eye or a broken nose, I had to quit the team."

"Sounds like good motivation not to let that happen."

"Haven't lost a fight yet. Did get a black eye once, but it was nothing makeup couldn't cover."

Amy was nothing like she thought the girl would be when she'd first joined the team. She always wore skirts and dresses, even outside of school hours, and her hair was done up in a different style every day of the week. She wore makeup and talked with a high-pitched voice and laughed with a girlish giggle. But she could throw a punch and dodge them just as easily. Amy was smart, practical, and most of all, *nice*. At least to the people she cared about.

That didn't give her a complete pass in Mandy's book. She might not bully any of the other kids at school, but she'd also stood by and done nothing while Roy King did. It wasn't quite as bad as being the perpetrator, but it was close. Part of Mandy felt guilty for becoming friends with someone who had watched Roy push her friend around, and the other part felt bad for only pretending to be Amy's friend. Then again, was it really pretending if they actually got along?

Mandy had been holding off on the question all week so she didn't look too interested. Now seemed like the perfect time. "What does your mom do?"

"I don't know. She's, like, an analyst or something for the Treasury Department."

"Oh wow. That sounds pretty interesting."

Amy rolled her eyes. "It's not. She's crazy about money and numbers and all that other crap. I have to write her a persuasive essay every time I want to go shopping to get new clothes."

Mandy bit back the comment teetering on the tip of her tongue. Okay, so Amy was smart, practical, nice, and a little spoiled. That didn't make her a bad person, though Mandy couldn't relate to her issues with buying clothes. It was something Mandy only thought of in practical terms: Would this outfit make her stand out too much? Were the materials good enough in quality to last years? Could she run and punch and kick in it?

"Anyway, what about your dad?" Amy asked. "No one knows what he does."

"Oh," Mandy said, scrambling. "He's a salesman."

"Really? And he can afford to send you here?"

"He's a really, really good salesman." Mandy needed to steer the conversation back to information that would be relevant to her investigation. "I can't be the only person without a parent who works for the government or something."

"Definitely not." Amy popped the last bit of her cake into her mouth and dusted off her hands. "But maybe the only one in sales."

Mandy forced herself to laugh, then tapped her pen to her lips. "Hey, have you heard anything else about Vinny Ortiz?"

Amy leaned forward, conspiracy shining in her eyes. "No, but I heard my mom talking about his dad. Apparently, he went missing, too."

"Really?" *Mark that down in the suspicious category.* "What happened?"

"No idea. I just heard my mom talking to Roy's dad on the phone."

"Are they friends?"

"More like business associates." Amy's eyes narrowed. "Why?"

Shrugging, Mandy tried to sound cavalier. "I caught him glaring at me during my first match."

"Probably because you gave his son a black eye."

"I'm still waiting for Roy to get his revenge."

Amy shrugged and returned to the stack of papers in front of her. "Roy is a big baby. I wouldn't worry about him too much. He can fight, but he'd rather go crying to his dad." Amy shuddered. "Now there's someone who scares me."

"Mr. King? Why?"

"He's just super intense. He's been over for dinner a few times, and my parents always make me eat in my room when he's there. He has some serious connections. It's the only reason my mom deals with him."

"What kind of connections?"

"Any kind you can think of." Amy leaned in again, but this time there was fear in her eyes. "You know Jory's dad?"

Mandy had to search her catalogue of names for a moment before it came to her. "Lochlan Reid?"

Amy nodded. "I heard he's not really a lawyer."

That piqued Mandy's interest. She tried not to show it on her face. "Oh, really?"

"Really." Amy leaned in closer. "I heard he's actually with the CIA."

A shiver ran down Mandy's spine. Now that was some good information to have Marcus look into.

25

MONARCH HUNCHED OVER HIS DESK, MINDLESSLY TRACING THE WOOD grain. The sun was setting behind him, yet he couldn't bear to turn around and watch the sky turn a mottled purple and pink. The comfort of his office felt like a joke these days. His focus was entirely on the phone in front of him. But this time, when he picked it up and placed it to his ear, he didn't dial Reagan's number.

"This better be good," the voice on the other line said.

Monarch had made his decision the second his fingers touched the number pad. "I have concerns."

The voice on the other line was silent for a moment. "It's good you brought this to me."

Baron was an old friend. Not since childhood, nothing that intimate and embarrassing, but since their college days. They'd never been close, with Monarch having gone off into politics and Baron entering the FBI to fulfill his patriotic duty. They viewed the world from different ends of the telescope—Monarch, up close, taking in every detail; Baron, a step back, examining the full picture—and yet they had both ended up on Reagan's payroll. That's what had cemented Monarch's belief in Mr. Reagan to begin with.

But no longer.

"What are your concerns?"

"Who, rather. Logan and Duvall. They're getting too close."

"Mr. Reagan is aware of this."

"Yes, I know. But I don't believe Reagan understands the full scope of the situation."

Baron laughed. It was a long, loud chuckle that would've drawn heads if they were in a restaurant or bar. "Mr. Reagan knows everything. You don't have to worry."

"They know about the meeting."

"And?"

"And?" Monarch couldn't contain his anger this time. He let it seep into his words like lava cascading down a hill, burning everything in its wake. "They'll try to stop it. They're getting closer. It's only a matter of time before they learn everything."

"Have you ever considered that's part of the plan?"

Monarch blinked and his anger dissipated as though it had met with the cool sea. To him, Logan and Duvall were thorns in his side. Reagan had hinted at the idea that they could be useful, but Monarch never believed they were actually part of the plan. Why hadn't he been told as much?

Baron must've heard Monarch's thoughts in the silence. "You need to trust in Mr. Reagan."

"I do," Monarch answered automatically, though he wasn't sure he believed it anymore.

"If you did, we wouldn't be having this phone call."

Monarch winced, glad to be in the privacy of his own office. The phone call was a mistake, not only because he felt like a chastised child, but because it hadn't dissuaded his own thoughts on the matter. Perhaps Reagan was using Logan and Duvall for some purpose he was not aware of, but that didn't mean the purpose served their greater goal. For the first time since he'd gotten into bed with the enigmatic figure, Monarch believed Mr. Reagan had made the wrong call by allowing Logan and Duvall to live.

Baron sighed, but Monarch couldn't tell if it was in exasperation or resignation. The latter was far worse than the other. "I know Iris Duvall.

She won't give up until she solves this or she's dead. Eventually, she'll make a mistake. That's when we'll make our move."

Monarch knew Baron was right. It wasn't his only purpose in the grand scheme of their plans, but it was one he was uniquely situated for. Duvall still trusted him, and they would use that to their advantage.

But the creeping feeling in Monarch's gut told him it would be a mistake to wait that long.

"You're right," he said, forcing relief into his voice. "We're so close now, I'm just getting paranoid. Even the jitters before my wedding day weren't this bad."

Baron didn't laugh. "You saw what happened to Vincent Ortiz when he didn't do as he was told."

"My faith in the plan has not wavered. I'm as committed as I ever was."

"Good. Make sure it stays that way." The silence between them was as heavy as cement shoes. "I'd hate to see you end up like him. There is no room for dissent, not even from you."

"I understand."

"Soon, we'll have everything we've been working for all these years."

"Looking forward to it."

Now more than ever, he was convinced he had to take matters into his own hands. He wouldn't let Reagan's arrogance ruin the future he worked so hard to preserve.

26

BEAR AND IRIS' PLAN WENT FELL APART IN UNDER SIXTY SECONDS.

Granted, it would've taken divine intervention for them to pull it off without a hitch, but Bear had hoped that after everything they'd been through the big guy would throw them a bone.

The address Oscar Bergin had given them was for a private airstrip on the outskirts of Chicago. The date had been set a week out, giving plenty of time to scope out the area and come up with a plan. The fact that the landing strip was a wide-open field did them no favors in the cover department, even though the meeting was to take place at one in the morning. The floodlights surrounding the building would make it difficult to approach without being seen.

Difficult, but not impossible. They'd caught a break when they realized there were no security cameras. It seemed like a hole in the operation to Bear, but he wasn't about to knock on the door and lodge a complaint about it.

The night before, they'd slipped inside and planted mics in the back office and in a few discreet places around the hangar. If a plane was running during the meeting, the mics wouldn't be able to pick up anything, but it was still a safer bet than trying to listen in the old-fashioned way.

Except that's exactly what they had to do.

From the tree line, Bear and Iris had used binoculars to spot the participants arriving. A man in a silver sedan pulled up first, followed by two black SUVs which arrived in a cloud of dust, holding seven men total. Ten minutes later, two box trucks arrived and pulled into the hangar. Silence from the mics told them they were waiting on someone else, and sure enough, an eighteen-wheeler disappeared inside the building. Then their mics went dead.

They'd had a contingency plan, but Bear didn't like it. The night before, they'd left the window to the office open just enough for Iris to slip her fingers through the gap, yank it up, and climb inside. She'd made it look easy, but Bear's bulk meant he had to squeeze himself through like fitting a sausage inside its casing. Something scraped along his side, and he emitted a low growl of annoyance. Getting in was fine, but getting out in a hurry would be almost impossible.

"Don't like this," Bear whispered as soon as he was inside.

Iris cut him a look that clearly said, *What choice do we have?*

Fair enough, Bear thought.

They'd searched the office the night before and found nothing of use. The landing strip was legitimate, and it was possible that whoever owned the hangar either didn't know about the meeting or didn't *want* to know. There had likely been a hefty sum of money in it for the owner if he took a vacation day and returned tomorrow like nothing had happened. Or maybe he was one of the men inside.

A small window looking out into the hangar allowed them to survey the situation before attempting to get any closer. The two box trucks and the eighteen-wheeler were lined up to make transferring their contents easier. More than a dozen men were inside, separated into two groups. There were those transferring boxes from the smaller trucks to the bigger one, and those who stood around in a circle looking high and mighty about it.

The hangar was too open for them to get any closer, but that ended up working in their favor. The acoustics of the room amplified the men's voices enough for Bear and Iris to hear the conversation clear as day. It was their first and only break so far.

Bear watched through the window, careful to keep his head as low as possible while keeping eyes on the group closest to them. All four men wore suits of either gray or navy blue. Four of them looked handsome enough to be actors. They were probably politicians. The fifth guy was at least a head taller than the others and watched the loading of the boxes with keen eyes. It wasn't hard to figure out he was their security, especially with a weapon strapped to his side.

The last man was the most interesting one. He was at least twenty years older than the others, in his sixties or early seventies, with gray hair and large glasses. His back was hunched, though he looked spry enough. He twitched more than the others, and Bear had to wonder if he was paranoid because he'd never done this before, or if he'd done it too many times.

"Remind me again why we can't just fly these to Miami?" one of the politician-type men said. "We've got access to private planes."

The old guy was already shaking his head before the other man finished speaking. "Way easier for something to go wrong."

"But it's a twenty-hour drive."

"And the weapons will get there with time to spare. That's all that matters."

Bear exchanged a look with Iris. The boxes were full of weapons, and they were going to Miami. Bear doubted that was their final destination. He wouldn't be surprised if they packed them on a plane there and flew them to South America. Were these the LAWS Ortiz had warned them about, or something else entirely?

"You sure your contacts will be there?" a different man asked.

"Been doing this for twenty years," the old man said. "They haven't let me down yet."

"First time for everything."

The first man slapped the other one on the back. "Come on, Richards. You've got to stop being so pessimistic."

"Don't use names," the old man snapped. "Never use real names. You have no idea who might be listening."

The four politicians exchanged looks. The first spoke again. "That's why we have the jammer." He held it up with a little shake. "No one can hear us."

Bear and Iris had to duck down as the old man twisted his head in one direction and then the other. "They're not fool-proof. Trust me on that."

"Okay, okay. No real names. Got it."

"When do we get our money?" a third man asked. He had beady eyes that bore into the backs of the men moving the weapons from one truck to the next.

"Like I said before," the old man said. "Upon delivery."

"How long does it take to fly from Miami to Venezuela?"

The old man slashed his hand through the air. "You'll get your money when you get your money. If you have a problem with that, I suggest taking it up with Mr. Reagan."

The group fell silent, exchanging glances. Mr. Reagan's name held the weight of fear, but he'd never seen it like this. However big these guys thought their britches were, they were nothing compared to their boss.

The old man checked his watch. "I trust you can handle seeing this through?"

The first man held out his hand. "Consider it done."

The old man eyed the other man's hand warily, then shook it once before dropping it. He didn't give the others a chance to offer their goodbyes before turning on his heels and walking out the front of the hangar.

Bear didn't hesitate. Didn't even bother to tell Iris what he was doing. He knew he had one shot, and he was going to take it. There was no way they'd be able to take on all the men inside the hangar and get away with the weapons. So, he'd do the next best thing.

He heard a little sound of protest from Iris as he squeezed out of the window and dropped to the ground below. Wasting no time, he sprinted to the corner of the building and spied the old man's car. The guy was halfway there and moving fast.

Keeping his steps light, Bear dashed along the side of the building, willing himself to move quickly and quietly. The old man had no idea what monsters lurked in the night, and the second he inserted his key into the car door, Bear was there, wrapping an arm around his neck and squeezing.

27

MANDY WAS JUST WRAPPING UP HER WEIGHT TRAINING WHEN AMY motioned her over with an urgent wave of her hand. Mandy set her dumbbells down and crossed the room. She ignored the way Roy King and his lackies glared at her. She could handle Roy, no problem. But if they all decided to jump her, she'd be in trouble. Not for the first time, she wondered if Amy would be on her side. Or would she sit back and watch, not wanting to cross Roy herself?

"What's up?" Mandy said, bending over to stretch her hamstrings.

Amy copied her movement. "I overheard my mom talking last night. Vinny's dad came home."

"Oh?" Mandy straightened in surprise, then started stretching her arms to cover the movement. "Do you know where he was?"

"No idea. She sounded relieved, but, like, in a weird way."

"What do you mean?"

"Like, not relieved that he was back home safe and sound, but relieved that they knew where he was. Does that make sense?"

"I think so. Are they all friends?"

Amy shrugged. "Not really. I mean, they talk sometimes, but they've never invited him over for dinner, you know?"

Mandy could read between the lines. "Anything on Vinny?"

"Not that I could tell." Amy had to pause while one of the boys from their team walked by, and she scrunched up her nose against the stench of sweat. "They were more interested in his dad. I wonder what's going on?"

Mandy had some theories, but she wasn't about to tell Amy what they were, considering they probably involved her mother. It was clear that Raymond King was the ringleader, but since she didn't know where Mrs. Stonewall fell within the rankings, she wasn't about to share her thoughts with the woman's daughter. Just in case.

Before Mandy could come up with a believable lie, someone cleared their throat behind her, and she turned around to find Coach Foley, his eyes hard and his hands on his hips.

"Ms. Davis," he said. "Can I speak to you for a moment?"

Everyone was watching. Mandy blushed but nodded her head and followed her coach out into the hallway. It had sounded like Mr. Foley was angry or disappointed in her, but she couldn't figure out why. She might've missed out on a set or two while she talked to Amy, but that was no reason to pull her out into the hallway.

"Mandy, I've noticed that you and Amy have become much closer over the last week or so."

"Yeah, I guess so."

"I hope you're not leaving your other friends behind as a result?"

"You mean Etta and Charlie?" When Coach Foley nodded, Mandy continued, not sure why she felt so nervous. "We still see each other all the time. They don't mind."

"Did they tell you this?"

"Yes." They hadn't, but Mr. Foley didn't need to know that. As a matter of fact, she couldn't figure out why he was so interested in the first place. "We're all going to hang out this weekend, actually."

That was a lie, and Mr. Foley seemed to know it, but he didn't call her out. "You have a curious mind, Mandy. You ask a lot of questions."

"I like learning new things."

"I'm not the only one who's noticed."

She tilted her head to the side. Mr. Foley looked back through the window into the gym, and she followed his gaze, finding Roy and Amy deep in conversation. Not for the first time, she wished she could read lips.

Mandy's gaze returned to Mr. Foley's face, and they locked eyes. It was as though the overhead lamps had shifted and brightened. She saw her coach in a different light. The sharpness of his eyes. The impassiveness of his face. The way he fisted his hands on his hips. He wasn't mad at her, but the tension in his body betrayed his true feelings. He was scared for her.

He was warning her.

Mandy nodded her head. "I understand."

Relief flitted across his face before he tamped it down. "Good. That's good."

Warmth spread through Mandy's chest, followed by a cold dread. She looked up to Coach Foley as much as she looked up to her therapist, Ms. Antoinette. They were both looking out for her in their own way. Mandy had been too preoccupied to realize how obvious she was being whenever she asked Amy for information. Amy seemed none the wiser, but Roy constantly watched her. And maybe not because he hated her, but because his father had asked him to.

"You know you can talk to me, right?" Mr. Foley said, bringing her back to the present. "Whatever is going on, I might be able to help."

Mandy swallowed back the temptation to dump everything on him. It was bad enough that she'd gotten her friends involved in all of this. Having an adult on their side could be helpful, but she'd play that hand when it was necessary, and not a moment sooner. As much as she trusted Mr. Foley, the more people in on their operation meant the more people who could compromise them, either on purpose or by accident. No, it wasn't worth it.

"Thank you." She looked down at her shoes so he couldn't catch the indecision in her eyes. "I appreciate that."

Mr. Foley patted her on the shoulder, then pushed back through the door and into the gym, but Mandy let it swing shut without following in his wake. She watched as Roy and Amy laughed about something, and a sudden guilt gripped her chest and squeezed. She knew she was making the right decisions to get to the bottom of Raymond King's scheme, but she didn't have a good feeling about it.

She was risking her old friendships with Marcus, Etta, and Charlie, and her new one with Amy.

She was drawing the attention and concern of Coach Foley.

And she hadn't talked to Bear in a while. If anyone would understand how she was feeling and how important it was to keep up her double life, it would be him. For what felt like the millionth time in the past few days, she wondered where he was and what he was doing. Was he safe? Was he any closer to figuring out who Mr. Reagan was and stopping him?

As Mandy turned around and headed back to the locker room on her own, she felt more lost than ever.

28

BEAR HAD THROWN THE OLD MAN IN THE BACKSEAT OF THE CAR AS SOON as he passed out from lack of oxygen. By that time, Iris was right behind him, gun drawn and climbing into the back with the stranger, even as a string of curses escaped her lips.

"What the hell, Logan?" She twisted so she could point her gun at the man. He was already stirring. "I mean—*what the hell?*"

Bear climbed into the front seat and pressed the button to start the car. Throwing it into drive, he forced himself to tap lightly on the gas pedal as he drove away, not wanting anyone inside the hangar to realize they'd captured the old man.

Bear checked his rearview and pressed down on the gas a little harder. "We need answers. This guy seemed to know what was going on."

"We have no idea who he is. This could blow up in our faces."

"Or it could be exactly what we need to get to where we need to go next."

"I swear to God—"

Iris' words cut off as the old man groaned.

Bear tilted the rearview mirror down so he could see the man's face. "Rise and shine, cupcake."

The man groaned again, then blinked his eyes open. He startled when he noticed the gun, then went stock-still as he took in Iris. "Ms. Duvall?" He sat up slightly but made sure not to move too fast. His gaze drifted to Bear's eyes in the mirror. "And Mr. Logan?"

"I'm so sorry," Bear said. "You know who we are, but we don't know you."

"Jackson Carter," the man replied.

"Is that your real name?"

"It's the name on the driver's license in my wallet."

"That's not a real answer," Iris said.

"It's as real of one as you'll get from me."

"Who are you?" Iris said, drawing attention back to her gun.

"Afraid I can't tell you that." He shifted again in his seat, and Bear had to wonder if he was uncomfortable or just gauging Iris' reactions to his movements. All the guy had to do was force the gun away and get Iris to pull the trigger. Then Bear would be dead, and the other two would be through the windshield. "How much of the meeting did you hear?"

"Enough," Bear said.

"Thought so."

"Venezuela, huh?"

"I'm gonna stop you right there," Carter said. "I'm not telling you a damn thing. Kill me if you have to. It'll be a better death."

"I wouldn't bet on that." Iris leaned a fraction closer. She hadn't been a fan of this plan when Bear first enacted it, but she played her role well now. "I can make it painful."

"Not so much worried about the pain," Carter said with a shrug.

"A better death," Bear said, "than what Reagan would give you, you mean."

Carter sneered. "They said you were smart."

"They?"

Carter waved his hand but froze halfway through the movement when Iris moved the barrel of her gun from his chest to his head. "The ones who know who you are. Monarch. Baron. Reagan."

"Do you know who Reagan is?" Iris said.

"Not a clue. And I intend to keep it that way. They say the sooner you know his identity, the sooner you end up in a shallow grave."

"You talk about him like he's the boogeyman."

"He might as well be."

"He's flesh and blood," she said. "And I intend to prove it."

Bear's gaze flicked to his side mirror, and he noticed for the first time that one of the black SUVs was in hot pursuit. He moved the rearview mirror to its original place and spotted the second vehicle not far behind the first. "We've got company."

Iris twisted in her seat to look out the back window, then ducked low when a bullet shattered it. She cursed. Bear swerved. Slammed down on the gas and urged the vehicle to go faster. The gravel road kicked up dust and rocks, jostling them around.

Iris turned back to Carter. "I'm with the FBI. I can protect you. Your family."

Carter laughed, holding onto his seat for dear life as he bounced around. "You have no idea what hornet's nest you kicked, do you? The FBI know exactly what's going on. So do the NSA. The CIA. All of them. Nowhere is safe. You're either with Reagan, or you're against. And if you're against? Well, you're not long for this world. I might be old, but I'm not ready to go out just yet."

Bear swerved as another bullet hit the car, this one knocking off the passenger side mirror. Something finally clicked in Bear's mind. They knew Reagan had sold the drugs to generate money and influence. What they hadn't known until today was how that money was being used. But the meeting had given them that answer—weapons. They were sending the weapons to Venezuela, and Bear would bet his life that the CIA was behind it. After all, this was nothing they hadn't done before. It'd been Nicaragua back in the eighties.

The United States had a vested interest in making sure Venezuela had a stable government they could work with, which currently wasn't the case. This wasn't out of the goodness of their hearts, but because of the oil reserves found in the country. It all came down to money and power, and the U.S. was a fan of both. Enough to break some laws in order to get what they wanted.

Could Mr. Reagan be in the CIA? Was Reagan even one person? If he was, could it be someone Bear already knew?

"Daniel Thorne." Bear moved the rearview mirror back so he could look into Carter's eyes. "Do you know the name?"

Carter opened his mouth to answer but Bear never found out what he would say. The next bump in the road launched all three of them in the air. Bear smacked his head on the roof, Iris slammed into her door, and Carter's head cleared the top of the backseat.

It was the moment their pursuers had been waiting for.

One second, the man in the backseat was alive and well, if not terrified for his life, and the next, his brains were splattered on the seat in front of him.

29

MARCUS SHOULD'VE BEEN ASLEEP HOURS AGO. UNLIKE HIS MOTHER, Uncle Brandon didn't check on him in the middle of the night to make sure he wasn't on his computer. That's why Marcus had begged his mom to go back to his uncle's house for the second weekend in a row. His mother had seemed suspicious at first, wondering what the two of them could've been up to. She also seemed to be relieved to have yet another Saturday and Sunday to herself.

Marcus wiped away the blurriness in his eyes and stuck his hand in the greasy, salty, delicious bag of chips at his side and shoved a handful into his mouth, not caring about the mess he was making down the front of his shirt. What he did care about was maintaining the cleanliness of his keyboard, which is why he kept a crumpled-up paper towel next to him. He used it again before returning to his screen.

Thanks to his uncle's information about the realities of hacking, Marcus figured the best way to get into private emails was to send an official-looking PDF file in the hopes one of his targets would download it, unknowingly putting malware on their phone or computer and granting him access.

Raymond King, their primary target, hadn't fallen for the trick. And considering it had been almost a week since Marcus had sent out the original email, he didn't think the Senator would change his mind anytime soon. The PDF was probably sitting in his junk email or had been deleted altogether.

Lochlan Reid, their secondary target, also hadn't downloaded the PDF file. Marcus was more nervous about sending him the email because of the latest intel they'd received from Amy: There was a chance that Mr. Reid wasn't a lawyer, but a CIA agent in disguise. It felt like something out of a spy movie, and Marcus had a hard time believing it. But those were the kind of people Bear and Mandy happened to run into on the regular. There was a chance the information could be true. None of his research had proven that theory, but it wasn't like the guy would post something like that in a Facebook update.

They hit paydirt with their third target Marissa Stonewall, Amy's mother. She worked for the Treasury Department and was the only one who had downloaded the PDF file. Marcus had gotten an alert as soon as she did so. That had been hours ago. He was still searching through everything he had at his fingertips. She'd opened it on her phone. He had access to both her personal and professional email, as well as text messages and phone records. There was a lot to go through, but he already had enough information to bring to Mandy.

It hadn't taken long to notice a pattern of codenames, like Monarch and Baron and Bishop. He hadn't been able to find any proof of who these people were. It didn't take a genius to notice that they were all different names for people with power. People like, for example, *kings*.

Marcus looked over at the scribbled notes by his side. He'd written *Monarch = Raymond King?* and circled it three times, sure that he was onto something there. One of the other ones could've been Reid's codename, but he couldn't even begin to guess which one. There was still one other name unaccounted for and that could belong to anyone.

There were tens of thousands of emails and messages to comb through. Marcus had spent hours guessing at other codenames and had come up with nothing. He'd used a thesaurus to help pick out as many regal synonyms as he could.

Marcus froze as he stared down at another note on his piece of paper. He'd written the word in a rush and hard trouble making it out.

After a few seconds, he recognized it as *regal*. But it sure looked like Reagan. Marcus' heart pounded. He typed the name into his search bar. His finger hovered over the enter key. He licked his lips and pressed the down.

"Reagan," he whispered to his empty room, "means little ruler or little king."

He stared at the search result for a solid two minutes, trying to piece together all the information he had in front of him. There had already been enough to give to Mandy with the codenames and talk of secret meetings. Nothing incriminating had been sent through email or text message, but enough could be inferred, especially if Raymond King really was going by Monarch.

But if Reagan was involved, then this situation just went from bad to apocalyptic.

Marcus' finger shook as he switched back over to Mrs. Stonewall's inbox and typed in the name *Reagan*, one agonizing letter at a time. He took a deep breath and held it as he hit enter. Then it whooshed out in an involuntary gasp as a single result was returned.

I have an associate, Monarch had written, *named Mr. Reagan, who has an interesting proposal. Meet tonight at the game?*

It was late, but Marcus knew this couldn't wait. He had to call three times before Mandy answered with a sleepy grunt.

"Wake up," he said, not bothering to hide his terror. "We have a problem."

"What is it? What's wrong?"

"I got into Stonewall's phone."

"That's amazing! That's—"

"She's part of Reagan's circle. She's working for him, along with Raymond King and a few others. Whatever they're doing, it's related to Reagan."

Mandy was silent for so long that Marcus had to check twice to see if they were still connected. When she finally answered, her voice was low and deadly serious. "Are you sure?"

"The name is in her emails. Just once, but it's there."

"Oh my God."

"What do we do? Should we call your dad?"

"It's not a coincidence I ended up at Eastern Blue Ridge." Mandy voice shook. "Iris suggested it. Which means she knew about the connection."

"Why would she do that? She can't be working for him, can she?" Marcus' heart seemed to race even faster than before. "I thought she wanted to find him even more than your dad?"

"She does. At least, that's what we thought." There was a rustle on the other end, and Marcus imagined Mandy shaking loose the thoughts cascading through her mind. "I don't think Iris would intentionally put me in danger, but she knew what she was doing. She must've thought I would uncover something here. She was using me to gather more information. Either that, or..."

Marcus waited for Mandy to continue, and when she didn't, he filled in the blanks. "Or she put you there as an insurance policy to make sure your dad did what needed to be done."

"King and the other parents don't know who I really am," Mandy whispered, as though they could hear her right now. "They would've done something about it by now."

"Let's hope that's true." A shiver went down Marcus' spine, and he found that all the blurriness clinging to his vision had dissipated. Even though he knew he was safe, he had no interest in falling into the vulnerability that was sleep. "What are we going to do?"

Marcus heard Mandy draw in a shaky breath before she answered. "Wake up your uncle."

He looked at his door, as though Brandon was just on the other side and not asleep in his bed down the hall. "And tell him what?"

Mandy hesitated for only a moment, and even though he couldn't see her, he could imagine her with perfect clarity. The determined set of her shoulders. The furrow in her brow. The glint of resolve in her eyes. When she spoke, her voice came out steady and sure.

"Tell him everything."

30

BEAR'S FOOT PRESSED THE GAS PEDAL ALL THE WAY TO THE FLOOR, AND YET he still couldn't shake their tail. Both SUVs were within feet of him, but they'd stopped shooting. Maybe because they knew Jackson Carter was dead, or it was only a matter of time before Bear reached the highway and drew the attention of the authorities.

The chilly night air whipped through the shattered window and bolstered the adrenaline in his veins. His fingertips were frozen, but they caused no discomfort. He had more pressing matters to deal with, including the fact that Iris had kept up a steady stream of curses since their prisoner bit the bullet.

"We're so screwed," she said.

Bear didn't disagree, but pointing out that they'd be hard pressed to get out of this mess wasn't doing them any favors. Better to keep his eyes on the road and lose their pursuers before dealing with the dead body in the backseat. After that, they'd dump the car, pick up a new one, grab Raine, and get the hell out of there.

Once they had time to breathe, they'd figure out their next step.

"He's got a phone and wallet on him," Iris said. "ID confirms his name is Jackson Carter."

"Could be fake." .

Before Iris could agree or disagree, a ringtone sounded from the back of the seat. "Someone's calling him," Iris said. "Name's Monarch."

Bear was silent as the phone rang out. The caller didn't leave a voicemail. Another chime indicated someone had sent him a text message.

"Facial recognition won't work," Iris said. Bear glanced over his shoulder to see her put the man's finger to the front of the phone. The lockscreen unveiled the home screen beneath and Iris pressed onto the Messages app.

"Who's it from?"

"Monarch. It says, *Pick up, Ms. Duvall.*"

The phone rang again, and Bear and Iris swore in unison.

"Might as well see what they want."

The ringtone cut off as Iris answered the phone, putting the caller on speaker. "Who is this?" she asked.

"You can call me Monarch," the man answered. He had a strong, clear voice. There was a hint of amusement there, too.

"Well, that doesn't seem fair. You know my real name. I'd love to know yours."

"Perhaps another time. I presume Mr. Logan is also listening in?"

"Are you an associate of Mr. Reagan's?" Bear asked.

There was a chuckle. "This isn't that kind of phone call, Mr. Logan."

"Then what kind is it?"

"The kind where I give you an ultimatum." The man's voice turned hard. "Pull over and allow my men to take you into custody. In return, I will not kill the Ortizes. Simple as that."

There was nothing simple about it, and they all knew it. "How do I know they're still alive?"

The sound of a door opening gave way to voices crying out in pain and panic. Bear couldn't make out any distinct words, but he recognized Ortiz's voice, along with a woman's and a young boy's.

"Bear," Iris said.

"I know."

"Two for the price of three," Monarch said. "Seems like a good bargain to me."

"How do I know you'll keep your word?"

"You don't. But something tells me you don't want their blood on your hands. Do we have a deal?"

Bear gripped the steering wheel until his knuckles turned white, then he swore loudly and slammed his foot down on the brake. The tires squealed, and Iris hit the back of his seat with a thud and a cry of surprise. Rocks kicked up into the tire wells, and dust floated through the shattered window. Behind them, the two SUVs skidded to a stop.

Three men emerged from the first vehicle, guns drawn, telling Bear and Iris to get out of the car with their hands up. Exchanging one last look in the rearview mirror, the two of them did as they were told. Neither put up a fight as two of the men took Carter's phone from Iris, then secured both their wrists in front of them with zip ties. The third man, the one who had been acting as security guard, kept his gun trained on them the entire time. Bear could've fought and probably won with minimal injury to himself and Iris, but there was no doubt in his mind that Monarch would kill the Ortiz family without batting an eye. It was a risk to go with these men, but that only meant the reward could be greater.

Two men emerged from the other vehicle and climbed into Carter's car, driving off to presumably take care of it and the dead body. Bear didn't have to do the deed, but that small consolation hardly made him feel any better. His prints were all over that car, and so were Iris'. If Monarch or Reagan wanted to frame them for Jackson Carter's murder, they wouldn't have a hard time doing it.

Then again, Monarch probably thought it was unnecessary considering he had them in custody.

That was a mistake.

A sharp command from the security guard had the two men behind Bear and Iris pulling hoods out of their pockets and fitting them over their heads. The material was scratchy and smelled like it'd been sitting in a basement full of mildew for months. Iris coughed to Bear's right. He fought at the scratching in his throat and resisted the urge.

A pair of strong hands led Bear stumbling toward where the first vehicle had stopped. The man emptied Bear's pockets and then shoved him into the back. After a moment, Iris landed next to him, her elbow digging into his thigh. He gritted his teeth against the pain until she sat up straight.

"So," Bear said as soon as he heard the other men climb into the SUV. "Where are we heading?"

The click of a gun was their only answer.

31

It was a little under an hour when the driver put the SUV in park. That was no indication of distance. For all Bear knew, they could've been driving in circles for the past forty-five minutes and were just a mile or two down the road from where they'd started.

Someone pulled Iris out first, then grabbed hold of Bear's arm to drag him out. He fought the urge to struggle, though he did wrench his arm free once he was back on his feet. It earned him a punch to the gut. He'd expected it and had tightened his stomach muscles. A small whoosh of air left his lungs as a result, but their captors didn't get anything more satisfying out of him.

"Where are you taking us?" Iris asked. "Where are the Ortizes?"

"You'll join them soon enough."

With his eyes covered and the smell of the hood still invading his nostrils, Bear had to rely on his hearing and the orientation of his body to picture his surroundings.

He could tell by the crunching and rocky terrain that they were crossing a gravel driveway. The rustle of leaves and faint chirping of crickets hinted they were still outside the city. The lack of traffic was no indication of how far they were from the road, considering it was still the middle of the night, but Bear had noted when they'd transitioned from smooth asphalt to the bumpy gravel. Wherever they were, the driveway had been long and winding.

The cool night breeze cut off as soon as they stepped inside a building. A sharp warning from one of the men indicated there were descending stairs in front of Bear. He. took his time going down one at a time, hoping to drag this out as long as possible and take in as much information as he could. Memorizing the way into the building would be his only chance to get out with everyone alive.

They reached the bottom of the stairs. Bear heard a door slide open, followed by faint crying and shushing, and then a soft gasp. Iris' cry of surprise as she was shoved inside the room was Bear's only warning that the same was about to happen to him. Every instinct in his body told him to fight, but he ignored those thoughts. A better time would come.

The door slammed shut behind him, and the room was silent once more.

"Vincent?" Bear called out. "Are you in here?"

"Y-Yes." There was a shuffling noise. "Mr. Logan?"

Bear almost sagged in relief. Their captors had done half his work for him. "Can you take our hoods off?"

More shuffling followed, and the scrap of fabric over Bear's head disappeared. The room was small and dim, and it only took his eyes a second to adjust. As Vincent shambled over to Iris to remove her hood, Bear took in the figures of a woman and a young boy. Vincent's wife stared up at him with a mixture of hope and terror, while his son kept his eyes down on the floor. Tears stained his cheeks, and his shirt was covered in remnants of yellow vomit.

"Does anyone ever come visit you? Do they come on a schedule?" Iris paced the room, looking for anything that could help them. With no windows and only one light fixture fitted into the ceiling, there wouldn't be much they could use. A single cot with a ratty wool blanket and a toilet in the corner were the only other additions to the room.

"Once a day," Vincent Ortiz said. "It's hard to tell time in here, but I think it's around noon. They feed us, and that's about it. Every once in a while, someone else will come in, try to get me to talk." He looked at Bear. "I told them everything I knew. My family—I couldn't—"

"I know." Bear would've patted the man on the shoulder if his hands had been free. "You did the right thing."

Vincent sagged against one wall but managed to remain standing. "Thank you for coming for us."

"The man who called us," Iris said. "Monarch. Do you know his real name?"

Vincent looked to Bear when he answered. "Raymond King."

"The man who wanted you to use Victoria Industries for the system. Good. I'd been wanting to meet him, anyway."

The door swung open behind Bear.

"Is that so?" a voice asked, the same voice from the phone. "I'm glad to hear that. The feeling is mutual."

Bear turned to see Raymond King standing in the middle of the door frame. Despite the late hour, his hair was perfectly coiffed. He wore a freshly pressed light gray suit, and his hands were deep in his pockets. He was the picture of smug reassurance.

Big mistake.

Without hesitation, Bear brought his zip-tied hands up over his head and then drove them down and back, using the momentum to break the plastic surrounding his wrists. King's eyes went wide as Bear charged him, landing a kick in the middle of the man's chest. It sent him flying backwards, ass over teakettle, with a grunt of pain and surprise.

Mrs. Ortiz cried out in surprise. Bear knew Iris would protect the family. There had been another man standing in the hallway, and he now charged into the room, his gun drawn. Bear landed a jab to the man's nose and felt bones break under his knuckles. The man yelled out. Bear spun him around and wrapped an arm around his neck then lifted him off his feet and jerked hard to the left. The man went limp in his grasp and the gun fell from his hand. Bear snatched it off the floor and stuck his head out in the hallway. Another man ran toward him. Bear raised the pistol and squeezed off a single shot. The guy collapsed to the floor and didn't move again.

Bear glanced over his shoulder. Iris had freed herself from her own zip-ties and had gathered the family behind her. She locked eyes with Bear and nodded once. There was no need to discuss the plan of action. Their number one priority was getting everyone out alive.

As Mrs. Ortiz clung to her son, and Ortiz clung to his wife, Bear turned back toward the hallway in time to see Raymond King stumble to his feet and take off down the hall. Bear lifted the gun once more and pulled the trigger, but King stumbled to his right just in time to take the bullet to his shoulder inside of center mass. King cried out in pain and disappeared around the corner.

Bear wanted nothing more than to follow the man and demand answers, but he couldn't do that and keep the Ortiz family alive at the same time.

"On me," Bear said.

Bear kept his gun at the ready as he crept down the hall, Iris and the family close behind. He stopped long enough for Iris to pick up the weapon of the fallen guard. His confidence that they'd get out of there alive increased tenfold.

As they reached the intersection of hallways, Bear stuck his head around the corner, raised his gun again, and fired three more shots. Two guards fell where they stood.

"Go," Bear said. "I'll watch our backs."

"King—"

Bear nodded and took off in the direction King had gone. He came to a set of stairs and heard the faint sound of an engine growing more distant. Blood on the ground led to fresh tire tracks.

Iris came up the stairs behind him.

Bear didn't look back. "He's gone. But he's injured. We'll have another chance."

Iris looked like she wanted to argue, but she turned and headed back down and led the family up the stairs and into the middle of the night. Two quick shots indicated she'd come up against some resistance, but there were no cries of pain or devastation.

Another guard skidded around the corner, and Bear felled him before he took another step.

Not knowing how many more men were inside the building, Bear backed away from the hallway and up the stairs. Outside in the dirt were two of the men who had captured them, including the security guard. Both had received a bullet in the head.

Iris waved from one of the SUVs, and Bear sprinted across the gravel driveway, wrenched open the passenger door, and threw himself inside. He'd barely settled into his seat before Iris tossed him his phone and slammed on the gas.

The group was silent while Iris peeled away from the compound, throwing up gravel and dust in their wake. They had no pursuers, and Bear had to wonder if they'd decimated Monarch's forces in the span of only a few minutes. Was anyone else left?

That was the least of their worries now. First, they had to ensure Vincent Ortiz and his family were safe for the foreseeable future. Then they'd collect Raine and find their own place to stay under the radar while they figured out their next step.

But the next step was impatient. It came to Bear in the form of a phone call from Mandy. He picked up on the first ring.

"What's wrong? You okay?"

"I'm okay." Mandy sounded breathless. "Are you?"

Bear didn't like the urgency in her voice. "I'm good. What's going on?"

"You know Marcus?"

Bear's heart squeezed. Had something happened to the kid? "Yeah, of course."

"Turns out, you also know his uncle."

As the adrenaline left his system, Bear felt dizzy and confused. Why was Mandy calling him in the middle of the night about Marcus' uncle? "Mandy—"

"Hey, Bear," a familiar voice said. "Been a while."

"Brandon?" Bear relished in the relief flowing through his body. "The hell, man? You're Marcus' uncle?"

"Small world, I guess." Brandon's voice didn't hold its usual humor. "Sorry to be calling in the middle of the night like this, but it couldn't wait."

"You in trouble?"

"No, no. Nothing like that. Not yet at least." Brandon took a deep breath. "But Mandy and Marcus have some information they wanted to share with you."

"About what?"

Mandy was the one to answer this time. "About Mr. Reagan."

32

DARKNESS LINGERED AS MANDY MADE HER WAY TO THE GYM. AFTER everything they had discovered the night before, there was no way she could sleep. So she figured she'd get in a short workout without anything else to do before dawn. Pummeling the punching bag was better than pummeling someone. With her luck, it would wind up being Roy King's. Then she'd be in real trouble.

Her arms ached as she continued throwing punches in the dim room, but she barely noticed the pain. Sweat gathered on her brow and a tingle crept up her back thanks to the pressing darkness, but she didn't want anyone to know she was here. Yet there was something about the desolate loneliness of the pre-dawn day that made her feel like she was cresting a hill, only to look down on a valley of destruction before her.

Mandy could feel that they were on a precipice. Last night, Bear and Brandon had shared a moment together, catching up amidst the chaos of the night. She had heard stories of Brandon, had talked to him briefly before looping her dad into their call, but hearing Bear talking to him even over the phone felt like sitting around a fire and watching friends banter the night away. A warmth had spread through her, if only for a few minutes.

Afterwards, Bear had told them what he'd been doing for the last few hours, and as scared as she'd been for her dad, she was overjoyed at the news that Vinny was safe and sound, if not a little traumatized. She wondered where the Ortizes were now. It was probably better she didn't know. Vinny wouldn't be coming back to school anytime soon, and she debated whether she should tell Amy.

As soon as the thought crossed her mind, she brushed it away. Coach Foley had warned her to be careful. Now that they knew Raymond King was the enigmatic Monarch, just as Marcus had guessed, she trusted Roy King even less than before.

Mandy wondered if Roy's parents would pull him out of school, or if they'd act like nothing was wrong. Raymond was injured. Would he risk showing up to take his son away? Would he order someone else to do it for him? Between that and the bullet wound, plenty of people would be asking questions, and neither Monarch nor Reagan could afford that right now.

Mandy took a break to shake out her arms and bounced from foot to foot while blinking the sweat out of her eyes. She was tired and invigorated at the same time. A combination that made her feel reckless. But her brain fired on all cylinders thanks to the extra intake of oxygen. She could go nine rounds with Roy King without taking a single punch.

After Bear had finished telling them about his night, Mandy filled him in on everything Marcus had discovered, including the connection between Raymond King and Reagan. Bear had already learned that little fact for himself, but it had connected some dots he hadn't previously known were on the same board. Vinny Ortiz had been taken from Eastern Blue Ridge Academy. The same school Mandy attended.

The same school Iris had suggested Bear enroll his daughter in.

Bear had gone deadly quiet on the other line, and then told Mandy to hang up and get some sleep. She'd protested, wanting to hear what he'd say to Brandon and eventually Iris, but his tone brokered no argument.

Then he told her to pack her bag and be ready to move.

The thought made Mandy's hands curl into fists, and before she knew it, she was back at the punching bag, hitting it harder than before.

Grunts and screams of frustration erupted from her mouth. She didn't care if anyone heard her.

Even just a few weeks ago, Mandy would've dropped everything if Bear had suggested he'd pull her out of school. But now she was too invested. She'd already involved Etta and Charlie in this whole mess, and Roy had seen her talking to Amy. They could all be in danger now.

More than that, Mandy had proven herself useful. Sure, she was pissed at Iris for suggesting she come to this school, knowing full well who was in attendance, but it had also allowed Mandy to gather information Bear wouldn't have been able to find on his own. He might've already known about Raymond King's connection to Mr. Reagan, but what about Marissa Stonewall and Lochlan Reid?

Mandy dropped her arms, finally too exhausted to land a proper punch. She was still debating whether she'd skip classes and try to sleep or just pretend everything was normal when she pushed through the door back out into the dim hallway.

She didn't even see the figure in black until the person cupped one hand around her mouth and the other around her waist.

Adrenaline surged through Mandy's veins, and any fatigue she'd felt moments ago was wiped away. She stamped down on the figure's foot with all her weight, then threw back her bony elbow until it connected with the person's ribs.

The deep grunt that followed told Mandy it was a man, and the way he squeezed her tighter told her he was much bigger than she was. But Bear had trained her for this, and few people were bigger than him. If she could escape Bear, she could escape anyone.

She was too short to throw her head back and connect with the man's nose, so she reached down and grabbed at his crotch, digging her nails through the soft fabric of his pants and squeezing as hard as she could. Fear overrode any disgust she felt at touching him there, and the fact that it forced the man to let go of her made it all worth it.

Mandy took the opportunity to sprint away, but the man recovered faster than she thought. He grabbed hold of her hair and pulled her to a halt. She cried out in pain. He tried to stifle her with his hand over her mouth, but she bit down until she tasted blood and he let go.

Now that there was some distance between them, Mandy spun around and connected the heel of her hand to the man's nose. It didn't land straight on, so didn't break it, but it surprised him enough that he stumbled back.

Mandy stepped closer and brought her leg up as hard as she could, connecting with the man's already sore groin and dropping him to his knees. One more kick to the face sent him sprawling back. It was now or never if she wanted to escape.

She sprinted down the hallway, listening for pounding footsteps behind her. When none came, she figured she'd incapacitated the man enough to escape. She sprinted through the grounds and didn't stop running until she made it back to her room. There, she locked her door and sank to the floor in exhausted relief.

Now safe, Mandy tried to remember everything she could about the man. He was at least six feet tall and white, with dark eyes. Maybe green or brown. Perhaps even hazel? The mask hid any defining features. There was no way she could pick him out of a lineup with any sort of certainty.

Mandy pounded her fists into her thighs. She should have been happy to have escaped, but it would've been better if she could've gotten the identity of her attacker. That would've helped Bear even more.

Mandy sighed and thumped her head against the door behind her. Wanted to tell Bear about what happened, but she was already on the verge of being pulled out of school.

And then what? Etta and Charlie would be on their own. So would Amy. And they would risk missing out on more information.

No, the sooner they figured out who Reagan really was and what he was up to, the better.

Until then, Mandy would just have to be even more vigilant.

33

Iris drove fifteen minutes before Bear told her to pull over. She tried to argue that they should put more distance between them and Monarch's facility, but one look at Bear's face must've convinced her otherwise.

Bear gritted his teeth against the pain in his body as he stepped out of the car. He ignored the whip of the early morning wind. The sun was still below the horizon, but the edges of the sky were turning paler by the minute. Soon it would be a new day. Normally he was grateful to reset the clock and start over from scratch. But today, his problems had increased tenfold in the matter of just a couple hours.

Monarch knew both Bear and Iris' identities and had already proven he had no qualms about kidnapping a child to achieve his goals. If Bear hadn't acted when he did, all five of them would be dead. Sooner or later, Monarch would come for them again.

It felt like his head wasn't screwed on tight enough to think properly. The information Mandy and Brandon had relayed to him coursed through his mind at lightspeed, too fast to truly comprehend. But one fact stood out above the others.

Iris knew Mandy's school had a connection to Reagan.

Bear turned as Iris climbed out of the vehicle and shut the door behind her. She approached him as though he were a wild animal. Bear reluctantly gave her a modicum of credit. It didn't look like she would deny the charges against her.

She stopped just out of arm's reach.

Smart.

Bear worked his jaw until he thought his voice came out as neutral as he could get it. "Why?"

"I thought it was the best course of action."

Iris' calculated tone grated against his eardrums. He could only get three words out amidst the rage building in his veins. "She's my *daughter.*"

"I know." Iris put her hands up in surrender, but Bear noticed that her stance was wide and at the ready. "I know, and I'm sorry."

"Don't lie to me. You're not sorry. You'd do it again in a heartbeat."

Iris' lips drew down into a frown, and for the first time, Bear thought she might be apologetic for what she had done. But not remorseful. "You're right. Reagan is too important. We needed every asset we could get."

Bear didn't hold back the roar of his anger. "She's not an asset. She's *fifteen!*"

Iris took a step back, her eyes wide and her hands stretched out to either side. "Isn't this what you trained her for?"

"I trained her so she could protect herself. Not so she could end up like me."

"She's not in any danger."

"Can you prove that without a shadow of a doubt?"

"She's your daughter. She's always going to be in danger."

"Don't you dare turn this around on me. Besides, weren't you just saying a second ago that she's not in any danger?"

"My point is, she's not in any *more* danger than she normally is. Raine had told me about Vincent Ortiz. I figured she could keep an eye on his son, befriend him, maybe get some inside information. From everything I read about Vinny, I figured they'd hit it off."

"That wasn't your decision to make. You should've consulted me."

"I didn't because I knew you would say no."

"That, I believe."

"I care about Mandy, too. She's a good kid. Smart and resourceful. Observant. I knew she could help us connect the dots. And she did."

"You had no right to use her like that without my consent. Without *her* consent."

Iris looked away, and for a second, Bear thought he saw her blinking away tears. When she turned back to him her voice was just as steady as it had been before. "I know. But I have people in place there, watching out for her. I promise you, she's safe."

"Did you know about Monarch? About how his son was at that school too?"

"No," Iris said. "I didn't know anything about Raymond King, I swear."

"We need to get her out of there," Bear said. "She's too close to it."

"Look, I'm not going to stop you if that's what you want. But she's just another student at that school. That's why we registered her under a different last name. Why we *both* decided you shouldn't show up there in person. If Reagan knew where she was, she'd be gone by now."

"Is that supposed to reassure me?"

"I'm just stating facts here. Mandy would've told you if something was wrong. We've got eyes on us. If you move her now, and they find out where she was, she might be in even more danger. Not to mention her friends. And they're far less valuable than Mandy is."

"You're not building a good case for yourself, Iris."

"We're so close," Iris said, her eyes pleading. "She'll be safe for another couple days. I'll check in with my people twice as often. Let's finish this thing with Reagan, then we can go our separate ways."

Bear locked eyes with her. "We're done after this, Iris. I mean it. Lose my number."

Iris looked away and nodded. "I understand."

Bear felt the tension rising in his muscles. All he wanted was to get to Mandy and take her as far away from here as he could. But Iris had a point—Reagan would find them sooner or later. She'd been at that school for months. There was no reason to think another couple of days would hurt.

"And if something happens to her, I'll kill you."

Iris looked back at him. "I know."

Bear watched the sun crest the horizon and inhaled the crisp morning air for a moment. "So, we've got Raymond King, Lochlan Reid, and Marissa Stonewall." Bear didn't miss the way Iris exhaled and softened at changing the subject. "One group keeps coming up again and again."

"The CIA. But how do we prove it? What's our next move?"

Too easy.

"Get Thorne out of jail."

Iris' jaw dropped. "How do you expect me to do that?"

Bear was already headed back to the car as he said, "I don't care. Just get it done."

34

BEAR HAD MANAGED A FEW RESTLESS HOURS OF SLEEP BEFORE IRIS WOKE him with the news that it was time to collect their prisoner. The look on her face indicated she didn't think this was a good plan, but they were running out of options. He didn't know what strings she'd had to pull to make this happen, but he didn't bother asking. All that mattered was they got their man. Bear knew the way Thorne's brain worked. He'd given up a small lead to show good faith, but there was no doubt in Bear's mind the man knew a hell of a lot more than he was letting on.

Neither of them had any delusions about Thorne's true goal. He'd try to escape, and they'd try to stop him. It would be a fun game for Thorne, until it wasn't. Sooner or later, Thorne would try to make his final move and disappear forever. It was a risk Bear was willing to take to keep his daughter off Reagan's radar and out of danger.

She's your daughter. She's always going to be in danger.

Iris' words bounced around Bear's head in a cacophony of noise while the pair of them made their way to Kentucky, first on a plane and then in yet another rental car. The actions were rote, a distant thought in Bear's mind. He was too occupied by thoughts of Mandy's safety to care that Raine had been terrified when he'd told her to stay in Chicago and find somewhere safe to stash the Ortizes, or that Iris had tried to start a dozen conversations with him before giving up entirely after she was met with angry silence.

His mood didn't improve when he pulled up to the prison and saw Thorne waiting for him, dressed in a gray suit and flanked by two guards. The man gave the pair of them a cheery salute, stretched his arms in defiance of the gloomy winter sky, and sauntered over to their vehicle. The smile never left Thorne's face. Bear had the very rational urge to see how many blows to the man's head it would take to wipe it clean.

"Morning, folks." Thorne slid into the backseat and sat in the center, like Bear and Iris were his chauffeurs for the day. He stuck his arm between the seats. "Ms. Duvall, I don't think I've had the pleasure."

"You haven't." She ignored his hand.

Bear snorted. He didn't meet her gaze, but some of the animosity drained from the air. A bigger threat was now in the backseat of their car, and the two of them would do well to stand united against him.

"Where can a man get a hearty breakfast around here?"

Bear tossed him a sleeve of powdered doughnuts from the gas station down the road. He had known Thorne wouldn't wait more than thirty seconds before making additional demands, just as he'd known it would give him immense pleasure to see the package bounce off the man's chest and into his lap. "Breakfast of champions. Start talking."

Thorne scoffed, holding up the doughnuts with his thumb and fore-finger as though it were poisoned. "I think not."

"I'm not messing around here, Thorne. Start talking, or I'll call the guards back over."

"We both know that isn't true." He tossed the package on the floor at his feet. "I've waited nearly two decades to bargain for my freedom. I saw you less than two *weeks* ago. Which of us, I wonder, has the patience to hold firm?"

Bear ground his teeth together and counted to fifty before throwing the car into drive and jamming on the gas hard enough to illicit a small *oomph* from the backseat. Thorne would see this as a point in his favor, but Bear was willing to play the game until he got what he wanted. Then Thorne would be back where he belonged.

Twenty minutes later, Bear pulled into the parking lot of the oldest, greasiest diner he could find. It was a relic from another era which seemed to have been left behind by all but a few faithful customers. The food was cheap for a reason, but you would've thought Thorne was dining in a three-starred Michelin restaurant by the satisfied noises he made while devouring four full breakfast platters on his own.

"Right," Thorne said through a mouthful of bacon and toast, which he washed down with his second cup of coffee. "Tell me what you know."

Bear and Iris exchanged looks, and he nodded for her to give him the rundown. As she spoke, Bear watched every movement Thorne made, from the way he cut his sausage to the way he chewed his omelet to the way he winked at the waitress when he asked what she'd recommend for dessert. It might've looked like he wasn't paying attention, but Bear could tell with every minor cock of his head and twitch of his lips that Thorne was cataloguing each bit of information they gave him.

Thorne wiped his mouth and patted his stomach once Iris had finished her story. "Well, it's not like this is the first time something like this has happened."

"You're talking about the Contra scandal back in the eighties," Iris said.

"That's just one example, but it seems to be the most relevant. That was not the first and only time the CIA has broken the law in order to get what they want, and it won't be the last."

The conversation paused when the waitress placed the bill on the table and Thorne slid it over to Bear with a saccharine smile.

Bear waited for the server to leave before speaking for the first time in nearly half an hour. "How high does it go?"

"It's been a while since I was in the game." Thorne scratched at his chin. "Who's in charge again?"

Iris scoffed. "You're saying the Director of the CIA is behind all this? Margaret Caldwell is a lot of things, but she's not stupid. She wouldn't allow the CIA to be caught with their pants down in the same place twice."

"You're so sure that's true, but wouldn't this be the best way of

avoiding suspicion? Caldwell and her minions are not common crimi-
nals. They're the best in the world at what they do."

"Do you have any proof?" Bear asked.

"I wouldn't be alive if I did."

"How do you expect us to trust you, then?"

"I don't." Thorne slid out from the booth and stood with a stretch. "I
don't much care if you do trust me. I listened to your story, I answered
your questions, and now it's time for me to head out."

Bear matched his movements, towering over the other man. "You're
not going anywhere, Danny-boy."

Bear had waited for the perfect moment to grab Thorne's arm and
slap the sleek metal cuff around his wrist. It looked like a high-tech
watch, but by the way Thorne's eyebrows shot up, he knew it was a
tracker.

Iris held up her phone with his beacon blinking from the middle of a
map. "You really need to give us more credit."

"I told you from the start," Bear said, "this is temporary. You get your
few days of freedom, and then it's back to your lonely ass little jail cell.
We both know you'll attempt to escape. And we both know I'll hunt you
down, just like I did last time."

Thorne sighed, drawing it out with a bit of theatrics, then sat back
down. "You're even less fun than you used to be, Bear."

Bear ground his teeth against his nickname in that man's mouth.
"We have less than twenty-four hours before that truck full of weapons
makes it to Miami for the exchange. I want to know where it's taking
place. The *exact* address."

"I require some assurances first."

"This is not a negotiation."

"Then I have nothing to say to you. You might as well take me back
to prison."

Bear raised an eyebrow. "Is that what you want?"

"Obviously not. But everything I know about Mr. Reagan indicates
he doesn't make mistakes. You know anything about him at all because
he *wants* you to know."

"Why?" Iris asked.

"Beats me. He's playing a sick little game with you, and you should be careful who you trust."

"That's rich coming from you," Bear said.

"I'm not the one you have to worry about. You already know who I am, what I'm capable of. It's the people you've put your full faith in that you have to suspect."

Iris leaned forward. "What do you know?"

"A great deal. But you won't know any of it until you've convinced me that I can trust you with my safety. If I start asking questions that raise eyebrows, it'll be my head on the chopping block. And frankly, I'm not interested in risking my neck in order to save yours."

Bear signaled for the waitress to bring another round of coffees. "Let's negotiate."

35

MANDY MANAGED FIVE SOLID HOURS OF SLEEP THAT AFTERNOON. WHEN she rose, her muscles were relaxed. She stretched and thought ahead to her match that evening.

Etta and Charlie were still helping her with her investigation, even after Mandy had told them about getting attacked. They'd both promised to double-down on their efforts to aid her, no matter what it took. She appreciated the front they were putting up when they both jumped whenever there was a loud noise.

Mandy wished she could tell them how much that truly meant to her, but overt displays of emotion made her feel like insects were crawling around under her skin. Besides, the moment passed as soon as Charlie said he had the mics ready for her to use that night. It shouldn't have taken as long as it had, but Charlie had made some tweaks to the devices, creating an object perfectly curated to what they'd needed with leftover parts he'd found around the A.V. Club's headquarters. That way no one would get in trouble for stealing school property, and it would be better suited for the situation.

Charlie had gone into a long-winded explanation of how the device worked, not noticing when both Mandy and Etta's eyes glazed over. They let him talk, knowing that he enjoyed the minutiae of his work and took pride in what he'd created. It wasn't a new invention by any stretch of the imagination, but even Mandy could recognize the genius of building the little recorder from scrap parts.

It was small enough to be hidden under the seats of the bleachers. The mic was strong enough to pick up surrounding voices and dampen the background noise. Charlie would still need to run it through a couple of programs to amplify the right voices and reduce others. Even better, Charlie had paired small earbuds to the device so Mandy could listen in live while the files were sent to her computer so she could review them later. First, she had her match to deal with.

For the first time since Coach Foley asked her to join the boxing team, Mandy wished she could be anywhere else. So far, her time had been spent honing skills that were already above and beyond those of her peers. Coach Foley pushed her harder than anyone else and she had seen the results of a more regimented routine than anything she'd gotten with Bear. Her jabs were more accurate, her hooks more devastating, and her footwork fancier than ever.

The problem was staying focused. She could blame it on her ADHD, but even she knew it was more than that. She couldn't stop thinking about whether Bear was okay or if he were bleeding out somewhere, all alone. Sometimes she wished he would call. And then she realized she was glad he hadn't because what if this time was the last time? What if he was calling to tell her goodbye, and that he loved her, and to find Jack, the only person he'd entrust with her care?

But it wasn't just what was going on with Bear—it was also what was going on right under her nose. She'd all but proven that Reagan was tied to this school, and thanks to Iris, she was able to do something about it. Mandy was shocked that Bear hadn't shown up on her doorstep to drag her away from this place as soon as he found out. The fact he hadn't proved how entrenched they all were. Everyone played a part.

She shook herself from the nihilism, slipped through the back door to the gym and climbed the bleachers to the top. A few students were already in place, though they were on the far end, laughing and chatting like they lived in a perfect world free of monsters and megalomaniacs. What a life that must be.

Pretending to survey the arena before her, Mandy made her way up to the top corner where the parents usually gathered and slipped her hand under the bench to stick the recorder in place. They'd had to come up with a contingency plan in case the parents chose to sit elsewhere tonight. It involved Etta clumsily shuffling through groups of people, falling, grabbing the recorder, and then repeating the process to stick it in place closer to their target audience. Mandy crossed all her fingers in the hopes that it wouldn't come down to that.

Mr. Foley and the rest of the team entered just as Mandy stood and made her way down the bleachers, limping on a non-existent sprained ankle. When she got to the bottom of the bleachers, she winced, caught her coach's eye, then shuffled over to him at an aggravatingly slow pace.

He looked her up and down as she approached. "What happened to you?"

"Sprained my ankle during some warmups this morning." Mandy shook her head and gave him an embarrassed smile. "I don't think I can fight tonight. I'm so sorry."

Coach Foley stared at her long enough that it became uncomfortable, but when she didn't squirm under his gaze, he just gave her a sharp nod. "What were you doing up in the bleachers?"

"Thought I'd sit up there and watch," she said, the lie coming out easier than the truth would have. "But it's too far away. Is it okay if I sit on the bench?"

"Yeah, okay." Mr. Foley gave her another long look before turning away and gathering with the team.

Mandy sat down on the bench, trying her best to look disappointed. When no one was watching, she slipped an earbud into place and covered it with her hair, hoping she'd remember not to toss it over her shoulder and give herself away. The other earbud was with Etta, who'd sit up in the bleachers and listen in just in case Mandy missed something important in the moment. Charlie would be down by the ring. He would film the match and try to catch the parents in his frame whenever he could.

It was a good plan, but not foolproof. The mic could short out or not pick up what they needed to hear. The parents could grow suspicious, not only of Mandy but of her friends. Roy King could spot the earbud. Or Amy could talk her ear off and not let her listen to the conversation. And those were only the most likely of scenarios. There were plenty Mandy hadn't even considered.

Marissa Stonewall arrived first, followed by Lochlan Reid. Mrs. Stonewall waved to her daughter from their usual spot at the top of the bleachers, and Mandy breathed her first sigh of relief since she planted the mic. If nothing else, at least Etta wouldn't have to move the mic right under their noses. Even from the other side of the gym, Mandy could see that her friend was just as thankful as she was.

A crackling in her ear almost made Mandy jump, and Charlie sent her a silent apology from where he stood a couple dozen feet away. He'd turned on the device as soon as the parents sat down, not wanting to waste the battery in case it drained faster than expected. The voices were distorted and tinny, but she could hear almost every word being said, no matter how quietly they talked. Once Charlie cleaned up the audio, it would be even easier to dissect everything. Mandy resisted the urge to smile in triumph.

But if she thought everything would go her way that day, she was sorely mistaken. Ten minutes into the first match, Mandy realized Raymond King wouldn't show up. She looked for him throughout the crowd, in case he chose to sit elsewhere, but she did not find him among the sea of cheering faces.

Not that she was surprised. Bear had told her about how he'd shot the man in the shoulder. Showing up to his son's boxing match the next day with his arm in a sling wouldn't be good for his image. Even if no one knew how he'd been injured, the cowardly would whisper behind his back and the brave would ask him to his face. You can only lie so many times before the truth slips out, one way or another.

For better or worse, Stonewall and Reid were doing fine without their de facto leader. Their heads were bent close enough together to make it obvious they were speaking in whispers, but not so close that the people around them would become suspicious. Over the last few weeks, Mandy had observed that most of the other parents and students often avoided looking at them altogether. Whether it was because they could sense they were up to no good or because they were smart enough to keep their eyes averted from those of a higher station, she had no idea.

"Have you heard from him?" Stonewall asked.

"No," Reid replied. "Called twice. Straight to voicemail. Something must've happened."

"He should've just kept his head down."

"Like you're not beaming on the inside. You've been waiting for him to screw up so you can take his place."

"I have no interest in *taking his place*," Stonewall replied. Mandy couldn't see her facial expression but could imagine the tilt of her upturned nose as she spoke. "We each have a role to play. If he endangered the plan—"

"It'll be fine," Reid said. "It's not like we're not all replaceable."

"Speak for yourself."

There was silence for a few minutes while the crowd cheered for the end of one match and the beginning of another.

"You know they've become a problem," Stonewall said. "We can't keep ignoring it."

"They're not *our* problem," Reid said.

"If Logan gets any closer, it'll be more than just a problem. It'll be a death sentence."

Mandy sucked in a breath, drawing the eyes of several teammates, and coughed to cover it up. Only when the others looked away did she allow some alarm to flicker over her face before tamping it down and focusing again on the conversation buzzing in her ear.

"Reagan isn't worried," Reid said. "So we shouldn't be either. One phone call and everyone Logan has ever called a friend will turn on him. Everyone has a price."

Stonewall scoffed and said, "You of all people should know."

"Hey, if I'm gonna commit treason, I might as well get paid for it."

After that, the pair of them talked of nothing concrete. Mandy's head was miles away, somewhere west of her with her dad, hoping against hope that he was okay. Reagan had considerable reach, but was he aware that one phone call could end it all for them? If he suspected, did he truly believe it?

With a shaking hand, Mandy pulled out her phone and texted Marcus.

She was getting tired of being afraid. Of running away just to protect herself.

It was time to fight back.

36

On a typical day, Monarch would take pride in his rich wood desk that he kept to a mirror finish. He'd soak up the warmth of the sun on his back from the wide windows behind him. Breathe deep the smell of lemon cleaner and coffee, which shouldn't blend well together but somehow, over the years, had come to symbolize the start of a fresh, new day.

On this day, he felt no such comforts.

The coffee ring to the left of his keyboard had been missed. The sky was bleak and cloudy. The coffee burnt. His shoulder throbbed in time with his heartbeat. Unable to go to a hospital, he'd knocked on his friend's door in the middle of the night, offering a blank check in exchange for a couple stitches and some painkillers.

The wound was closed with the kind of precision that only came with decades of experience, the bandage tight and unmoving. He'd never been shot before and found it infuriatingly cumbersome. He had to be careful not to twist too sharply or else the stitches wouldn't stay in place and he'd bleed through his collared shirt. He decided it best to keep his jacket on today.

It had been almost twenty-four hours since the disaster of an operation that had gotten him shot. His one consolation was that the weapons were at least halfway to Florida by now. The next step of their journey would be well underway.

But Riley Logan and Iris Duvall should've died, buried in an unmarked grave next to all three members of the Ortiz family. Instead, they were all in the wind, and his cover was blown. The shadow of the anvil that hung over his head grew denser with every snap of the thread holding it aloft.

He'd been a loyal servant to Mr. Reagan for years, and there was no reason to think that had changed. This was the first true mistake he'd ever made. Surely that wasn't reason enough to throw him to the wolves?

Staring down at the phone sitting in the middle of the desk, Monarch jumped when a polite knock sounded from his office door. It was late enough that all his employees should've been long gone. He made a mental note to give his assistant a raise, considering she had four kids and a worthless husband at home.

"Come in." Monarch flattened his expression into one of harried annoyance. Whoever it was, he'd answer their question and send them on their way.

The doorknob turned, allowing a slim figure into the room. She wore a red dress that left nothing to the imagination, and her brown hair was cut into a bob that did nothing to soften the sharp angles of her face. Her bangs made her look younger than her years, but he really had no idea how old she was. Younger than him, to be sure.

The woman shut the door behind her with a sharp *click* that made Monarch sit up a little straighter. On black stiletto heels, she crossed the room like a model, with one foot in front of the other, hips swaying to a beat only she could hear. She wasn't a tall woman, but her back was so straight and her shoulders so rigid, it seemed like her head was inches away from brushing against the ceiling.

"Mr. King," the woman said, her voice deep and sultry, like a lover come calling. "How's your shoulder?"

He was in trouble. She had never once used his real name in any of their conversations except the very first, all those years ago. The concern in her eyes was a lie—merely theatrics to make the pinnacle of her visit land all the harder.

"It's fine." Monarch hated the way his voice sounded like that of a prepubescent teenager's, high and broken. He cleared his throat. "I was expecting a phone call."

"Nonsense." The woman poured herself into the chair opposite him like molten rubies, and he couldn't stop the way his eyes trailed up her thigh as she crossed her legs at the knee. "I wanted to see you with my own eyes. Make sure you were doing as well as you'd said."

It wasn't hard to bite back the retort on the tip of Monarch's tongue. He could count on one hand the number of times he'd met *Mr. Reagan* in person. Each and every time, she had sent a shiver down his spine. Like a black widow spider, she was deadlier than she was beautiful—more beautiful than anyone else he'd ever laid eyes on.

He had seen firsthand what she was capable of, especially regarding the men who'd dared question her abilities or resolve. He'd gained the privilege of being her righthand man not only because he was loyal, but also because he never questioned her judgement. Not once.

Not until yesterday.

"Tell me," she said.

He didn't need to ask her to clarify.

He told her about the weapons exchange. How Logan and Duvall had kidnapped Jackson Carter. He would have given the order to kill Carter if he'd been on site.

He told her about how he'd called Carter's phone, knowing Iris was in the backseat and would find it eventually. With robotic detachment, Monarch explained how, instead of killing Ortiz and his family as ordered, he kept them alive long enough to use them as bait for Logan and Duvall. Two birds with one stone, he said. Or rather, five birds with one gun.

He didn't tell her that he had figured out the young girl who had given his son a black eye was Logan's daughter. She went by a different last name, but he had access to more than just the school's records. He'd used the information for his own benefit, but the man he'd sent to kidnap her had failed. His best bargaining chip was gone. He refused to admit another defeat to the woman in front of him.

"It wasn't as easy as you thought it would be." She had a gentle look on her face that could've been interpreted as an *I told you so*, if she wasn't above such a thing.

It took Monarch a moment to realize she wasn't talking about kidnapping the girl but about trying to take down her father. What was the point in denying it?

"No," he said. "It wasn't."

Reagan remained impassive, though her interest sharpened like a piece of broken glass. "How did he escape?"

"He surprised me. Stole my man's gun. Killed everyone."

"Everyone but you."

"Yes."

"Because you ran."

Monarch ground his teeth together. "Yes."

"That was smart."

"It was?" He hated how he craved her approval.

Her eyes widened, innocent as a newborn fawn's. "A tactical retreat can be just as useful as a surprise attack."

Monarch wasn't relieved. He had known her too long to believe her sweet words. "I can make it up to you. I'll find them. I'll take care of it."

"Who?" Reagan asked, tilting her head to the side.

"Logan. Duvall."

Reagan's laugh was girlish. It didn't match the darkness of her eyes. "I did warn you to leave Logan alone. You're lucky you escaped with your life. It's the Ortizes I'm most concerned about. Vincent owes Logan not only his life, but the lives of his family. He will do whatever he can to ensure our operation fails. And we have little hope of finding them now that Logan has sent them away to safety."

"I can—"

"You can't." Reagan dropped her femme fatale façade for the first time since she entered Monarch's office. "You can't, and you won't."

Without waiting for a reply, Reagan uncrossed her legs and stood, her body no longer molten, but now as hard as diamonds. She strode across the room and uncorked a bottle of fifteen-year-old Whistle Pig Rye and poured two fingers into a glass. She carried the glass back across the room and sat it down on the edge of the desk.

If Monarch had been a stronger man, he would've taken his punishment in silence. But the strength of her anger made his knees weak, and he couldn't help but ask the question that had been on his mind since the moment he escaped from the compound.

"Are you going to kill me?"

Reagan's reply was quiet, but not gentle. "No."

Monarch watched as she slipped a hand down the front of her dress and removed a small packet of white powder. With a flick of her wrist, she dumped it into the whiskey and tucked the empty bag back into her bra. Swirling the glass until the powder dissolved, she used a single finger to slide it across his desk until it sat in front of him. Normally a beacon of hope at the end of a long day, now the amber glinted up at him in warning.

"You said—"

"You can kill yourself."

He shook his head, losing what little nerve he had, and looked back down at the drink. "Why would I do that?"

"Because I plan to frame you for the murder of your wife and son if you don't. At least this way"—she gestured to the glass—"they'll get to live."

Monarch placed his palms flat on his desk. With a swipe of his hand, he could send it cascading to the floor. He could leap across his desk and wrap his fingers around her neck. He was bigger than her. Stronger, too.

And yet there was no scenario in which he won that fight.

"You promise?"

"I promise." There was no warmth in her gaze, but he chose to believe her sincerity. What other option did he have?

For the briefest of moments, he considered telling her about Mandy Logan. He wasn't above sentencing a child to death if it meant he got to live to see his own son grow old and have children of his own.

But no. Reagan would see him dead, one way or the other. Whether it was tonight, tomorrow, a week, or a year from now, the plan had never been to let him live.

Monarch took the glass in one hand and closed his eyes, picturing the faces of his wife and son and hoping someday they could forgive him for all he'd done and everything he'd never do.

Then he lifted the glass to his lips and tipped the liquid down his throat in one swift movement.

37

MARCUS WAS SITTING ON THE COUCH WATCHING YET ANOTHER *THE FAST and the Furious* movie when he got a text message from Mandy. The revving of engines covered up the buzz, and he managed to take a peek at it without his uncle noticing—at least until he sat up straight and held the phone an inch from his nose.

Bugged the seats. They mentioned my dad. King wasn't there.

Btw someone tried to attack me this morning. I'm fine. Don't tell your uncle.

It was only when a hand landed on his shoulder that Marcus realized he was hyperventilating. When he looked up at Brandon, he saw his uncle's mouth moving, but the sound was coming from a long way off, and he couldn't make out any of the words. His vision turned a sick sort of green with black around the edges.

"Hey," his uncle said. "Hey. Come on, don't pass out on me. Deep breaths. Slow. Slower."

The tightness in Marcus' chest eased. The frenetic thoughts subsided.

"There you go. Follow my lead." Brandon dragged in a deep breath, held it for a few seconds, then blew it out. "That's it. Give me a couple more like that."

He inhaled and held the air in his lungs before finally letting out an exaggerated sigh. He focused on nothing else but his uncle's commands and the rhythm of their shared breaths. After a while, his vision sharpened and his heartrate slowed. A cold pit of worry still lived in his stomach, but it shrank to the size of a grapefruit from a beachball.

"How're you doin', Champ?" Brandon asked.

Brandon hadn't called him Champ since he was five, but there was a familiar kind of comfort to the stupid nickname that Marcus would never admit out loud to anyone, not even Mandy. Especially not Mandy. She'd do nothing but call him Champ for the rest of her life.

"I'm good." He noticed the movie was still going on in the background, but it'd been muted. "S-s-sorry about that."

"Hey, it's no problem. That's why God invented the rewind button." Brandon's voice was light, but he was looking at Marcus as though he wanted to read his thoughts. "What's going on?"

"Mandy was at her match tonight. She bugged the bleachers."

"Did she now?" Brandon looked amused. "Like father, like daughter."

"Stonewall and Reid were talking about Bear. By name. Iris, too. And Raymond King wasn't there."

The laughter in Brandon's eyes was gone. "Not surprised by any of that. What were they saying?"

"Just that they needed to be taken care of. But that Reagan didn't seem concerned."

"His loss. But that's not anything we don't already know. Something else gave you a panic attack. What was it?"

Marcus swallowed back the bile rising in his throat. Mandy hadn't wanted him to tell his uncle about her getting attacked, but it's not like she made the best judgment calls. He'd lied for her plenty of times in the past. This felt different. It felt wrong to keep it from Brandon.

"She was attacked this morning," Marcus said, his breath hitching on the last word. "And I think it's my fault."

Brandon turned around. "Whoa, whoa. Attacked? What happened?"

"I'm not sure. She said she's fine. I believe her. She wouldn't lie about that."

"Did she tell her dad?"

Marcus licked his lips. His gut clenched against the lie he was about to tell. "Yes."

"Good." Brandon nodded. The relieved tension from the man's shoulders crawled across his lap and up Marcus' spine. "Why do you think it's your fault?"

"No one knew where she was until I sent that email. What if it wasn't a coincidence?"

"Hey, we don't know that for sure. If it's anyone's fault, it's mine. I should've been more careful. Should've taught you better. I knew you were up to something, but I just figured it was some light shenanigans. Nothing worse than I got up to when I was your age. I was wrong, wasn't I?"

"I'm sorry."

"You'll be better than me someday, kid. But it's up to me to make sure you get there."

Marcus was blinking away tears now, and he couldn't tell if it was from his uncle's compliments or his fear that he'd gotten Mandy in worse trouble than she already was. "How do we know it wasn't my fault?"

"I guess we don't. But Reagan is serious business. Not kid stuff. You did a good thing trying to help your friend. But this is bigger than you. And me. We both need to be more careful."

Marcus tried to take his uncle's words to heart, but he found it hard to swallow past the guilt that formed a lump in his throat. "How?"

"First thing's first. You need to pack your bags."

Marcus didn't bother trying to hold back his sob this time. "You're kicking me out?"

"What?" Brandon shook him a little bit until he met his eyes again. "Hell no. We're both packing up and getting the hell out of here. Just in case Reagan decides to try to ruin our night."

"Where are we going?"

The smirk that crossed Brandon's face look equal parts excited and menacing. "I've got a few options. Don't you worry."

38

BEAR STOOD WITH HIS EYES CLOSED AGAINST THE WARM BRICK FAÇADE OF A warehouse on the outskirts of Chicago, trying not to shiver against the cold breeze caressing his skin. The sky was a mottled gray, tinged with the type of gloom that promised rain—or possibly snow—later in the day. With any luck, he wouldn't be there to see it.

Thorne had made a few calls under the watchful gaze of both Iris and Bear and tracked the eighteen-wheeler full of weapons back to a distribution center outside the city. He was certain there would be a record of the shipment from Chicago to Miami—Reagan would want the truck to look as legitimate as possible. There'd be a manifest and a load of real product sitting in front of the true cargo. If that were true, they'd be able to find the truck's destination with enough time to get to Miami and intercept the exchange.

Bear and Iris had no choice but to rely on his information. Besides, Thorne would be right there with them, in as much danger as they were if it ended up being a trap. Iris thought Bear was being paranoid, but she didn't know Daniel Thorne like he did.

Bear did one more sweep of their surroundings. Overgrown grass and bushes desperately in need of trimming had allowed them to remain hidden until they were ready to launch their attack. Not that there was much worry about them being seen. No one wandered the property, and the single security camera dangled from a pair of wires, aimed at the ground. So far, luck had been on their side, but they had no idea what was waiting for them inside the warehouse.

"You can't possibly expect me to go in there without a gun," Thorne said.

It was not the first time he'd brought up the issue, and it probably wouldn't be the last.

Bear chuckled. "Lost your touch already? The Daniel Thorne I knew could talk himself out of any situation."

"And I still can," Thorne said. "But a gun is faster. And less dangerous. For me. At least give me a vest if I have to go unarmed."

"You've still got two fists, don't you?" Iris added, catching Bear's eye. "What more do you need?"

"Besides," Bear said, "no time for vests. Let's do this. Quick and dirty. In and out. Don't kill anyone unless it's in self-defense. Just incapacitate. We may need to question them. I don't think these guys are part of Reagan's network. I think they are just unfortunate enough to work here."

"You take all the fun out of it," Thorne said.

Bear ignored him. A quick nod to Iris had her turning around and leading them along the back wall and toward the rear entrance. They'd watched the building long enough to know it remained unlocked so the workers could take their smoke breaks. A group of them had gone back inside ten minutes ago. Now was the best time to catch them unaware.

Iris stopped next to the door. Thorne lined up behind her while Bear placed his hand on the knob from the other side. A silent countdown passed between them, and he yanked the door open with such force it bounced off the wall. Iris stepped inside, Thorne on her heels, with Bear taking up the rear, gun at the ready.

"FBI," Iris shouted. "Everyone down on the ground."

A dozen faces turned to look at the three of them. The warehouse contained four eighteen-wheelers and a handful of smaller cargo vans, along with a pair of forklifts. Pallets of boxes lined one wall, and the men had been in the middle of loading one of the trucks when the trio had entered. An office on the other side housed a bank of computers and a frightened man with a goatee who froze in the doorway. That office was their goal.

"FBI," Iris repeated. "Down on the ground. Now."

The room thawed. The dozen men loading and unloading the trucks scrambled. Iris swore and sprinted for the nearest worker. A gunshot rang out. The bullet passed inches from her and stopped her dead in her tracks. Another shot had her diving behind one of the empty forklifts.

Bear and Thorne threw themselves behind the tires of one tractor trailer as a pair of bullets headed their way.

"Stay with me," Bear shouted at Thorne.

"Trust me," Thorne said, his composure cracking. "I plan to use you as my personal shield."

A series of pops sounded from Iris' location, and he knew she was returning fire. Bear leaned around the wheel and squeezed off a shot, causing one man to drop his weapon and dance out of the way.

"This would be more efficient if you killed them," Thorne said.

"We don't know who they are or how they're involved," Bear said. "I'm not killing innocent civilians."

"In my experience, no one is truly innocent."

Bear ignored the comment. "We need to make it to that office."

"Lead the way."

Bear stood and sprinted to the end of the tractor trailer, leaning around the back, and cataloging the number of men in front of him with a single glance. Raising his gun, he shot the tire out from one of the cargo vans which had all three men spinning toward it in surprise. Bear used their distraction to sprint to the next truck, trusting Thorne would stay close enough to remain uninjured.

But as soon as Bear hit his mark, a figure jumped from the back of the truck and landed on his back, knocking him to the ground and causing him to lose his grip on his gun. It skittered across the concrete floor as the air whooshed out of his lungs. A knee in the middle of his back pinned him, and a death grip around one of his wrists wrenched his arm back until his shoulder screamed in protest.

Between one grunt and the next, the weight shifted off Bear and he could breathe again. Rolling over onto his back, prepared to fight for his life, he saw Thorne with his arm around the larger man's neck, squeezing until the man went blue in the face. Just as Bear thought Thorne had the upper hand, the man threw himself on the ground, sandwiching Thorne between the floor and his considerable bulk.

Bear scrambled to his feet, but Thorne was faster. As the other man twisted to wrap his hands around Thorne's neck, there were a pair of pops and the man shuddered then fell to the side. Kicking away from his adversary, Thorne rose to his feet, Bear's gun held between both hands.

"Damn that felt good." Thorne turned toward Bear and raised the gun, aiming it at his chest.

Bear took a step back, knowing that no matter how fast he was, he couldn't outmaneuver a bullet at this range. Thorne's grin widened, and there was a glint of something dangerous in his eyes.

But then Thorne let go of his grip on the gun, letting it swing from his pointer finger by the trigger guard. "You dropped this."

Heart hammering in his chest, Bear took the weapon in silence, knowing this was less a proof of trust than a reminder of how dangerous Thorne could be. That the man across from him was simply choosing to play along until he was dealt a better hand.

Iris rushed around the corner of the truck and nearly slammed into Bear. "What the hell are you doing? Get to the computers. I'll cover you." She looked down at the dead body between him and Thorne. "What happened to not killing anyone?"

"Wasn't my choice." Bear avoided Iris' eyes. He'd have to tell her what happened sooner or later, but now was not the time. "How many are left?"

"All of them," Iris said. "I've been trying to distract them so you could get to the office."

Bear didn't need to be told twice. He spun on his heel and sprinted for the back office. Thorne stayed close, nearly stepping on Bear's heels. He wove through trucks and around palettes. Bullets came close enough to spray dust and debris across them. Iris held up her end of the bargain and kept them safe.

The man inside the office turned the lock as soon as Bear was within arm's reach, but he didn't slow his approach. He dropped his shoulder and slammed into the thin wooden door, taking it off its hinges. The man inside screamed and crawled under the desk, but Bear hauled him up by his collar and shoved him back into his chair.

Turning to Thorne, he pointed at the man. "Make sure he gets what we need."

"With pleasure," Thorne said.

The man whimpered in protest.

Bear squatted next to the busted off door, keeping one eye on Iris and one ear on Thorne's instructions to the man. Every once in a while, there'd be another whimper, but Bear assumed by the lack of fists meeting flesh that Thorne was getting what they needed.

Meanwhile, Iris was doing more than her fair share of keeping them alive. Running back and forth, diving like a maniac behind anything that could shield her from bullets, she was distracting at least half a dozen men at a time. Whenever they would get too close, Bear would fire a warning shot and they'd back off, allowing Iris to move again and pop up where they least expected her.

At least six more dead bodies lay on the ground, unfortunate casualties of their little operation. Taking out the whole warehouse of men was the more efficient way of going about this, but it also meant more evidence stacked up against them. If these deaths could be traced back to them, there was no doubt in his mind that Reagan would use that to his advantage. They had to get away clean.

"Got it," Thorne said. "Got the address and time."

"Can we make it?" Bear asked.

"If we leave within the hour? We might have a few seconds to spare."

Bear cursed. They had been lucky so far, but it seemed as though their luck might be running out. "On me," he told Thorne. "Let's get out of here."

39

Mandy knocked on the door to Amy's room, filled with anticipation and concern. She'd received a text message twenty minutes ago asking her to come over so they could talk about something important.

Amy opened the door with a meek smile, which Mandy returned as she stepped inside. The other girl was a little taller than her, with hair so straight and shiny, Mandy swore she could see her reflection in it. Not for the first time, Mandy wondered if they were truly friends, or if the truth about why she'd started talking to Amy would come between them one day.

Was that day today?

"Thanks for coming." Amy closed the door behind her. "Sit wherever you want."

Amy's room couldn't have been more different from Mandy's. Where Mandy's was sparse and practical, Amy seemed to have filled hers with everything she could fit inside her parents' car from her bedroom back home. Dozens of purple pillows were artfully arranged atop a pink bedspread that looked softer than anything Mandy had ever slept on. Posters hung across the wall, a mix between Amy's favorite bands and a few well-known paintings. There was even a sofa, topped with more pillows, next to a desk that looked cluttered and yet still meticulously organized.

Everything matched, and Mandy had to wonder if Amy's room back home looked even better than this. A pang of jealousy coursed through her body, but she wasn't sure why. It's not like she and Bear were poor. In fact, she'd bet a considerable amount of money that Bear had more savings tucked away than Amy's parents combined. But they moved around too much for her to have a room filled with this much stuff.

Maybe that's what had made her envious. The permanence of it all.

Mandy sat on the sofa. It was more comfortable than it had any right to be. She waited until Amy sat down in the desk chair to her right before asking, "What did you wanna talk about?"

Amy took a deep breath and stared down at her folded hands resting on her lap. "Look, I'm not stupid. I know you're not my friend because you like me."

Mandy's spine straightened. "That's not true—"

Amy shook her head. "It's okay. I was the new girl once, too. I know how mean everyone can be. I know what you have to do to survive in a place like this. I'm not proud of the way I've turned the other way when Roy and his friends bully the other kids."

"Maybe that's what I thought at first," Mandy said. "But I do like hanging out with you. Really, I do."

Amy finally looked up at her. "Really?"

"Yeah, really." Mandy laughed a little. "I'm sorry if I made you feel like it wasn't real."

Amy held Mandy's gaze. "You ask a lot of questions. I'm not the only one who's noticed."

"I'm a curious person."

"I believe that. But it's more than that, isn't it?"

"I just—I mean—"

"I think"—Amy swallowed before continuing—"I think my mom might be...*involved* in something."

If Mandy wasn't sitting as rigid as possible, her spine would've straightened more. "What do you mean?"

"It sounds crazy."

"I like crazy. Hit me with it."

"I-I think my mom might be"—Amy lowered her voice— "involved in a conspiracy."

Mandy blinked in surprise. "What makes you think that? Did you hear her say something?"

"It's a lot of little things, you know? I've caught her in a few lies, saying she's going to one place and then saying she came back from another. She always blows it off." Amy licked her lips, her eyes growing wider. "I snooped through her office once. She's got this hidden safe behind a painting. I don't know how to open it, though."

"Could she be hiding something else?" Mandy didn't want to suggest the obvious, that maybe Mrs. Stonewall was having an affair, because that would be hard for anyone to believe of their parents.

"Maybe, but there's more." Taking a deep breath, Amy turned to fully face Mandy now. "She has two cell phones, and she was on the weird one when I heard her talk about being worried that someone would find out what she was doing. She said she could only turn a blind eye for so long before someone got suspicious of her. Sometimes, when I'm home, I notice the same SUV driving by multiple times a day."

Now Mandy was really interested. "Do you have any idea what she's doing?"

"I don't really know what her job is, other than the fact that she works for the Treasury Department," Amy said. "But I'm scared. And I see the way you watch my mom and Mr. King and Mr. Reid. I can tell that the footage for the matches isn't just for us. You're studying our parents too, aren't you?"

Mandy winced. She thought they'd been less obvious about that, especially with Charlie cutting the footage that didn't center on the matches. "Are you mad?"

Amy shook her head. "No, but"—she looked like she was holding back tears—"I don't want my mom to get into trouble."

"Look, I—" Mandy broke off, not sure she should make any promises.

But what Stonewall and the other parents were involved in was so much bigger than Mandy and Amy. It was bigger than all the families involved. Whatever Reagan was planning was big enough to put the whole country in danger. It was her responsibility to find out what that was, even if it meant she bore the brunt of the consequences in the end.

"I'll do what I can to keep your mom out of this. I don't think she's in charge of whatever's happening." Mandy convinced herself that it wasn't a total lie. "But I need to know what you know."

Amy nodded, wiping away her tears. "I really don't know much. But she mentioned Venezuela. Does that mean anything to you?"

Mandy's stomach twisted into a knot. "As a matter of fact, it does."

40

REAGAN SAT ON A BLUE VELVET COUCH, STILL IN THE SLINKY RED DRESS she'd worn to speak with Monarch. She'd removed her heels and tucked her feet up under her body, knowing that the position not only showed off her toned thighs, but it would make her look like the picture of relaxation.

Underneath the surface, she was anything but.

Her muscles were tight with anticipation, and she had the urge to pick at the skin around the bed of her thumbnail—a habit she had kicked many years ago when she'd realized it was nothing but a tell for her anxiety. Now she couldn't afford even that small gesture of comfort. She was mere days away from seeing her goals completed, and nothing and no one would stand in her way.

A knock sounded at the door. She reached over to pick up the tablet on the plush carpet of the apartment. Turning on the screen, she called out, "Come in," in a bored voice.

Baron entered the room with a tranquil expression on his handsome face, though she saw the way his eyes scanned the room, looking for threats in every dark corner. "Did you see the news?"

She turned her screen so he could see the headline she'd been pretending to read. "Raymond King found dead in office. Investigation ongoing."

"Do I need to keep an eye on anyone involved?"

"No. I think the evidence will be fairly straightforward."

"They'll question the bullet wound in his shoulder."

Reagan shrugged. "I think that'll only help the case for suicide."

Baron made a noncommittal noise that indicated he wasn't sure he agreed but showed he was smart enough to keep that thought to himself. She'd always appreciated the way he pushed against her, not because he wanted to prove his way was the right way, but because he wanted their plan to succeed. He had a lot to gain from it, after all.

"Besides," Reagan said, "we have a bigger problem in need of your attention."

"Logan and Duvall." Baron slid into the matching chair across from her.

"We need to slow their progress. Put them on a watchlist."

"Are you sure—" Baron cut off when Reagan raised a single eyebrow at him. "I think we're playing with fire here."

"Oh?" Reagan sat up, setting her tablet down next to her and crossing her legs at the ankles. "Do tell."

Baron huffed "They're not yet aware of everyone working for us. If we put them on a watchlist, it will become apparent."

"They'll find out soon anyway. We need to get ahead of them."

A muscle in Baron's jaw clenched, but he remained silent.

Forcing Monarch to drink the drugged whiskey had not been as satisfying as she'd hoped, and she ached for a proper fight. "Go on. Tell me what's on your mind."

"We should've killed them when we had the chance. I warned you that—"

"*You* warned *me?*" Reagan pushed to her feet like a dancer preparing for her big number.

Baron remained seated, apparently refusing to become her sparring partner. "I didn't mean—"

"I know Riley Logan better than you ever will." Reagan crossed the room and stood within arm's reach of the man. "You've studied his files and read all the reports, but I've seen what he's capable of with my own two eyes. I have not underestimated him. I *will* see him dead when the dust settles. But not before he plays the role of pawn in my little game."

"I look forward to it."

Reagan took a step back, knowing she wouldn't get the fight she was looking for.

Baron cleared his throat and said, "Duvall is proving more resourceful than expected."

"Have you found Logan's daughter yet?" Reagan asked, already knowing the answer.

"No." Baron didn't look away as he said it, though she could see the disappointment and shame in his eyes. "Not yet. But I will."

"I expect nothing less from you. Just like I expect you to ensure the exchange goes off without a hitch."

For the first time that night, Baron looked concerned. "Reagan—"

"*Mr.* Reagan," she said. The name had done well to cover her tracks for many years, and she was oddly fond of it now. It inspired fear, even in those who knew the truth of her identity.

"*Mr.* Reagan," Baron corrected, "I'm happy to do this, but—"

"But?"

"But Logan and Duvall will find out where the exchange is taking place. They'll try to stop it."

"And you'll ensure they fail."

"My cover will be blown."

Reagan sighed. The fight had gone out of her. "A necessary complication now that Monarch is dead. It can't be helped."

Baron hesitated, but in the end he nodded. "Understood." He got to his feet and buttoned the jacket of his navy-blue suit. "Is there anything else I can do for you?"

"Don't disappoint me." Reagan didn't bother to watch for his reaction to the threat. She picked up her tablet and leaned back until she was propped up by her elbow. "I'd hate to lose another member of the team."

"Understood."

With nothing left to discuss, Baron left the apartment, closing the door behind him with a soft *click*. Reagan lifted her gaze to watch him go, wondering if it would be more difficult to kill him than Monarch.

41

BEAR CALLED IN A FAVOR AND GOT A FRIEND OF A FRIEND TO FLY THEM down to Miami in his private plane . It wasn't first class accommodations, which Thorne had pointed out at least three times, but they could have a conversation without worrying about being overheard. Not to mention this was much faster than going through security at an airport, and easier with a convicted felon in tow.

Bear's phobia of flying sat just under the surface of his skin, boiling up whenever they hit any kind of turbulence due to the few storm cells they passed through as they left Chicago. He tried to ignore the way Thorne watched him white-knuckle his armrests, knowing the man would use any sign of weakness against him.

There were only eight seats in the cabin. Thorne sat across the aisle from him and Iris, her nose buried in a tablet she'd bought at a local electronics store moments before they were due to meet their contact at the airstrip. They'd left Raine in the hotel room back in Chicago.

"I think we should call for backup," Iris said. They were halfway through their three-hour flight, and this was not the first time she'd mentioned it.

"We can't risk it," Bear replied, not for the first time. "We have no idea who could be on Reagan's payroll."

Iris' gaze slid to Thorne. "Lucky for us we have someone who can verify that."

Thorne held up his hands. "I don't know every person Reagan has under his thumb. I'm not exactly risk-averse, but even I think that would be a poor choice given what we're heading toward. It'd be naïve to invite an unknown player to the plate without assurance they're not batting for the other team."

Iris returned her gaze to the tablet. "Good thing you don't get a vote, then."

"Well, I do." Bear's voice came out sharper than he intended. "And I say we can't risk it."

"You're siding with him?"

"I'm not siding with anyone. I just want to give us the best chance to walk away."

Iris lowered the tablet to her lap in a huff and leaned forward, her eyes caught between desperation and anger. "We barely got out of the last place alive. We need someone to watch our backs. They'll know we're coming. It's a death sentence."

"It would be a death sentence to bring someone along only for them to stick a gun to our heads once we crossed the point of no return."

"That's exactly what I just said," Thorne said. "Of course, if you gave me a gun—"

"No," Bear and Iris said in unison, not even bothering to look at him.

"Worth a try," Thorne mumbled, and returned to picking invisible lint off his pants.

"Is there anyone you trust to back us up?" Iris asked.

"No one who can get here in time. We're all we've got."

"And we're not exactly the A-Team," Thorne said, his voice too innocent to trick anyone. "More like—what's that movie where one of them betrays the group? Ah, *The Losers*."

Iris' gaze narrowed in on him. "What's that supposed to mean?"

"Well, there's me." He gestured to himself. "The former CIA operative and current convicted felon. No one's rooting for me."

"Tell me something I don't know."

"Then there's Mr. Logan." Thorne waved a lazy hand in his general direction. "You've known the man for what, a couple months? He, apparently, had no idea who Mr. Reagan was prior to meeting you, and yet he found himself embroiled in the HealTek conspiracy, not to mention everything that went down in North Carolina."

Bear felt a shiver run down his spine but kept his voice even. "How do you know about that?"

Thorne shrugged. "I've kept my eye on you. Not easy, I'll admit, but not impossible. No one can disappear completely, no matter how many friends they have within clandestine agencies."

Bear noticed the way Iris studied him, but he spoke directly to Thorne. "Those were coincidences. We know how vast Reagan's network is. It was only a matter of time before I ran into one or two of his operations."

"Perhaps." Thorne turned his attention to Iris. "Then there's Ms. Duvall. Current FBI agent who has been chasing Mr. Reagan for how many years now? And it's only since meeting Mr. Logan that you've come this close."

Iris' eyes narrowed. "What does that have to do with anything?"

"A smart operative looks at the situation from every angle. Perhaps it's a trap, and you're the one leading him blindly into it."

Iris scoffed. "For what purpose? There've been at least a dozen times I could've taken him out on my own. Why would I go to all this trouble?"

"You tell us."

"There is no us," Bear said, though he hated the way he was considering Thorne's words.

"I'm just talking out loud." Thorne crossed his legs and leaned down to rest his chin in his hand to continue staring at Iris. "I find it highly convenient that you've known about Mr. Reagan for all these years and yet you're still alive. Why do you think that is?"

Iris went stiff in her seat when Bear asked, "What's your connection to Mr. Reagan?"

Iris recoiled as though she'd been slapped. "I don't see how—"

"Answer the question, Iris." Bear shifted in his seat in case the conversation escalated. He adjusted his tone. "Maybe the information will help us look at this from a different angle."

Iris sighed, deflating like a balloon that had finally given up any chance of flying away on the wind. "It was years ago. I was a rookie. Naïve, to say the least. There was this young woman. Her name was—" She faltered for a moment, like she hadn't said the name out loud in years and the shape of it scraped painfully against her throat. "Bridgette."

"Who was she?"

"A young woman in trouble." Iris looked out the window and watched the clouds pass by as though she could see her memories in them. "She'd been mixed up in a drug operation. We got her out when we took it down, but she was ranting and raving about how we might as well have killed her ourselves. She was out of her mind. I don't know if it was drugs or fear or some combination of the two."

"Were they protecting her?" Bear asked. "Is that why she didn't want to leave?"

"Part of it. A little while later, when she calmed down a bit more, I found out she was after information. That was the first time I heard Reagan's name."

"What kind of information?"

"There was an undercover agent who had been embedded in that cell for over a year. She'd been tasked with finding out who it was, or else Mr. Reagan would kill her whole family. She said she had a little sister, just ten years old."

"Do you know why he wanted to know?" Bear asked.

Iris shook her head. "Never got a chance to find out. I promised Bridgette I would keep her family safe, but before we could do anything, she disappeared."

"Do you think she's still alive?"

Iris shook her head, the pain evident on her face as though this had happened just a few hours ago instead of a few years. "A couple days later, I received a message from Reagan telling me her blood was on my hands. It's been a wild goose chase ever since. His name pops up every-where, but no one knows who he is or what he's truly after."

"You couldn't have known." Bear wanted to reach out and comfort her, knowing that would do nothing to assuage her guilt.

"Doesn't change the outcome though, does it?" Bitterness tingeing her words. "

"Who was the undercover agent?" Thorne asked.

Bear and Iris looked at him. "Why would I tell you that?"

"Could be important. Doesn't matter now anyway, right? That was years ago."

Iris looked to Bear, who shrugged. "Might be useful."

"Richard Peake."

Bear remembered the name. "The one covering for you."

Iris nodded. "After I found out what happened to Bridgette, I told him about Reagan. He didn't think it was a big deal—until we started hearing the name over and over. He stopped going undercover after that. Doesn't seem to miss it."

"What did Reagan want with him?"

"No idea. He didn't want anything to do with the case. Stayed out of it best he could. Helped me out on occasion, but whatever Reagan wanted out of him, he must've gotten somewhere else."

A ping from Iris' tablet interrupted their conversation. Picking up the device, her brows furrowed, and then she looked up with concern. "Raine just sent a headline. Raymond King is dead. Apparent suicide."

"How convenient," Bear said. "Guess he made one too many mistakes."

"Monarch seemed pretty high up in the grand scheme of things. Wonder who replaced him?"

"Maybe we'll find out when we get to Miami."

"You're right. We can't trust anyone. But I trust you. And I hope you know you can trust me too." She shifted in her seat, as though the next words out of her mouth caused her physical discomfort. "There's nothing I want more than to find Reagan and make him pay for his crimes. I know I didn't kill Bridgette directly, but I promised to protect her. Just like I promised to protect my cousin. And now they're both dead. Along with dozens, maybe hundreds of other people who made the mistake of crossing his path. Whatever way this plays out, Reagan won't be the last one standing."

One way or another, Reagan wasn't going to walk away from this. She just hoped they wouldn't meet the same fate along the way.

42

Marcus didn't know what he was expecting when his uncle told them they had to pack up and move to a new location, but it wasn't a fully furnished apartment just under an hour away from Brandon's house. The place was immaculate. Simple but comfortable enough. There were plenty of canned goods and snacks for them to eat. Marcus wondered when Brandon had last been there. The place was free of dirt and dust.

None of that made Marcus feel any better, though. Part of him was glad Stonewall had opened that email and granted them at least a little more information. He was still racked with guilt over the possibility that he could be the reason why Mandy had been attacked.

Earlier, his uncle had told him to keep his computer on as they drove in the opposite direction. Brandon had him leave it hidden in the stall of a bathroom at a fast-food restaurant while they drove back the way they'd come from. Marcus would've felt worse about losing his computer if his uncle hadn't promised he'd get him a better one.

That was the one thing Marcus couldn't understand—why his uncle wasn't angrier with him. Instead, Brandon seemed to come alive under the pressure. His eyes held excitement. He seemed all too eager to be able to use his safehouse. Even now, he hummed as he turned on his workstation, and when he asked Marcus to draw all the curtains, there was something akin to a giggle of excitement in his voice.

"Look, Uncle Brandon—"

"I told you, it's fine."

"Yeah, but—"

Brandon turned around to face him, clasping his hands in his lap and giving Marcus a goofy grin. "You didn't know any better. We avoided any major detection. Mistakes have to be made for you to learn. I'm just glad I'm here to show you the right way to do this."

Marcus gulped. "To do what?"

Brandon's face sobered. For the first time in as long as Marcus could remember, his uncle looked sincere. Pained. As though thinking back on a memory that hurt to hold in his head. "To help your friends. You and Mandy remind me a lot of me and Jack and Bear. We've been through a lot together, and I can see enough of myself in you to know you're not gonna quit. Am I right?"

"If my mom knew—"

"What your mom doesn't know, won't hurt her." Brandon turned back around. "As long as we're careful, anyway. Our secret, okay?"

"Our secret."

"Good. Pull up a chair."

Marcus did as he was told. "What are we doing?"

"You were smart *and* lucky when Stonewall opened that email and downloaded your PDF. Good job, by the way. It looked legit." Brandon tore his gaze away from the screen for a moment. "But while my IP address is difficult to track down, it's not impossible."

"That's why you had us drive so far and leave the computer."

"Right. They'll chase that while we chase them." Brandon's fingers flew over his keyboard, too fast for Marcus to keep up with. "I'm interested in how Stonewall is involved with Reagan. What does he want with someone who works with the Treasury Department?"

"Could she be, like, printing money for him or something?" Marcus felt stupid as soon as the suggestion left his mouth, but Brandon just shook his head, no judgement in his voice.

"Not her department. And not as easy as you might think. Not as hard either if you've got the right scheme going. But no, I think she's up to something else."

A sharp *ping* rendered Brandon frozen as he looked at the message that popped up in the corner of his screen. Leaning forward, he switched windows and typed out a few phrases. Another screen popped up. When he swore loudly, Marcus' stomach clenched.

"What's wrong?" he asked.

Brandon took a deep breath and let it out before answering, and Marcus got the sense he'd done that to regulate his voice. "Bear and Iris have been put on a watchlist."

The pain in Marcus' stomach twisted. "Is it because of me?"

"No, no." Brandon patted Marcus twice on the knee but never looked away from his screen. "No, this is separate. I monitor several different channels for my friends so I can tell them when someone has their eye on them. Give them a heads up, you know? Bear popped up on this one, right alongside Iris."

"What kind of list is it?"

"It's a database the government uses for terrorists and anyone who's a threat to national security. And it looks like—" Brandon's fingers typed out a few commands. Then he sat back. "This isn't good."

Marcus leaned forward, but he couldn't make sense of the information on the screen. It looked like another language.

"The Director of the CIA placed them in the database."

"Yeah, that's doesn't sound good."

Brandon opened a new window, typed in a string of letters, then hit enter. He read from the screen. "Margaret Olivia Caldwell. Let's see what's you've been up to."

Marcus tried to follow along as Brandon explained some of what he was doing. But if anything took longer than a few seconds to explain, he just brushed it off and said he'd get into it later. Marcus knew a lot about computers for a kid his age, but he was like a newborn baby compared to his uncle.

"Looks like Director Caldwell has been busy," Brandon said. "Traveling overseas more than usual the last couple of months. A few trips to Venezuela. Interesting." He kept scrolling. "And look at this, several foreign bank accounts in her name, totaling—well, a lot more money than you and I will ever see in our lifetimes. She's definitely up to something. I wonder—"

When Brandon didn't finish his sentence, Marcus leaned forward, looking from his shock still uncle to the screen and back again. "You wonder what?"

Brandon turned to Marcus, who could see the gears turning through the man's wild eyes. "I think we might've just found Reagan's real identity."

CHAPTR FORTY-THREE

Mandy sat in her room, headphones blocking out the entire world while her laptop screen glowed bright in the sea of darkness around her. She had closed her curtains and turned out all the lights to minimize distractions while she focused on the screen.

On her best days, Mandy's mind wandered at least a dozen times each hour and she had to force herself back to the task at hand. It felt worse when she was bored out of her mind and caught herself daydreaming of taking down Reagan singlehandedly while her dad cheered her on from the sidelines. Whenever her fantasies became a little too ridiculous, she'd force herself back to the present. Sometimes she had to go back and relisten to whatever conversation had set her mind adrift in the first place.

Right now, she didn't have that problem. Mandy's eyes were glued to the audio waves running in front of her, just blue squiggles against a white background, but she stared at it like she could read words within its designs.

"Only a few more days," Stonewall said, her voice tinny and distant. Charlie had cleared out as much background noise as he could, so the voices on the tape were distinguishable but distorted. If they found something important, they would send it to Brandon or Iris to clean up with better tech than Charlie had available. "Only a few more days, then we're done with all of this."

"Are you sure about that?" Reid asked, his voice not as lazy and disinterested as Mandy was used to hearing. "Or is it a few more days until he asks something else of us?"

Stonewall's next words had a bite to them. "And what's he asking of you, hm? Is he asking you to look the other way while the CIA breaks a dozen sanctions? I could go to prison. You understand that, right? I'll never see my daughter again."

"They'd let her visit you," Reid said, and Mandy could imagine the shrug he gave her while saying it.

"Some consolation that is. That'll help me sleep better at night."

Mandy listened for a few more minutes, but the pair of them remained silent while the crowd cheered around them. Pausing the audio, she made a few notes in her document, detailing the timestamp where she'd heard Stonewall's confession, and then switched over to a separate window, which she only used in private browsing mode.

Thanks to Amy, Mandy knew that not only did Stonewall work for the Treasury Department, but she was also part of the Office of Foreign Assets control. Mandy had pretended to know what that meant, but now she did her due diligence and went to their official website to read about their mission.

OFAC administered and enforced economic trade sanctions based on U.S. foreign policy and national security goals against targeted foreign countries and various regimes, terrorists, and other criminal organizations. More searching returned the results Mandy was hoping for, and her heart hammered in her chest due to a dangerous combination of fear and excitement.

Marissa Stonewall oversaw sanctions against the Venezuelan government.

That's what she was talking about when she said she looked the other way while the CIA broke those sanctions. Mandy didn't totally understand every detail of what was going on, but she knew the weapons heading to Miami were eventually going to Venezuela.

Mandy wrote the information down and saved her document a dozen times before she was certain it wouldn't disappear from her computer. This was hardly the smoking gun they were looking for, but it was yet another step in the right direction.

And maybe, if Mandy played her cards very, very right, she might even be able to use this information to blackmail Stonewall into helping her. That way, she could do her part in taking down Reagan without further betraying the trust her friend had put in her.

Mandy, like Bear, didn't particularly enjoy relying on luck to get the job done, but sometimes you didn't have much choice at all.

43

Bear pulled into view of the hangar outside Miami just as a plane took to the runway. Chances were low they could ground it at this point, but they had to try. As they drove closer, he spotted a second plane being loaded.

Bear threw the car into park and shoved open his door. "Thorne, with me." He turned back to see Iris already climbing behind the driver's seat. "Do what you can, then meet us back here."

"Be safe," she said, already shifting into gear.

"You too." Bear shut the door for her and stepped back as she pulled away.

"I suppose you're the only one who gets a gun," Thorne drawled as Bear pulled out his weapon.

"You'd suppose right. On me."

Thorne rolled his eyes but didn't argue, choosing instead to follow in Bear's footsteps and use him as his human shield. For his part, Bear pretended like Thorne wasn't there. He had to worry about himself and himself alone. Bear had no doubt Thorne could handle his own self.

With two deep breaths to calm his adrenaline-filled heart, Bear steadied his weapon and leaned forward, taking in the scene before him. A dozen men were running around, shouting orders, and cursing as they tripped over one another in a rush to get the crates of weapons loaded from the eighteen-wheeler onto the second plane. Whether they had spotted Iris in the car was anyone's guess. Either way, they weren't waiting around to be caught with their dicks in their hands.

Two men seemed to be calling all the shots.

"Priority number one is grounding the plane," Bear told Thorne. "Number two is capturing one of those men."

"I don't know about you, but priority number one for me is staying alive."

"Either back me up, or stay the hell down, Thorne."

"Fine, fine." Thorne threw up his hands in surrender. "Just trying to be honest."

Bear turned back to the hangar and stepped around the corner, feeling Thorne move with him. Unlike at the distribution center, there was no doubt in Bear's mind that every single person in front of him knew about the illegality of their operations. It didn't matter who they were or who they had waiting at home for them—these were the people knowingly carrying out Reagan's plans.

Stepping around the corner and raising his gun, Bear squeezed off three shots and felled two men before the rest of the crew became aware. There were shouts of surprise and a mad scramble to duck for cover.

Then the shooting started in earnest.

Bear dove behind a stack of boxes on a pallet, but when the bullets tore right through it, he was forced to move deeper into the hangar until he came to a pickup truck parked along the wall. He dashed from one wheel to the next, leaving room for Thorne to take cover. Once again, Bear refused to feel guilty about leaving the man to his own devices. They'd both been in worse scrapes than this.

He'd only spent a maximum of two seconds looking over his shoulder when he felt the vehicle rock and looked up to see a man towering above him from the bed of the truck. He pointed a gun at Bear's head. Big mistake. Bear reached up and pushed the man's wrist aside while he yanked on the guy's arm. The force of the momentum sent him careening over the side, where he landed on his shoulder. Bear gave him a chance to twist around to face him before he put a bullet in the man's head.

After Bear let go of the man's wrist, Thorne reached down and picked up the man's weapon, released the magazine to check how many bullets were left, and then reloaded. By the time he was done, Bear had swung his weapon around to point it at Thorne's head.

The other man simply rolled his eyes. "Really? This again?"

Bear opened his mouth to answer that he'd *never* trust the other man, no matter how much time had passed since Thorne had betrayed him, but he didn't get a chance. Thorne's eyes shifted and he raised his gun and squeezed the trigger. Once. Twice. Three times.

Bear didn't flinch despite the ringing in his ears causing him physical pain. He looked over his shoulder and noticed a man lying dead on the ground, his blood already pooling around him. Bear looked back at Thorne.

"A thank you would suffice."

"Not a chance."

"One of these days, Logan, you and I will be friends again."

"That implies we were friends in the first place."

Thorne clutched his chest. "You *wound* me."

"If only."

He had to admit he was grateful for Thorne's assistance in moments like this, but he'd never say that out loud. Thorne was a liability, and there would come a time when Thorne would choose himself over Bear.

Then they'd all be screwed.

Until then, the man was here to watch Bear's back.

"Let's do this," Bear said.

"With pleasure," Thorne said. "It's been too long."

Men like Thorne became soldiers because they enjoyed the power it brought them. Bear had joined for many different reasons. He wouldn't deny there had been a few deaths he'd relished in. Every person on that short list had deserved what had come of them a thousand times over. But in this moment, with every man he took down, numbness overrode every other emotion.

Meanwhile, Thorne looked like a dog who'd been finally let off his leash.

He ducked and rolled, popping up to fell one man, then another. His movements were light and fluid, power backing each action. Thorne might've been out of the game going on fifteen years, but he'd forgotten none of his training.

Sprinting from the pickup truck to the side of a van, Bear surprised a pair of men who'd been fighting over the driver's wheel. Two quick shots put that argument to bed forever, and now Bear was a dozen steps closer to the two men in charge.

Both were tall and muscled, not like the average man in the hangar. No, these were government men. The first had a rugged look of self-assurance, while the second took everything in with hooded eyes, despite the carnage raging around him.

Bear took aim, but his focus was stolen by the second plane. Shouts rose as the last of the LAWS were loaded into the back, and the men in charge of transporting them raced away as the plane began to roll. Bear set off after it.

There was no reality in which Bear could run faster than a plane, but the pilot was being too cautious before takeoff, giving Bear time to raise his weapon, aim, and squeeze off three shots. They landed exactly where he'd hoped, and the pilot slumped in his seat. Bear waited for a co-pilot to emerge from the back and take over, but no one did.

Looking out to the airstrip, Bear noticed Iris racing back toward them. His eyes shifted to the distance, and he saw the other plane in the sky, heading southwest toward Venezuela. Any revelry he'd felt over grounding one plane washed away. They might've stopped half of the shipment, but they still failed.

Tires squealed as a black SUV peeled out of the hangar. Bear caught a glimpse of the man with the hooded eyes behind the wheel. Bear lifted his weapon and pulled the trigger but missed.

Bear turned to find Thorne in a standoff with the other man. Both were within six feet of each other, guns aimed at the other's head. As Bear took a step forward, the other man's gaze shifted to him, causing the slightest movement in his gun. One look at Thorne told Bear what would happen next.

"Thorne, no!"

But it was too late. Thorne pulled the trigger and the other man dropped to the ground, a bullet between his eyes.

Bear ran up to Thorne and yanked the gun from the man's hand. For his part, Thorne didn't resist. Bear looked down at the body, but there was no doubt the man was dead, his eyes staring blankly up at the ceiling of the hangar.

"We had him. He would've dropped his weapon."

"I wasn't about to take that risk. I saw my opening, and I acted. You can't fault me for that."

He could, but before Bear could say as much, he heard a shocked gasp behind him. Iris rushed past him to kneel at the man's side. Her hands hovered over his chest, as though she wanted to touch him to ensure he really was dead, but she didn't dare. She looked up at Bear with fear and confusion.

"What happened?" she asked.

"He was one of the men leading the group," Bear answered. "The other got away."

"You're sure?"

"He was in a black SUV—"

"No, I mean, you're sure he was leading them?"

Bear tried not to let his annoyance show on his face. "He was calling the shots. Why?" He looked down at the body. "Who is he?"

Iris returned her own gaze to the body. "That's Richard Peake."

Before Bear could let the implications sink in, his phone buzzed. Pulling it from his pocket, he answered Brandon before it went to a second ring.

"What is it?"

"I know who Reagan is." His voice was breathy with anticipation. "And better yet, I know where *she'll* be tonight."

44

REAGAN STOOD IN FRONT OF THE FULL-LENGTH MIRROR AND SCRUTINIZED her image. Many years ago, she'd learned from her mentor that every part of herself could be used as a weapon. Not just your hands and feet. Not just your mind. But your hair. Your clothes. The angle of your eyeliner. The tilt of your head.

Her mentor had been a bastard. She wished she'd been able to stick a knife through his heart years ago. But he hadn't been wrong. He had taught her many valuable lessons, and she even took a few of them to heart.

Today, she wore a sleek black dress that was as simple as it was elegant. Sitting just above her knees and dipping low enough to show a hint of cleavage, she wore a string of pearls to accentuate it. Her stilettos were modest compared to most of her other shoes, though they enhanced the muscles in her calves as much as they lengthened her legs to supermodel proportions.

Moving her gaze up to her face, she leaned closer to the mirror, ensuring her makeup had not smudged. A deep red lip was bold without being scandalous while her eye makeup remained dark and smoky. It was sensual and dangerous, even otherworldly, but still approachable. The perfect balance.

Taking her ring finger and dragging it along the curve of her eye, she wiped away an errant spot of mascara that no one would've noticed but her. Then she lifted her hands to her hair and smoothed her sleek bob until it lay exactly where she wanted it.

Satisfied, she straightened and took in the whole effect one more time. She'd use everything at her disposal to get what she wanted. After years of working her way to the top, she was finally in the right place at the right time. Her patience and tenacity had proven stronger than the weakness of her cohorts. And in less than a day, the whole world would learn what Mr. Reagan was capable of. Even better, she'd remain hidden, pulling the strings and watching everyone dance to the beat of her drum.

A shrill ring interrupted her thoughts. With one last look in the mirror, she crossed the room to her bed like she was sauntering down a catwalk. The white comforter on her bed was unwrinkled except for where she had tossed her phone on top of it. It let out a second ring before she had the chance to look down at the name on the caller ID. Disappointment flared as she picked it up, though her face remained a mask of disinterest as though the person on the other end could see her.

"Bishop," she said by way of greeting. She didn't bother to mask the tone of her voice. She knew what this call was about.

"Baron is dead." Bishop sounded like he was whispering into the phone, and she imagined him cupping his hand over the receiver so no one would read his lips.

She reached out a hand and examined her nails. "Who killed him?"

"A man named Daniel Thorne. He's working with Logan and Duvall."

"Did any of them see you escape?"

"No. My identity remains intact."

"Good."

"Baron's death complicates things."

The flare of annoyance ignited into a flame and spread throughout her body, but she didn't bother voicing it. "I'm aware. But at least congratulations are in order."

"Congratulations?" the man asked.

"You've become Mr. Reagan's second-in-command."

There was a pause, like Bishop was contemplating whether he even wanted the job. Not that he had much of a choice. He'd wind up dead if he didn't accept. "When will I speak to Mr. Reagan directly?"

Reagan would've laughed if she'd been in the mood. Monarch and Baron had been the only ones to know her true identity. She was certain she could trust Bishop, but with them closing in on their target, it was better to play it safe.

"Soon," she said. "I'll relay the information to Mr. Reagan. For now, it's your job to ensure nothing else goes wrong. We cannot afford any more mistakes."

"What would you have me do?"

Reagan rolled her eyes. You'd think being an undercover CIA operative would've afforded him a brain to think with. This was why he hadn't been part of the inner circle. Now, she had no choice. "The weapons?"

"They grounded one plane. The other made it into the air. It's on its way."

Reagan clenched her jaw. Losing even half the weapons was a risk. "Unfortunate, but we knew it could happen. Tell me, Bishop, do you have any plans tonight?"

Bishop gulped back whatever answer almost came out of his mouth. "N-No. What did you have in mind?"

"There's a charity event being held at the Smithsonian. I'd like you to attend. Eyes only. Report back when you're done."

"Yes, ma'am. Is there—"

Reagan hung up before he could ask any more questions. A surge of anger coursed through her body and she threw her phone at the mirror on the other side of the room. The glass shattered, but no shards fell to the ground. Even her phone remained intact. There was something immensely dissatisfying about that, but at least she didn't have a mess to clean up.

Stepping close, she viewed her distorted reflection, and for the first time, she felt as though it showed her what she looked like on the inside. Broken and jagged, held together by sheer force of will. Nothing and no one would disrupt her plans.

She'd make sure of it with her dying breath.

45

MANDY LEANED AGAINST THE COOL CONCRETE WALL OUTSIDE THE PACKED gymnasium. It felt nice against her skin, which was flushed from her warmups. Coach Foley had scrutinized her when she said she'd forgotten her gloves in the locker room. Her heart hammered as she raced back to her locker and retrieved her equipment. The gloves now hung around her shoulders like an ostentatious necklace.

If her coach had any suspicion she was lying, he didn't show it. But he probably would now as she lingered in the hallway far longer than it took to retrieve her gloves. Her target was running late, and Stonewall parked her car on the other side of the school and would enter through the doors at the end of this hallway. It was only a matter of time—

Sure enough, one of the doors flew open as though it had been torn from its hinges in a hurricane. Cool air billowed past Mandy, ruffling the ends of her ponytail and making goosebumps erupt along her arms. It evaporated the sweat from the back of her neck and made her wish she'd brought a hoodie to toss over her tank top and shorts.

Stonewall didn't look up as she stormed down the hall, her high heels echoing loudly in the empty space. She didn't stop until Mandy pushed away from the wall and stepped into her path, wondering if the woman would even notice her or if they'd have a full-on collision.

Coming to a halt at the last second, Stonewall peered at Mandy with an air of annoyance that flickered into recognition before becoming haughty. Looking down at her nose at Mandy, she arched one perfect eyebrow in what Mandy could only interpret as a challenge.

"Can I help you?"

Mandy plastered on her biggest, most insincere smirk. "Oh, I really hope so. I have a question I hope you can answer for me."

Her eyebrow raised another fraction of an inch. Any further and it would disappear into her hairline. "I'm late to my daughter's match. Maybe another time."

Stonewall stepped to the side and Mandy mirrored her movements, blocking her path again. She dropped her. "It can't wait."

"Do you have any idea who—"

"—you are? Actually, I do." She tilted her head to the side. "Do you know who *I* am?"

"My daughter's *friend*, I presume."

"That's right. Your daughter's friend. And I'm concerned about her."

For the first time since they came face to face, Stonewall's mask flickered, revealing concern and confusion. But a second later, she pulled it back into place. "If you've done anything to hurt her—"

"It's not what I've done." Mandy took a step further into Stonewall's space. To her credit, the older woman didn't step back. "It's what you're doing."

"I have no idea what you're talking about."

"I think you do." Mandy had thought long and hard about how she would confront Amy's mother. There were a lot of ways she could play this, but she decided to go for the jugular. There was nothing like a direct attack to see how an opponent would react. "Look what happened to Mr. King. Do you think you're going to fare any better?"

The woman went white as a ghost and swayed a little on her feet. "What happened to him was a tragedy. But he did that to himself."

"It was murder. And we both know it."

"You don't know what you're talking about, young lady. He killed himself."

Mandy just shrugged. "If you say so. I don't have any proof to the contrary. But"—Mandy chose this moment to take another step forward, and Stonewall reacted by backing up—"I can tell you I do have proof of you committing treason."

The woman's cool demeanor shattered, and now she looked around the hallway like a rabbit caught in a trap. "What are you talking about? I've done no such thing."

"Your conversations with Mr. King and Mr. Reid suggest otherwise. Looking the other way while the CIA ignores the sanctions on Venezuela? You could get in a lot of trouble for that, Mrs. Stonewall. What would your daughter think if you were carted off to jail?"

"Don't you dare bring my daughter into this."

"I didn't. You did. And she's going to pay the price for *your* crimes. Do you want that to happen?"

Stonewall's hand twitched, and Mandy got the impression that she wanted nothing more than to slap her across the face. "If you think I'm afraid of you, *little girl*, you're more naïve than you look. You have no idea the kind of people I deal with."

"Like Mr. Reagan?" Mandy asked. She enjoyed the way Mrs. Stonewall gasped in surprise. "Yeah, you haven't been as careful as you thought. And now a fifteen-year-old *little girl* has you by the balls." Mandy shrugged. "Metaphorically speaking."

"What do you want?"

"Help us take down Mr. Reagan."

"Who's us?"

"I'm not telling you anything until you hold up your end of the bargain."

Stonewall snorted. "You're in dangerous waters."

"Monarch is dead," Mandy said pointblank. "It won't be long until you follow in his footsteps. Stone walls don't last forever."

"Are you threatening me?"

"I'm doing what I have to take down Mr. Reagan. I don't want Amy to get caught in the crossfire, and something tells me you don't either. But you put her in danger. Now it's time to get her to safety."

Stonewall looked down at Mandy, assessing her. If Mandy were anyone else, she wouldn't have seen the moment the woman decided to make her move. But Bear had trained her for this, and though it was only the twitch of an eye and the curling of a fist, Mandy saw it coming from a mile away.

Before Stonewall could make her move, Coach Foley came around the corner, causing the two of them to jump apart as if they had been caught passing notes in class.

"What's going on out here?" Foley looked between Mandy and Stonewall.

"Coach Foley," the woman said, back to her stoic and sensual self. "Have we kept you waiting? My apologies. I've just been chatting with Mandy here."

Mandy didn't flinch when the woman placed a hand on her shoulder, nor did she make a sound when she dug her fingernails into the sensitive skin along her neck. "Yep. Just talking." She held up her gloves. "Ran into her after I came out of the locker room."

"We're about to start," Coach Foley said, still studying the two of them. "I imagine Mr. Reid has saved a seat for you, Mrs. Stonewall."

"Perfect." Stonewall squeezed Mandy one more time before slipping past Coach Foley. "It was nice talking to you, Mandy. I look forward to our next chat."

"Likewise."

Coach Foley waited until Mrs. Stonewall disappeared around the corner. He even waited until he heard the door to the gymnasium slam shut behind her. When he looked down at Mandy, he appeared as though he were searching for answers in her eyes. "Are you okay?"

"Yeah," Mandy waved a hand, laughing a little. "She's not as scary as she seems. Amy exaggerates."

Coach Foley continued studying Mandy's face. Then his eyes drifted to her shoulder.

His gaze returned to meet hers. "You know you can talk to me, right? About anything."

She didn't like the scrutiny in his eyes. He saw too much. "I know. But right now, I have a match to win."

46

BEAR, IRIS, AND THORNE HAD DRIVEN HALF AN HOUR TO A DIFFERENT private airstrip and jumped on a plane to get back to D.C. in time to attend a charity event at the Smithsonian. Thorne was convinced he could get credentials together in time to get them in without causing a stir, and with no other options at their fingertips, Bear and Iris had to agree.

Bear didn't like it, but they had more pressing issues to discuss. While Thorne was wheeling and dealing in a seat across from them, Iris and Bear had leaned over her tablet, studying up on Margaret Caldwell. Bear had tried to bring up Richard Peake, but Iris had shut down the conversation. What was done was done, she said. That was a problem best left until after they took down Reagan.

Bear let it go for the time being. There would be plenty of time to deal with that later—if they survived the next few hours.

Brandon had called in a friend to meet them with the appropriate attire for the charity event. It was nothing flashy, but Bear felt a world away from the events of the last few hours in his tux. Thorne had elected for a royal blue suit with black trim, though Brandon hadn't bothered shelling out the money for the shoes he'd requested. Iris was in a sparkly black gown that accentuated her figure without restricting her in case this all went sideways. She wore low heels, but Bear knew she was no less dangerous than if she'd been wearing combat boots.

The courier had also delivered three sealed envelopes containing their invitations. The charity event had a price tag of ten grand per invitation. Bear didn't ask whether Thorne had paid it.

The same man who'd dropped off their wardrobes and invitations also doubled as their chauffeur. How had Brandon managed to arrange all this in just under three hours? Bear always knew the guy was a miracle worker, but he'd really gone above and beyond this time. And it had allowed Bear the space to worry about their target rather than whether they'd stick out like a sore thumb at the party.

The driver pulled to a stop in front of the red carpet leading to the entrance of the museum. Someone opened the door, and Bear slid out first, followed by Iris and then Thorne. All three of them adopted an air of casual indifference, which was more natural for Thorne. He led the way while Iris took Bear's arm and leaned in close.

"You sure about this?" she whispered.

"No," Bear said. He watched Thorne's every movement as the man waved at passersby even though there was zero chance anyone knew who he was, considering where he'd been the last decade and a half. "But what choice do we have?"

"Don't like being unarmed. We should've snuck in."

They'd already had this discussion. It would've taken far longer to plan a way inside without being noticed by security or any of the guests. The list wasn't long, and he was already worried they'd stand out by virtue of being a couple of unknowns amongst a group of millionaires.

"Best way in is through the front door," Bear said. "We'll figure out the rest as we go."

If Iris still had doubts, she didn't voice them. As Thorne approached the entrance, he made a show of pretending as though he'd forgotten his invitation before slipping it out of his pocket and handing it over. The guard wasn't amused. He waved him through without issue, if not annoyance. Even though it went against every instinct in his body, they'd removed the cuff from around Thorne's wrist so it wouldn't set off the metal detector, but Brandon had the tailor slip a smaller one into the seam of his pants.

As Thorne walked away, Bear picked up his pace, shoving his and Iris' invitations into the guard's hands. It took the man an agonizing amount of time to double-check that the invitations were real, but after a few moments, he waved them through. The metal detectors didn't give either of them any trouble, but Bear didn't breathe a sigh of relief.

He'd lost sight of Thorne.

Bear used his considerable height advantage to scan the crowd, not caring that several heads had turned in his direction to place his face. No one would be able to, but that was hardly a relief. High society liked to gossip.

A flash of blue caught Bear's attention and he stalked forward, pressing close to Thorne as the other man lifted a glass of champagne from a passing tray.

"I told you to stay put," Bear said.

"Yes, you did," Thorne said. "But I never agreed to it."

"I swear to God, Thorne—"

"You're here on my invitation, *literally*. I've had multiple opportunities to kill you and haven't." His eyes turned ice cold. "Give me a little slack, will you?"

"He's right." Iris grabbed a glass of champagne for herself. She held it to her lips, but she didn't drink. "We have more important things to focus on tonight."

She was right, but old habits die hard. If Thorne wanted to give them the slip, this would be where he'd do it. Besides, Reagan was more important. They'd hidden that tracker on Thorne for a reason.

"Anyone spot Caldwell?" Bear asked.

"Upstairs," Iris said, finally taking a sip of champagne. She made a face but kept the glass. "Two o'clock. She's got company."

Bear followed her direction and spotted the woman on the second floor. She was dressed in black, the angles of her face made sharper by the short, round cut of her hair. From here, Bear couldn't read the expression on her face. Her body language indicated she was tense, despite her ease and amicable conversation.

"Let's move," Bear said, grabbing a glass of champagne for himself.

Bear used his considerable bulk to weave through the crowd with ease. Only the security guards lining the room were built like him, but none held champagne in one of their massive hands. A few people watched him as he passed. They were either too busy or too intimidated to ask who he was and what he was doing there. All the better for him.

Bear gestured for Thorne to ascend the stairs before him. The man complied and took Iris' arm before Bear had a chance. She didn't put up a fight. Bear was forced to follow in their wake. Thorne looked perfectly at ease as he complimented the women and shook hands with the men they passed.

"Keep it in your pants, Thorne," Bear said. "We're supposed to lay low."

"Not possible with you here," Thorne said out of the corner of his mouth.

Bear ignored him, turning his attention back to Caldwell. She'd extricated herself from her group and held a phone to her ear. The tension he'd seen earlier in her body had doubled. She didn't even try to hide the scowl on her face, every line filled with anger and annoyance.

They'd come up with several possible scenarios and plans to get Caldwell on her own, but they hadn't landed on one in particular. The situation could go a number of ways. There was no point in locking themselves into one option if it wouldn't fit the scenario. Playing it by ear seemed like the smartest move.

Still, Bear hadn't expected Caldwell to look up and lock eyes with him. Before he knew it, four men surrounded him, and the press of a gun in his back made him go stiff.

One of the men leaned in close. "Nice and easy, big man. No need to make a scene. Let's take this somewhere private, okay?"

Going to a secondary location was dangerous.

"Sure, man." Bear kept his hands in view but didn't raise them to avoid suspicion. "Whatever you say."

Bear had lost track of Iris and Thorne. He felt a little more at ease when the same man said, "You two, follow us."

At least they were in this together.

Caldwell hung up her phone and led them through one of the sturdy doors most people never got to walk through. It led to a hallway lined with priceless artifacts, the only sounds the echoing of everyone's shoes bouncing off the marble. No one spoke and for once, Bear had no interest in pushing anyone's buttons.

Near the end of the hall, Caldwell entered a room to the left, and Bear was pushed through the entrance. Before he had time to take in more than a few glances at the various paintings and eighteenth-century furniture lining the room, Caldwell stopped and turned to face him. That same sneer was still on her face.

"Riley Logan, I presume," she said. "Bold to attempt a move against me in such a public space. It's obviously a distraction, so why don't you give up your boss' real plans, and I'll see about giving you the chance at parole in, say, fifty years?"

Bear went still. His chest constricted as if he'd been cast in concrete, and he found he could barely breathe let alone think straight. They had talked about the possibility that Caldwell could get the jump on them, but never in their wildest dreams did he think it'd play out like this.

She was surrounded by her own men. There was no point in keeping up the charade. Unless—

Unless Caldwell wasn't Reagan after all.

Bear turned his head to look at Iris, to see if she'd come to the same conclusion as he had. But as he took in the group beside him, he noticed everyone was dressed in black. The blue suit was nowhere to be seen.

Thorne had escaped.

47

MANDY FELT GOOD. EVERY NERVE IN HER BODY BUZZED AFTER HER MATCH. The adrenaline had barely subsided. Her opponent only managed to land a couple good hits before she knocked the other girl down. She'd gotten up again, but not for long.

There were no words to describe the rush she felt whenever she stepped out of that ring a winner. She was no stranger to fighting, but boxing was about technique as much as it was about assessing your opponent and either outsmarting or outlasting them. Fighting for your life and succeeding was satisfying, to be sure, but Mandy had done that out of necessity. Winning inside the ring was *glorious*.

Mandy was riding high as she made her way back to her room. Confronting Stonewall without telling anyone else was probably not smart, but she'd needed to talk to the woman face to face. Would she back down when she learned someone knew of her crimes, or would she go on the offensive? Mandy already had her answer. Either Stonewall didn't care about her family as much as she'd pretended, or she was more afraid of Reagan than she was of getting caught, going to prison, and abandoning her daughter.

Whatever Reagan was planning was big—big enough that it had taken years to set up and pull off. A lot of people could get hurt along the way. Mandy didn't want to cause Amy any pain, but sacrifices had to be made. It wouldn't be the first time Mandy lost a friend, and it likely wouldn't be the last. She'd even accepted that someday Marcus would no longer be a part of her life. She had to be realistic. Still, she hoped it would be a long time from now.

When she put her key into the lock and twisted, the customary *click* of the bolt sliding to the right wasn't there, and it only took a gentle push to swing the door inward. A shiver climbed down her spine. This wasn't right. Mandy had ensured her door was locked several times before she'd left for her match. Just like every other time she left her room.

That wasn't all. To most people, the room would look exactly the same as it had when she'd left earlier in the day. But to Mandy, it might as well have been ransacked.

The crease in her bedspread hadn't been there before, as though someone had leaned against it and didn't bother smoothing it out before they left. The book she'd left on the corner of her desk was turned slightly to the side so that one part of it hung over the edge. And then there was her computer which had been pushed a full two inches back from where it normally sat.

All exhaustion from her match was immediately replaced by adrenaline. Her muscles recoiled in response. Her room wasn't big. There weren't many places to hide. She checked under the bed and in the closet. Clear. She closed the door and locked it. Then she allowed herself to think of the worst that could've happened.

She walked over to her computer and sat down on the edge of her chair. It felt as though the intruder had left behind a disease she could catch through simple contact with the surfaces they had touched. Her fingers shook as she opened her laptop screen and breathed a sigh of relief that it was still intact.

The need to put in her password didn't make Mandy feel any more at ease. She didn't know as much about computers as Marcus, but there were ways to get past that. She typed in a string of numbers and letters and waited for her desktop to load.

The cursor shook as she dragged it across the page with unsettled fingers against the mousepad. She clicked through a series of folders where she'd kept the recordings and notes hidden along with copies of the pertinent emails Marcus had sent her from Stonewall's inbox.

Gone. It was all gone.

Mandy stared at the empty folder in shock, blinking rapidly as though that would clear her vision and reveal what she wanted to see. But no amount of wishing and hoping would bring it all back.

Her phone vibrated against her leg, startling her into a jump. She dragged it out of her pocket to see Charlie calling. True fear hit her for the first time, and she didn't even bother covering it up.

"What's wrong? Are you okay? Are you hurt?"

"No." Charlie's voice shook. "No, I'm not hurt. Why? Are you okay?"

Mandy tried to slow her breathing, but it remained shallow enough that she knew it would lead to a panic attack if she wasn't careful. "I'm fine. What's going on?"

"Someone broke into my room. I didn't even notice at first, but when I went to work on some more of the videos, they were gone. I'm so sorry, Mandy. Everything is gone."

"It's okay." It was easier to reassure someone other than herself. "We'll find a way to get it back."

"I don't know how. Even my emails have been wiped clean. They went through it with a fine-tooth comb."

Mandy checked her own inbox and swore. "The same happened to me." She took two deep breaths and gave herself exactly ten seconds to freak out before she took action. She silently counted backward from ten, telling herself to panic with every beat. Before reaching zero, she sighed, and her mind stilled.

"You there?"

"I'm here. Here's what we're going to do. I want you to call Etta and make sure she's okay. Hang out in the library until they kick you out. Get some other people to go with you. Form a study group or something. Don't go anywhere alone. Not even the bathroom. Then you and Etta go back to her room and stick together until you hear from me again."

His breaths were ragged through the phone. "I'm scared."

"I know. I'm sorry I dragged you into this."

"You didn't. We knew what we were getting into." Charlie let out a shuddering breath. When he spoke again, he sounded a little calmer. "You gave us a choice. We knew the consequences. I was just hoping we'd never have to face them. We're lucky this is all that happened."

Mandy's imagination went to the worst-case scenario. Her gut clenched in response. "Talk to Etta. Go to the library. Stick together. I'll be in touch when I can."

"What are you going to do?"

"Talk to someone who can get the files back for us. He knows a lot more about this stuff than most people. If anyone can do it, he can."

"Okay." Charlie didn't sound convinced, but he didn't argue. "Mandy?"

"Yeah?"

"Stay safe."

"I will. I promise."

She knew she couldn't truly make promises like that. Anything could happen. But it would make Charlie feel better, and right now, she had to make sure he was worrying about himself and Etta, not her. She could handle the rest on her own.

Mandy barely had enough time to pull up Marcus' phone number before her phone buzzed in her hand. The caller was unknown. At first, she thought maybe it was Bear with a new number. Then she thought maybe it was someone calling to tell her something had happened to him.

She brought the phone to her ear. "Hello?"

The voice on the other end was distorted, and she couldn't tell if it belonged to a man or a woman. "You've been sticking your nose where it doesn't belong."

"I'd say I'm trying to kick the habit, but I don't want to add *liar* to that list, too."

"But you are a liar, aren't you?"

Mandy strained her ears to hear anything in the background that could give her a clue as to who the person was or where they were located. Static overtook the silence. "I don't know what you mean. I've never lied a day in my life."

"Another falsehood. Did you learn that from your father?"

Mandy sat up straighter. Goosebumps erupted across her arms. "I'm self-taught."

"I doubt that. Your father isn't a salesman. And your last name isn't Davis."

"Who is this?"

"I can't tell you that." The voice paused. "But I can tell you that I know who you are, Mandy Logan. I know who your father is. I know what you're trying to do. And I also know that you'll fail."

"I wouldn't be so sure about that," Mandy said, though it didn't come out as confident as she'd have liked.

"This is your one and only warning. Keep your nose out of other people's business, and you might live to see your friends again. Your father, however, is a different story. He's on borrowed time. And I'd hate to see someone as young as you follow in his footsteps."

Tears welled in Mandy's eyes and before she could think of what to say, the line went dead.

48

It felt as though the walls were closing in around Bear.

"There's been a misunderstanding," he said.

Caldwell raised an eyebrow. "Do you know how often I hear that?"

Bear closed his eyes. In all the time he'd spent chasing after Mr. Reagan, he had never envisioned this. Despite all his training, all his preparation, he was at a loss for the next steps. As far as he could tell, there was no getting out of this.

Iris cleared her throat and said, "Ma'am—"

"Agent Duvall." The woman shot her steely gaze over to Iris. "Given Logan's track record, I can hardly be surprised to find him working in Reagan's employ. But you? This truly shocks me. I knew your mentor. He'd be turning over in his grave."

"Director Caldwell, please." Iris sounded as desperate as Bear felt. "There's been a misunderstanding. The man we were with, Daniel Thorne—"

"Trust me, there will be plenty of time to discuss all the ways in which you've broken federal law. Thorne is the least of our worries."

"He won't be soon." It took everything in Bear not to fight past the men surrounding him. "My guess is he'll head directly for Reagan. I don't know if they've been in contact, or if he's just playing the cards he's been dealt, but once he leaves this party it'll be impossible to find him. He knows more about Reagan's network than we do."

Caldwell didn't argue the point. "Ortega, Munier, Pearson, and Gianelli, track him down. Be discreet. Take him to a separate room if you find him. Don't come back until you do."

The four of them shuffled out of the room.

"What's it going to take for you to talk?" Caldwell asked Bear.

Bear ground his teeth together. He'd tell Caldwell everything he knew if it would get him out of this room. He doubted it would, though. The clock was ticking. Half the weapons were on their way to Venezuela. Reagan wouldn't have put all his eggs in one basket. The other play here had to do with putting the smoking gun in Caldwell's hand. Reagan couldn't have done it alone.

"I'll talk," Bear said. "We both will. But only to you. The others have to leave."

"That's not happening—" one man said.

"You're out of your goddamned mind—" the other said.

"Deal," Caldwell said. "Everyone out."

One of the men took a small step forward. "Ma'am—"

"Handcuff them together. Hands behind their back." She opened her purse and pulled out a pistol. It might've been small, but the bullets were just as deadly at this close range. "Then sit them on the floor. Wait outside the door. No one comes in unless they hear my gun go off. And if they get one up on me? Well, then I don't deserve to be Director, do I?"

The men exchange glances, but no one could argue with her logic. "Director Caldwell—"

"Farro stays," she relented. "The rest of you, out."

Bear stiffened in surprise at hearing that name, but he didn't dare turn around and find the gaze of the man who had kicked this all off for them several weeks ago. He stood by while two men closed in on Bear and pulled his arms behind his back, securing them painfully in a set of handcuffs. He heard the same familiar metallic opening and closing of the cuffs happening to Iris. Then a third set was used to connect the two of them back-to-back, and they were shoved to the floor. Bear winced as his arms were pulled tight against Iris' weight.

After another brief pause, Bear watched as the rest of Caldwell's men filed out the door, shutting it behind them. A few seconds of tense silence passed. Caldwell tipped her head back with a heavy sigh and Farro stepped up to her side. She looked back down at Bear with relief in her eyes.

When she noticed Bear eyeing Farro suspiciously, she gestured to the man at her side. "If you trust me, you can trust him. He's been my eyes and ears for a lot of this."

"You said you were with the FBI."

"I lied," Farro said with a shrug. "Telling you I was CIA would've been a red flag. We couldn't afford that at that point in time."

"We were cannon fodder." Bear waited until Farro looked in his direction. "You knew where Silas Marino's information could lead, and you sent us out instead of one of your men."

"Not quite," Farro said. "But too many people were watching my every move. I needed someone else to get the job done. It was never our intention to put you in front of the firing squad."

"Plus, you didn't know if you could trust me."

"Ma'am," Iris said. "There's been a huge misunderstanding—"

"She knows." Bear kept his gaze trained on Caldwell. "Don't you?"

"Sorry for the theatrics, but I've already found one mole. There's no telling if the others are smarter than him. Better to play it safe." She checked her watch. "That said, we don't have much time. You show me yours, and I'll show you mine."

Iris sputtered, but Bear had already caught onto the game. He didn't know how much Caldwell and Farro actually knew, so he started from the beginning. "The short version is that Iris has been chasing Reagan for years. I've been on the case for a couple months. We've hit a lot of dead ends along the way."

"Until recently," Caldwell said.

Bear nodded. "Didn't seem suspicious at the time, since none of it was easy, but everything has been pointing to the CIA. Between the list of undercover operatives, the bank accounts in your name, and the weapons exchange with the Venezuelans, it wasn't hard to figure out who was behind it all. Or so we thought."

"Reminded you a lot of the Contra scandal, did it?"

Bear nodded again. His arms were starting to go numb. "It all adds up, with evidence to support it. But you're not Reagan. This has all been a distraction for us. And it's not over."

"Far from it." Caldwell sighed again, and this time Bear could see how bone-weary she was. "And no, I'm not Reagan. Can't say I blame you for looking in my direction. Especially after seeing your names on the watchlist. One of my men said it was a mistake, but by that point, I had a good idea of what was going on. And I knew someone would be coming after me sooner or later."

"This was a trap," Iris said.

Caldwell shook her head. "This was bait. And you took it, hook, line, and sinker."

"It's a good thing we did," Bear said.

Iris ground her teeth together so hard it made Bear's jaw ache in sympathy. "What part of this is a good thing?"

Instead of answering right away, Caldwell pulled out a key to the handcuffs and passed it to Farro, who walked over to them, stooped down, and began undoing their restraints.

"Because we just doubled our numbers."

When Bear felt the cuffs drop from his wrists, he brought his arms back around and rubbed at the sore spots. No doubt there would be bruises there tomorrow, but it was a small price to pay for the information they'd just gained. He stood and then helped Iris to her feet.

Iris looked ready to knock some teeth loose. "But we still don't know who Reagan is or where to find him."

Caldwell took her phone out of her purse and swiped through, then showed the screen to them. "You ever seen this man before?"

Bear peered down at her screen and was surprised to see the man who'd gotten away from the hangar earlier that day. "As a matter of fact, I have."

Caldwell nodded like she wasn't surprised. "Lochlan Reid. I've been suspicious of him for a while now, but it was only recently he started to truly get sloppy. Did you hear about Raymond King, the state senator from Virginia?"

"We did." Bear and Iris exchanged glances. "Might even know how he got that bullet wound in his shoulder."

Caldwell's eyes sparkled. "You'll have to tell me that story when this is all over."

"Consider it a deal."

"Reid should've been here with me tonight, but something came up at the last minute. I can't guarantee he's with Reagan, but it's an avenue worth checking out. My gut is telling me Reagan will need him to pull off whatever it is he's up to now that two of his closest allies are dead." She gestured to Farro. "I would apologize for the indirect assistance, but Reagan's proven to be a tough person to find. Farro was sure you could be trusted. I was a little slower to come around."

"No offense taken," Iris said. "But that still doesn't tell us *who* Reagan really is."

"I've got an idea," Bear said. "But I'm not ready to lay my cards down just yet. First, we need to get out of here."

Caldwell exchanged glances with Farro, who nodded. They had to make it look real.

"You're sure?" Farro asked.

"Come on, son," she said. "You know I can take a punch."

Farro at least looked hesitant about it, but he raised his fist and struck out at Caldwell's face with sickening speed. Bear didn't hear any bones crunching, but when the Director looked up again, a trickle of blood leaked from her nose and into her mouth, staining her teeth.

"Good enough. Now go. You've got a ten-second head start." She raised her gun and pointed it directly at Bear. "It'll be your ass if you're still in the way when I pull this trigger."

Bear didn't need to be told twice. The three of them headed for the windows on the other side of the room. Farro threw them open and didn't hesitate before launching himself over the edge, grabbing onto the banner hooked to the balcony on the way down and sliding to freedom. Bear and Iris only had time to exchange a single look before doing the same. Three shots followed, bullets flew over their heads, and Bear heard the crash of the door opening and the yelling of half a dozen agents over the roar of the wind.

But by the time his feet hit the ground, it was too late to catch him.

49

Marcus jerked awake when he felt his phone buzz in his hand. He hadn't meant to fall asleep, just to lay down on the couch across from where his uncle had stayed crouched over his computer for the last few hours. He only wanted to stretch out and maybe close his eyes. Before he knew it, he was waking from a deep sleep, drool lining his chin, and the time said a few more hours than he anticipated.

Heart thundering, he sat up and looked down at his phone. Trepidation wormed its way through him when he saw it was Mandy. They hadn't talked since before her match. She'd mentioned offhand that she might confront Amy's mother over what she'd heard on the recordings. He hadn't thought it was a good idea, but there was no stopping Mandy when she got an idea in her head.

He answered the call, hoping he didn't sound as groggy as he felt. "Hey."

"Hey." Mandy's voice was uncharacteristically somber. "Did I wake you up?"

"No," he lied. "What's up? How'd your match go?"

"I won. But that's not why I'm calling."

Marcus stood, now on full alert. "What's wrong?"

"Is your uncle there? Can you put me on speakerphone?"

Marcus did as he was asked. His uncle had turned around at the sound of alarm in his voice. "It's Mandy."

"Hey, Brandon. Sorry to be calling so late."

"Don't worry about it, kiddo. We're still in full swing over here," he said, eyeing Marcus. "What's up? Everything okay?"

"Have you heard from my dad lately?"

"Yeah." Brandon furrowed his brows. "Not too long ago. I'm due for another check-in here soon. I can let you know once I hear from him again."

"That would be great."

Marcus wasn't used to hearing her sound so melancholy. "Mandy? Did something happen? Are you okay?"

There was a deep sigh before she answered, and Marcus could hear the tears of frustration in her voice. "I confronted Stonewall before my match. I tried to get her on our side, but she doubled down. She looked like she wanted to hit me by the time I was done talking."

"Did she try?" Brandon's voice sounded harder than Marcus had ever heard it.

"No." Mandy didn't sound relieved by that, but from everything he'd heard about her, Marcus couldn't imagine the woman would've been much of a threat. "My coach interrupted us. I was almost late for my match."

"I'm guessing you won?" Brandon asked.

"Yeah. But when I got back to my room, I noticed some things were off. Someone broke in."

"Are you okay?" Marcus asked before his uncle could. "Was anyone in there?"

"They were gone by the time I got back. They tried to leave without making it obvious they were there, but I noticed a few things were moved."

Marcus knew about Mandy's obsessive-compulsive tendencies. They didn't talk about it much, but she'd get frustrated about her habits and vent to him. He didn't know what living with OCD was like, but they both shared symptoms of ADHD and anxiety, so he knew what it was like to feel out of control in that way. It was as aggravating as it was exhausting. He was glad she was in therapy for it.

"Did they take anything?" Brandon asked.

Mandy finally let a sob of frustration out and her voice sounded wet and choked. "All my recordings are gone. I'm not sure if they took them or deleted them. I even asked Charlie. The same thing happened to him."

"Is Charlie okay?" Marcus asked. He might not be best friends with the guy, but he didn't want to see him hurt.

"He's okay. And so is Etta. I told them to stick together and stay somewhere public for the time being. I don't think anyone will hurt them, but I'd rather not take a chance. If something happens to them—"

"It won't be your fault," Marcus said. "They knew what they were getting into when they agreed to help you. You can't blame yourself."

"Marcus is right." Brandon clapped his nephew on the shoulder. A look passed between them, and Marcus realized that he'd told Mandy the same thing his uncle had told him earlier. Why was it so much easier giving your friends advice than following it yourself? "It's not your fault. The fault lies with whoever did this. Do you think it was Stonewall?"

"I don't see who else it could've been. Raymond King is...gone. Possibly Lochlan Reid. But I was pretty direct with Mrs. Stonewall. She knew I had been recording them."

"And it wouldn't have been hard for her to figure out that Charlie and Etta were helping," Marcus said. "They were at every match."

"You did the right thing by telling them to stick with each other and be somewhere public," Brandon said. "Now, let's see what we can do about those recordings."

"You think we can get them back?"

"Depends on how they deleted them." Brandon went back over to his desk. "But I wouldn't give up hope just yet. Are you somewhere safe right now?"

"I'm still in my room," Mandy said. "The door and windows are locked, and I shut my curtains. I really don't think they'll come back. They already got what they came for."

Marcus followed his uncle over to his desk and pulled up the chair he'd been sitting in earlier. "We'll need remote access to your computer. I'll send you a link to download."

"Done. Let me know when you have that downloaded. Then we'll connect."

After a moment, Mandy said, "Downloaded. I'm all set."

Marcus was relieved to hear her sound more grounded. "Great, now just tell me the code it gives you, and it'll grant us one-time access."

Mandy gave them the code, and Brandon connected to her computer. "All right, I'm taking over your mouse. Let's make sure their little breaking and entering was all for naught."

With Brandon on the case, it didn't take much time at all to recover the missing recordings or the copies of Stonewall's emails. Whoever had broken into Mandy's room had been smart enough to permanently delete everything out of the trash bin, but they either didn't know you could still recover those files, or they hadn't had time to do anything more permanent.

"There you go." Brandon leaned back and wrapped his hands around the back of his head. "Everything should be back in order. And I don't detect any corruption."

Mandy exhaled. It sounded as though a weight had been lifted from her shoulders. "Thank you so much. You'll have to teach me how to do that someday."

"Hey, any time kiddo. Glad to see you're not as tech averse as your dad."

Mandy chuckled. "Few people are."

Marcus was about to volunteer his time to teach her anything she wanted to know about computers, but he was cut off by an alarm that sounded from Brandon's computer. His uncle clicked on the pop-up notification.

"What was that noise?" Mandy asked. "Is everything okay?"

"Not exactly," Brandon said. "It's Daniel Thorne. Looks like he gave Bear and Iris the slip." He clicked a few more things on his screen and pulled up a map. A weary sigh left his mouth. "And according to this, he's either in the sewer system, or he figured out we put a tracker in his pants."

50

REAGAN PACED BACK AND FORTH BEHIND HER DESK WITH MEASURED STEPS. It had been a long time since she'd felt the flare of nerves wreak havoc with her system. Now that she was on the cusp of achieving everything, anxiety spread through her whole system. Getting in a good workout–either in the gym or the bedroom–was out of the question at this point in the evening, so she was left to walk back and forth until she felt more in control of her body.

About half an hour ago, she'd gotten word from Bishop that Bear and Iris had been taken into custody by Director Caldwell. Reagan allowed her face to twist in a sneer. She didn't stop the growl that came out of her mouth. She had her reasons to despise all three of them, and if push came to shove, she wasn't sure she could decide who deserved her ire more. Part of her wanted to bomb the Smithsonian and kill them all in one fell swoop, but her real plans would be a thousand times more devastating.

Lights flashed as a car pulled into the empty parking lot below. The lamps in her office were dim enough that no one would see her through the window. She stepped away from it regardless. No one needed to witness her pacing. She had never presented herself as anything other than perfectly in control of every aspect of her life and plan. Tonight would not be the night where she proved otherwise.

Reagan turned back to her office. Her gaze skimmed over every surface to make sure it was all in place. Her mahogany desk was so clean it looked like a prop. It was true that she didn't spend much time here, but when she wanted to present a certain image, she liked to take her meetings in this room. The desk was part of the illusion. She'd spent plenty of sleepless nights sitting at it in the beginning, furiously typing away on her computer.

The rest of the office was simple yet elegant. The bookshelf was full of first editions. She had made sure she'd read every single one of them in case some hotshot waltzed in there and decided to quiz her on them. More than one had tried and all of them had left looking either ashamed or impressed when she'd turned it back around on them.

The rest of the room was full of tasteful art and comfortable furniture in muted earth tones. The large leather couch was her favorite piece in the room. Not only because she had spent many nights sleeping there in the early days of her plan rather than in her own bed.

A door opened and closed downstairs, and though Reagan's heartbeat didn't quicken, she could feel adrenaline pumping through her veins. She told herself it was just anticipation for what came next, but that was a lie even she couldn't swallow.

Still, she refused to hurry as she crossed the room and sank onto the couch, draping one arm over the back of it while she picked up her tablet with the opposite hand. She pulled up the news and skimmed the headlines, barely taking in the information they provided. All her senses were tuned into the two pairs of feet ascending the stairs, making their way ever closer to the room she occupied.

Though she couldn't make out the words through the thick door to her office, someone whistled their appreciation for the building before making a comment that went unanswered. The headlines blurred in front of Reagan's eyes as she focused on picking up every little sound she could as they drew nearer.

She was so focused that she almost jumped when a knock cracked like a gunshot against her door. Taking two breaths and crossing one leg over the other, she rearranged her face into one of bored indifference. In a voice that matched her expression, she said, "Come in."

The door opened. Bishop stepped inside. His usual casual expression was nowhere to be seen. In fact, he looked like he was barely holding it together. She trusted him to do what needed to be done, but she had realized early into their relationship that he wouldn't be in it for the long-haul. That's why Monarch and Baron had gotten top billing.

And look at what had happened to them.

Bishop gave her a stiff nod that was equal parts greeting and confirmation that he had completed the task she'd set before him. She had known as much when he'd pulled up to her building, but pleasure coursed its way through her system and chased after the adrenaline that still lingered there.

Bishop stepped to the side and allowed his guest to enter the room. Reagan couldn't stop her gaze from sliding to him immediately. It had been a long time since she'd seen him in person, and she wanted to see how much he'd changed.

Daniel Thorne had hardly aged in fifteen years. He was bulkier than she remembered, and his face had a few more lines, but otherwise he looked the same.

The piercing eyes.

The affable look.

The easy set of his shoulders.

"Thorne." She offered him a nod of her head and nothing more.

"*Mr.* Reagan, I presume."

Reagan looked to Bishop. "Leave us. Stay close. I'll be in need of your services later."

Bishop nodded, and without looking either of them in the eye, he backed out of the room and shut the door behind him. Reagan and Thorne waited until his footsteps retreated before they locked eyes again.

"When did you figure it out?" Reagan went back to her tablet.

"I had suspected for some time, but I'll admit, I wasn't sure until I laid eyes on you." Thorne looked around the room before his gaze returned to her. "You've grown up quite a bit. I'm proud of you."

Reagan flashed him a look. She didn't need his praise. She found that it rankled. "I didn't have much choice."

Thorne nodded as though he understood. She hadn't expected an apology from him, and she didn't get one. He sat down on the opposite end of the couch, matching her movements.

"You never reached out," he said.

"I figured you had everything under control."

"As did you, I suppose. You've built quite an empire in my absence. I assume you'll be kicking off the grand finale here any second."

"Let me guess." Reagan set her tablet down and gave him her full attention. "You want in?"

Thorne held up his hands. "I wouldn't presume. I'm here if you want me, but I'm under no illusion that you need me."

"I appreciate that. You understand why I'm not ready to trust you just yet."

"I'd be disappointed if you did."

"Do Logan and Duvall know you're here?"

"I slipped them before Caldwell's men took them. I assume their first conclusion will be that I fled their employ in order to walk straight into yours."

Reagan eyed his clothes. "You didn't pick those out, did you?"

"Hardly." Thorne picked at his suit jacket. "The color is divine, but the quality leaves something to be desired."

"Did you check for tracking devices?"

Thorne frowned, but it was playful. "Dear, I may have been out of the game for some time, but I haven't lost my touch. They'll be chasing me through the sewers for the next several hours if we're lucky."

"I've never much relied on luck."

"No one should rely on luck. We should be grateful for it nonetheless."

Reagan bristled, feeling once again like she was just a teenager, hiding in the shadow of her mentor. But then she relaxed. She no longer stood in anyone's shadow. If everything went according to plan, her legacy would be longer and darker than anything Thorne had ever dreamed possible.

"Speaking of Logan and Duvall," Thorne said. "What are your plans for them?"

"Don't you worry." Reagan pushed to her feet and really looked at Thorne for the first time in fifteen years. "They'll have front row seats to the show."

51

MANDY SLIPPED OUT OF HER ROOM AND LOCKED HER DOOR BEHIND HER with an annoyed twist of her wrist. Whoever had snuck into her room while she was gone had done so without breaking the door down. Who would have a key? That narrowed the list down to the entire school. It didn't exactly make her feel safer than if it was someone else who had managed to just pick the lock.

Their intention had been to delete the files, not lie in wait for her. Just because they hadn't attacked her after the match didn't mean she wasn't in any danger. And now that this mysterious person knew who she was? Well, it would be smarter to lay low. That's what Bear would want her to do.

But she couldn't wait for someone to make a move against her or her friends. She had to get to the bottom of this herself. There was no time to waste. Or the next phone call she got could be Charlie or Etta calling from the hospital.

Mandy checked the lock on her door three times before walking away. She was glad her habit had served its purpose. It annoyed her that she couldn't tell Ms. Antoinette about what had happened, to explain why her rituals were so important. She would just end up alerting the school and the authorities over the break-in, and then Mandy would have an even bigger problem on her hands.

No, there was only one person she could talk to, and even that was a risk. Normally, she didn't like relying on outside help, especially from people she didn't know all too well. But Coach Foley had proven he'd been looking out for her from the beginning. He'd looked the other way when she was caught fighting. He'd instead invited her onto the boxing team. Then had warned her that she was being too obvious in her questions to Amy, followed by interrupting her clandestine meeting with Stonewall. Maybe he didn't know what was really going on, but he'd proven that he had her back.

She hoped she wasn't putting her faith in the wrong person. Everyone knew Coach Foley stayed late after the matches to review Charlie's footage. Tonight would be no different. Most of the lights throughout the school were off, but a few were kept on so the staff could move around after-hours. Strictly speaking, she wasn't allowed out of her room at this hour, but so far, she'd been able to give the cleaning staff and the security guards the slip. Bear would be furious to find out how easy it was for her to go undetected.

She stood outside Coach Foley's office. Dim yellow light spilled through the gap along the bottom of the door.

Mandy tapped on the door with her fingertips. She was eager for him to open the door before someone caught her out in the hall. She didn't want to push her luck. Coach would have her back, but she didn't want there to be more witnesses to this meeting than necessary.

Ten seconds felt like an hour while she waited. Mandy heard shuffling on the other side of the door before it opened. Coach Foley looked exhausted, but his eyes sharpened as soon as he spotted who was waiting for him. He checked down the hallway in one direction and then the other then stepped to the side and gestured Mandy in. As soon as she cleared the door, he shut it behind her and turned to scrutinize her with a frown on his face.

"You shouldn't be wandering the halls this late."

"I know, but I...I couldn't sleep." Mandy had wanted to come right out with the truth, but a voice in the back of her head told her to be more cautious. "I feel really bad about being late to the match. It was irresponsible, and it won't happen again."

Foley studied her for a moment before gesturing to one of the chairs in front of his desk. Once Mandy sat, he walked around to the other side and sank into his own chair. "You're a good kid, Mandy. A good fighter. What you can do in that ring at your age is incredible. I mean that, really. You could go far if you decide you want to pursue boxing professionally."

"But?"

"But you don't seem dedicated to it. You enjoy it, that's plain to see, but you've got a lot going on inside that head of yours, don't you?"

"You could say that."

"You wanna talk about it?"

That was why she was here, but she found it harder to get started than she had imagined. "I'm just worried I'll get into trouble. Or that I'll get someone else into trouble."

Coach Foley nodded his head. After a moment, he clasped his hands in front of him on the desk and leaned forward. She'd never seen him so earnest. "I can't make any promises. If someone is hurt or in a dangerous situation, then I have an obligation to report it. That said, I promise I'll do the best I can to listen to what you have to say and help if I can."

Mandy nodded. It felt like she was on a rollercoaster—one minute she was weightless, and the next, the gravity of her situation slammed down onto her, forcing her back in her seat. "I've been recording conversations." Better to keep this simple and straightforward. And not mention Etta and Charlie at all. "Of the parents at the matches."

Coach Foley frowned. "Why?"

"I've had suspicions for a while that they're up to something. Something bad."

"What made you think that?"

Mandy sighed. This was why she hadn't wanted to tell him. It was all so complicated now, so wrapped up in everything Bear was doing to fight Reagan. Mandy needed help, but she couldn't tell Coach Foley about that. Not unless she really trusted him with her life. "I can't get into that right now but suffice it to say that I was right. They were planning something big."

"Okay." Coach Foley just kept nodding his head, like he was taking this all in on faith but didn't quite believe it. "What did you find?"

"That's complicated. Look, I just need you to know that someone broke into my room tonight and stole the files."

Coach Foley launched out of his chair. "What? Who? Are you hurt?"

Mandy shook her head until she felt dizzy. "I wasn't in the room at the time. They didn't even leave a mess. But everything is gone." She elected not to tell him that she got them back. When she opened her mouth again, something else came out. "But that's not really what I wanted to tell you."

"Okay." Foley eased back down into his chair. "What did you want to tell me?"

"I got a phone call from someone who used a voice modulator. They told me to keep my nose out of other people's business. They knew something. About me." She swallowed thickly, as though the words had lodged in her throat. "They knew something they shouldn't have. And I just felt like I should tell someone. And you said I could talk to you. About anything." The words were no longer stuck, but she was aware she was rambling now. "And so I came here. I didn't know what else to do."

"You did the right thing." Foley's gaze lifted to the ceiling, as though searching for the answer to all her problems. When he looked back down at Mandy, his face was set. "And I think that maybe they're right."

Mandy froze in her chair. "What?"

"I think you should stay out of it." Coach Foley's voice was gentle, but his gaze was unwavering. "Whatever you uncovered, it's dangerous. I know you can handle yourself, but this sounds bigger than any one of us."

Mandy's mind spiraled. "Okay."

"I'm glad you told me. Let me—let me investigate a few things and get back to you. In the meantime, why don't you lay low. Can you do that for me?"

"Yeah, of course." Mandy stood, trying to ignore the way her legs shook. "Yeah, I can do that."

"Get some sleep. I'll be in touch tomorrow."

Mandy blinked, and she was already across the room and opening his door. At the last minute, she looked over her shoulder. "Thanks, Mr. Foley."

"Any time, kiddo."

Mandy closed the door behind her and made it to the other end of the hallway. As soon as she was around the corner, she sprinted all the way back to her bedroom, only slowing down long enough to make sure she didn't get caught out of bed.

It wasn't until she'd slipped back into her room and closed the door behind her that she allowed herself to listen to the voice that had been screaming in the back of her head the entire time. It was that instinct that had been cultivated over years of experience and practice.

And it was telling her she'd just made a huge mistake.

52

MARCUS WAS IN AWE OF HIS UNCLE. BRANDON WAS A GENIUS WITH computers but seeing him work was like witnessing Rembrandt paint The Night Watch in real time. When Brandon added another line of code, it was like he was adding another layer of color and blending it in to form a portrait so beautiful that it nearly brought tears to Marcus' eyes.

Unfortunately, Marcus wasn't much help at a time like this. It was taking all his concentration to keep up with the basics, let alone try to remember everything Brandon was doing to replicate later. Even if he had the programming equivalent of tracing paper, Marcus didn't think he'd be able to come close to what his uncle was doing. Not for many, many years.

Marcus' job was to run back and forth to the kitchen to make sure Brandon had enough Diet Coke to fuel his brain. He'd also searched through the pantry and fridge and come up with what he thought was a decent meal. A can of soup for each of them, plus frozen garlic bread and a vegetable medley that he only added so when his mother asked him if he'd eaten anything green while he was at Brandon's, he wouldn't be lying. He'd even found some of those frozen chocolate eclairs in the back of the freezer that never seemed to taste quite right, no matter how long you let them thaw for. But it was better than nothing, and Brandon had fist-bumped him when he delivered them and eaten two without complaint.

Whether it was from his earlier nap or the adrenaline of their current situation, Marcus was wired. Or maybe it was from the four Diet Cokes he'd had over the last two hours. Unlike his mother, Brandon didn't tell him to slow down or to drink some water.

Occasionally, Brandon would pull his attention away from his computer long enough to explain at least part of what he was doing. As soon as Thorne had given Bear and Iris the slip, he'd done his due diligence by following the tracker, but he was sure the man had figured out it'd been in the seam of his pants. Sure enough, it had ended up at a water treatment plant downriver from Alexandria. Since chances were low that Thorne had flushed himself down the toilet, they could cross that possibility off the list—no matter how hilarious Marcus found the visual.

That meant they had to go back to square one. Instead of being dejected by the prospect, Brandon seemed to come alive at the challenge of tracking down Thorne in record time.

"Strictly speaking, a lot of this isn't legal." Brandon took his eyes off the screen for a few seconds. "But I have a lot of defenses to make sure no one can track any of my movements back to me. On the off chance they do, that's where someone like Iris comes in. You can get away with a lot of gray area stuff in the name of national security, as long as you have someone like her backing you up."

Marcus nodded. It felt like a master was passing down years of experience to an uninitiated apprentice. He didn't care about being out of his depth. He was just happy to be in the room.

"So, what are you doing right now?"

"Thanks to Iris' contact at the NSA, we've got access to the CCTV footage around the D.C. metro area. Right now, I'm running facial recognition software in the hopes of picking him up somewhere. Remember how I said it's easier when you have a better database?"

"Yeah."

"Well, let's just say the NSA keeps track of a lot of people, and since Thorne has been in the system for a while, we have a lot of data points to go off of." Brandon popped open his can of Diet Coke and sipped some liquid from the opening. "Plus, we have a solid timeline in terms of when he left the museum, so that narrows our window down quite a lot. It's much easier to go through an hour's worth of footage across the city than to watch an entire day."

"I thought Raine was kind of on the run from the NSA?" Marcus asked. "Didn't she figure out her boss was part of Reagan's network?"

"She does have to be even more careful than we do, but she's very good." Brandon had a wistful look on his face.

"Do you have a *crush* on her?"

Brandon scowled. "No. For one, I haven't given up on Kimberlee coming back again. And I'm too old to have a *crush*. I have a professional appreciation for her abilities. There's a big difference."

"Sure." Marcus had seen the way his uncle blushed. He pointed to the screen behind Brandon. "Speak of the devil."

Brandon whirled around, hitting a key on his keyboard to answer Raine's phone call. "Hey, good timing. The search is almost–yep, there we go. Just found him."

"Where?" Raine answered.

"In a black SUV heading across the river. It's like he wasn't even trying to hide. Cameras picked him up looking out the window. I've got a clear shot of the license plate too."

"This sounds too easy for Thorne."

"I don't disagree, but maybe someone's throwing us a bone. We've been running ourselves ragged. We were bound to get lucky."

"You're right." Raine didn't sound like she believed it. "I was just in touch with Iris. They got away. Farro dropped them off, and he's headed the other way. They're standing by for our next move."

Marcus leaned forward. "They're okay? I'll text Mandy with an update."

"No one's injured."

Marcus nodded even though Raine couldn't see him. He shot a text off to Mandy. The reply was instant, and he felt like he could feel her relief through the phone.

"You sound like you've got some bad news," Brandon said.

"I do. Remember the plane that took off for Venezuela?"

Brandon glanced down at his computer's clock. "It would've landed already, right? Were your contacts able to intercept it?"

"Yeah, they had no problem tracking it down. Except when they did, it was empty."

"What do you mean it was empty?"

"I mean it was empty." Raine's frustration overtook the dejection in her voice for the first time. "There were no weapons onboard."

Brandon slammed a fist against his desk, making Marcus jump. "It was all a diversion."

"That's what I figured. Found a private flight heading from Florida to Dulles. After about a half hour, a truck left, headed for Langley."

Brandon froze, then clicked through several of the windows on his computer, bringing up a series of maps. He adjusted them until he got the view he wanted. "That's where Thorne was headed. Which means—"

"That's where Reagan is."

Marcus felt a shiver crawl down his spine and lodge in his stomach. "Langley is where the CIA headquarters is, right?" He felt stupid for asking, but he needed to say something to chase away the tense silence.

"It's also where Caldwell's men took her after the party," Raine said. "After the shots were fired, everyone left. Her team ushered her into a car and straight back across the river."

"It was never about Venezuela," Brandon said. "That was always a distraction. Or a backup plan. Caldwell would've gotten in enough trouble selling drugs to fund the weapons to send oversea. What Reagan has planned is a thousand times worse."

"What?" Marcus looked to his uncle for answers. "What's Reagan planning?"

"He's going to use the weapons to launch an attack from Langley, and make it look like Caldwell hit the button."

"Attack who?" Marcus asked.

"Those LAWS have a limited range. The White House. The Pentagon. The Capitol." He pulled up a different map and typed in some commands. The area turned red, and he sank back in his chair. ""Hell, all of Washington D.C."

53

REAGAN PLACED THE PHONE BACK ON THE RECEIVER IN THE CENTER OF
her desk. Her hand lingered there for a moment. She had thought about
sending Thorne out of the room while she took the call, but she was
glad she hadn't, given the nature of the information she had just
acquired.

She would be a fool to trust Daniel Thorne to look out for anyone
but himself. It wasn't that he was incapable of being selfless, but she
couldn't rely on him to follow her lead. Not when she was this close to
achieving everything she had worked for after all these years. She
refused to fall back into old habits. She refused to let *him* take the credit
she deserved.

Besides, Daniel Thorne being self-sacrificing was part of the reason
she was in this situation to begin with. Years ago, he'd tried to right
some of his endless wrongs, and look where it got him. A decade and a
half in jail. Was it worth it? She didn't think so. He seemed like the same
old Thorne she had always known. Maybe he'd helped stop the vice
president's plot to kick off World War III, but it seemed like he'd only
delayed the inevitable. The world was getting more violent by the day.
What good had it done him to fall on his sword? She wouldn't make the
same mistake.

Reagan realized she was scowling when Thorne asked, "Trouble in paradise?"

"Quite the opposite, actually." She smoothed out her expression. "Did you know Logan had a daughter?"

"Mandy," Thorne said, with a nod of his head. "He keeps information about her pretty close to the vest, but from all I gathered, she's a smart kid. Tough, too. Been through a lot already. Reminds me of you."

Reagan did everything she could not to wince. "I'm not a kid anymore, Thorne."

"Can you blame me for being nostalgic? It's been so long."

Reagan had nothing to say that to that. She refused to get trapped into a conversation about the past. "Logan hid Mandy away where we couldn't find her. Do you know where?"

"No. He never mentioned it in front of me. Seems like there was some tension between him and Duvall, though. Mandy seemed to be the center of it."

Reagan raised a brow. "What made you think that?"

"Bear brushed her off more than once. I heard them whispering. No one mentioned anything important in front of me, but Mandy's name kept coming up."

"She's at Eastern Blue Ridge Academy. Not too far from here."

This time, it was Thorne's turn to raise his eyebrow in surprise. "I'm surprised she's not halfway across the world. Feels like something he would do."

"She wouldn't have been able to hide from us, no matter where she went. But I will admit this is much more convenient."

Thorne was silent for a moment, now looking at Reagan like he hardly knew her. "Convenient for what? What are you going to do to her?"

"What's necessary." Reagan stood and walked around to the front of her desk. She leaned against it and folded her arms across her chest. She would've done something about Mandy a long time ago, but it seemed Monarch had remained defiant even in death. "Don't tell me you're going soft in your old age."

"She's just a child. She has nothing to do with this."

"What does her being a child have to do with anything? That's never stopped you before."

"I've done what I had to do in the name of protecting my country. But I never enjoyed what I did. I never relished it."

"And you think I do? It's a necessary evil. I thought you of all people would understand that."

"I guess I'm still trying to figure out what you're trying to accomplish."

Reagan tried to ignore the flush of pleasure at Thorne's confusion. She checked her watch. "While I would love to sit here and explain it to you, I don't have that kind of time. My associate will do what's necessary to keep Mandy from interfering any further."

Thorne chuckled. "I suppose she takes after her adoptive father, after all."

Reagan scowled. "She's a child. She's been an annoyance, at worst. Now she'll be another piece of leverage."

Thorne looked like he had plenty to say about that, but he kept it to himself. "You've come so far, M—"

"Reagan." Straightening, she crossed the room and opened the door. "My name is Reagan. And if you want a front row seat to the event, I suggest you wash up. Maybe eat something. You're looking a little... peckish."

"Of course. I appreciate the invitation."

Reagan watched Thorne pass through the door, scowling at her over his shoulder, then closed it behind him. She turned around and stalked back over to her desk. Whatever she did next, she wouldn't let Thorne get under her skin. What she had planned was so much bigger than him. More grandiose than anything he'd done. By the time the night was through, he'd know that without a shadow of a doubt.

54

Mandy listened to a soothing soundscape to calm her nerves. She didn't know what she would've done if Marcus hadn't been keeping her up to date. Bear called her when he could, but he had bigger problems to focus on at the moment. She understood. That didn't make it any easier. As much as she'd been through prior to this, sometimes she just wanted her dad to hug her close and tell her everything was going to be okay.

But right now, it was up to her to make sure she stood on her own two feet and was ready for whatever was about to happen.

According to Marcus, the target was Washington, D.C. Not too far from her school. She had no idea if whatever Reagan was planning would end up hurting her. She couldn't worry about that now. Either her dad stopped Reagan or he didn't. And if he didn't, she might as well go down with the ship. She couldn't imagine a world without Bear in it.

Besides, she had her own problem to deal with at Eastern Blue Ridge Academy, and its name was Coach Foley.

She'd gone to him because he'd warned her at every turn to be careful. She thought he'd wanted to protect her. But after her impromptu meeting with him, and the warning he'd issued, she wasn't so sure. It's not like he'd been mean or particularly forceful. But an edge to his voice made her think he was saying *or else*. She hadn't told him about Mr. Reagan, but now he knew she was recording those conversations. She was more certain than ever that Stonewall was the one who'd called her, but she'd never even considered that Coach Foley might've been in on it too.

A chime from her phone had Mandy picking it up and staring at the screen. She hoped the text message was from Marcus with another update. She didn't get her wish in either department, but she didn't have time to be disappointed.

She unlocked her phone and her jaw dropped when she saw what Charlie had written.

Amy's mom just walked through the courtyard outside Etta's room, looking like she was going somewhere important. Then thirty seconds later, Foley went after her. Do you know what's going on???

She didn't, but that wouldn't be the case for long. She told Charlie and Etta to stay put and keep their eyes open. Mandy put on a sweatshirt and pulled the hood up over her head, hoping it would be enough to mask her face from any onlookers or cameras that might catch her. And especially from Stonewall and Coach Foley.

For the second time that night, Mandy slipped out of her room and walked quickly and quietly to her destination. She only had to stop and slip into the shadows twice to avoid being caught by security.

Still, she was going to lodge a formal complaint after she left Eastern Blue Ridge. They really had to step up their security if they wanted to keep kids safe. You'd think after Vinny's disappearance they'd be taking extra precaution, but it seemed like they were more worried about covering it up than making sure it didn't happen again.

Charlie had said he'd seen them walking through the courtyard and into the gazebo on the edge of the school property. It was a little distance from the Academy, and as Mandy drew nearer, she saw that someone had cut all the lights surrounding the structure. That was good for her, and for her targets. The sky was obscured by thick clouds. Her eyes were beginning to adjust but there were still plenty of spots where people could be hiding. She hoped she was the only one out here trying to do that.

The temperature over the last week or so had been getting colder now that they were inching closer to December, and she caught the first few snowflakes of the season falling in lazy circles toward the ground. The flakes felt as though they were burning her skin before melting. She was glad it hadn't been coming down any thicker, or she'd be leaving evidence of her escapades in the snow behind her.

Her sweatshirt wasn't warm enough for this kind of weather, and her socks were already wet from the damp grass. Her toes were freezing. The sooner she could figure out what Stonewall and Foley were up to, the sooner she could get back inside, get warm, and take action.

Mandy was glad the Academy had someone to keep the grounds clear of fallen leaves and branches that would crunch underfoot. The soft ground might give her away in the daylight, but right now, it was doing its best to cover her footsteps. She found a large oak tree to hide behind. She could just barely make out the conversation from her perch. Mandy had left her room right after Charlie had texted her, but the two adults had had some time to talk before she'd arrived.

"Monarch never told me you were part of the plan," Stonewall said.

Coach Foley was just a silhouette from where Mandy stood. It looked like he'd shrugged. "That was the point. I was only meant to be a backup in case something happened. Then he went and got himself killed."

Stonewall stiffened. "You mean he killed himself."

"That's the official story, but we both know what really happened. King screwed up. Reagan took care of the problem. End of story."

"Monarch," Stonewall bit out.

"He's dead. What does it matter now?"

"You said you wanted to talk," Stonewall said, a shiver in her voice. "What did you want to talk about."

"Mandy Davis," Coach Foley said. Mandy couldn't stop herself from gasping softly. "Rather, Mandy Logan. You figured it out, didn't you?"

Stonewall was silent for a few seconds. "Yes. She all but bragged about it to my face."

"She's been recording you."

"How'd you know that?"

"She told me. Been trying to gain her trust for months. Finally paid off."

Mandy bit her tongue to keep from cursing out her coach. She knew how dangerous it was to trust anyone, and she'd told him more than enough. He'd put two and two together to figure out her real identity.

"Did Monarch know who she was?" Stonewall asked.

"Yeah. He was sitting on the information. Don't think he ever told Reagan."

"Why not?"

Foley shrugged again. "Don't think he wanted to see the kid get hurt. Or he wanted to use her for leverage later. His mistake."

"One you're not going to make?"

"Not my call." Foley held up his hands. "I'm here for backup. Not looking for any glory. Can't blow my cover yet. I'm working an angle with Duvall. But Mandy told me someone called her with a voice modulator and threatened her. Was that you?"

"Couldn't let the brat get away with what she was doing. She's been causing enough problems. Besides, we can use her to get Logan to do what we want. He'll stay out of the way if we have his daughter in our clutches."

Foley was silent for a moment. "You called Reagan, then? Told him about the kid?"

"Yeah. I've got a pair of guys heading to the brat's room right now." Stonewall opened her phone, the light bright enough to make them wince. "They should be there any minute. I've got a car waiting to take her to meet Reagan."

"I was really hoping you'd say that." Coach Foley pulled something out of his back pocket, and Mandy's breath caught as she saw a hint of metal flash in the light from Stonewall's phone.

Stonewall gasped. "What the—"

"Marissa Stonewall, you're under arrest for attempted kidnapping and, well, a whole lot more that we'll figure out later."

Stonewall sputtered, but Foley already had one wrist locked up and was pulling her other arm around back to snap the second one in place. He slipped the phone from Stonewall's hand but kept it open so he could read the messages. Without looking up, he said, "You can come out now, Mandy. It's safe."

She hesitated for a moment, her mind spinning with possibilities. Could this be a trap?

No, if Coach Foley had wanted to hurt her, he wouldn't have put Stonewall in cuffs. Swallowing down her trepidation, Mandy stepped out from her hiding place. Stonewall glared at her as she approached.

"It's time I properly introduce myself," Coach Foley said. "My name is Special Agent Sean Flint."

Mandy sputtered. The name didn't sound familiar. The man must've known as much.

He looked down at her the same way Bear did sometimes, like a father just happy to have his daughter simply exist in the world. "Iris and I have been working together. You were never in any danger. I've been here the whole time."

55

BEAR AND IRIS FOLLOWED FARRO TO A CAR A FEW BLOCKS OVER FROM THE museum. Bear had no idea whether it had been intended for them the whole time, or if it would've been Caldwell's getaway vehicle if plans had turned out differently. None of that mattered now. The important part was that they were out, and they knew exactly where to go next.

Even better, Bear felt as though he finally knew who they were up against.

"Check under the seats for weapons." Farro tossed Bear the keys for the car. "Nothing fancy but should get you where you need to go."

"What about you?" Iris asked.

"Anyone who follows," Farro said, "I'll lead them away."

Iris stepped forward and placed a hand on the man's shoulder. "Thank you for everything."

He nodded. His eyes met hers, then Bear's. "Sorry I couldn't be more helpful in the beginning. I know you've been through hell and back. There were too many eyes on me. Had to keep the heat off you and hope that you ended up in the right place at the right time."

Bear gripped the other man's hand in a firm handshake. "By the skin of our teeth. But we did it. Appreciate it. When this is all over, I'll buy you a beer."

The glint in his Farro's eyes let Bear know he appreciated the offer. "I'm gonna need it. Stay safe. Sorry we can't be more hands on, but Caldwell knows she's being pinned for this. We've got to be as far away as possible. It's up to you now."

"Consider it done," Bear said.

"I'll hold you to that." Farro turned and jogged off into the dark.

Bear turned to Iris and tossed her the keys. "You're driving," he said. "I need to call my kid."

She didn't argue. As soon as she pulled away from the curb, Bear brought up Mandy's number. She picked up on the first ring.

"Bear? You okay?"

"I'm good, kiddo. How are you?"

"Good. Coach Foley is a special agent, and he arrested Marissa Stonewall. She stole the recordings I'd made, but I have them back now thanks to Brandon. She was going to send someone to my room to kidnap me and take me to Reagan. Coach Foley stopped it. Well, I guess his name is Special Agent Flint. Amy's never going to speak to me again, but her mom broke the law and she wanted to hand me over to Reagan, so I don't feel too bad about it."

It was everything Bear could do to keep up. "But you're okay? You're safe?"

"I'm safe. And we have evidence that we can tie to everyone who was a conspirator, not that there are a ton of them left now. But you need to find Reagan."

Some of the tension left his shoulders. Despite everything else going to hell around him, at least Mandy was safe. "And that's just what I'll do. What about your friends?"

"Everyone's good. Don't worry about us."

"I'm your dad. I'm always going to worry. Get some sleep if you can. I'll call you as soon as I'm done."

"Make sure you talk to Brandon," she said. "He has some news for you. I love you."

"I love you too."

Bear hung up. He looked down at the phone in his hands and replayed the conversation. When he looked up again, Iris was glancing at him out of the corner of her eye. "Coach Foley," he said. "You know him?"

Iris swallowed, like she was trying to dislodge the guilt that had built up in her throat. "Agent Flint. I'm sorry I didn't tell you. I still wasn't sure who to trust, but he and I go way back. I knew he'd keep an eye on her. He was updating me daily."

Bear looked out the window, watching as D.C. passed by in a blur of color and lights.

"Thank you," he said. "I appreciate you looking out for her."

"Of course." A moment of silence passed between them. "What now?"

"Now it's time to call Brandon." Bear selected the man's number and put his phone on speaker. "We're gonna end this."

Brandon picked up on the second ring. "Good timing, big man. You all good?"

"All good here. What've you got for me?"

"A lot." Brandon exhaled loudly, like he was still trying to comprehend the situation they were in. "Saw that Thorne gave you the slip. How'd that happen?"

"Caldwell's men surrounded us, he got away. Did he figure out where the tracker was?"

"Yeah. He flushed it. He's in the wind."

"As expected." Bear shook his head. Pulling the man out of prison to help them was always a risk. But he'd caught him once. He could do it again. "We'll cross paths again at some point."

"It's gonna be sooner rather than later. Reagan is planning something, and Thorne is gonna be there when it goes down."

"How do you know that?"

"Because Thorne wasn't exactly hiding after he left the museum. Cameras picked him up on way out of D.C. Wasn't hard to track the car to the other side of the river. Driver was Lochlan Reid—"

"CIA," Bear said. "Caldwell warned us about him."

"Followed them all the way to their destination. My guess is Reagan knew Thorne would be at the museum with you and sent Reid to pick him up. Now they're all gathering to watch the grand finale."

"We know what that is yet?" Bear asked.

"Yeah. Hang on, let me patch Raine in." Bear heard a click. "She's done a lot of the heavy lifting for us."

"Thanks," Raine said. "Iris?"

"How are you holding up?" Iris asked. "Any trouble?"

"None at all. At least not on my end."

"Glad to hear it. Brandon, send me Thorne's location. I'll head there now."

"What do you have for us, Raine?" Bear asked once they were en route.

"We tracked the plane to Venezuela," she said, "but it was empty when it got there. All a diversion. The weapons are still in D.C."

"Any idea what Reagan's planning?"

"Actually, yeah," Raine said. "Caldwell's men took the director to the same location. We think Reagan's going to hit D.C. with the LAWs and frame Caldwell."

Bear and Iris exchanged a look. "How much time do we have?"

"I don't know for sure." Raine's voice shook. "The weapons have been there for about an hour. To unload them, get them prepared, and send them out? I'd assume they'll be ready sooner rather than later. We're really racing against the clock here."

Bear felt himself go into mission mode. "Any chance the two of you can hack into the system and stall?"

"They're on a closed network," Brandon said. "We'll need you to get us access. Until then, our hands are tied."

"You can talk Iris through that?" Bear asked.

"Shouldn't be a problem. But what are you going to do?"

"I'll be the distraction," Bear said. "It's about time Reagan and I had a nice little face to face."

"And us?" Raine asked. "What do you want us to do in the meantime?"

"Call up the President of the United States," Bear said. "And the Pentagon, and the Capitol. The page program coordinator. Anyone who will listen. Tell them they're about to take it up the rear and they better be prepared."

56

BEAR NEVER ENJOYED WALKING THROUGH A PAIR OF DOORS WITHOUT knowing what was on the other side. But his job was to be the distraction while Iris circled around the back to look for another way in. And the best way to get everyone's attention?

Cause a little destruction.

If they'd had more time, he would've come prepared with more than a handgun and an extra magazine. But since he didn't, he'd have to rely on his wits and charming personality. And his two fists.

He kept out of sight. The two men guarding the front door didn't realize he was there until it was too late. As one turned to bring his gun up, Bear wrapped an arm around the other's neck and snapped it.

The first man charged just as the second one went limp in Bear's arms. Bear dropped the man to the ground and knocked the other man's arm away, preventing him from putting a bullet through his brain. But the guy managed to squeeze the trigger. The shot rang out and alerted everyone in the vicinity that something was going down.

Shouts erupted. Bear had limited time to take down his opponents before a second wave crashed over him.

He pulled his gun out and put a bullet between the eyes of the other man. The guy crumpled to the ground and twitched once before going still. In the back of his mind, he wondered if any of them were Lochlan Reid and whether Caldwell would be mad that she hadn't been the one to end his life.

A bullet pinged off the door. Bear dove back into the darkness. He ducked low and ran along the outside of the building until he came up against another pair of men. Like most of his opponents, they had no idea he was as fast or agile, and they only had time to shout in surprise before they headed to join their associates.

Bear headed back to the front door and tested the handle. Unlocked. He stepped to the side, pulled the door open and a volley of gunfire greeted him. Using the small gap where the hinges connected to the frame, Bear spotted his adversaries and memorized their locations. He stuck his arm around the door and squeezed off four more rounds. A cry and a thump told him he'd hit at least two of his targets.

Bear used the distraction of the wounded men to line up his shots. He took out the one who'd been wounded, along with the man who was trying to pull the guy to safety. The remaining man fled for cover, and Bear took a moment to take in the warehouse in front of him.

He had no idea what it had previously been used for, only that it was full of dusty machinery, plastic tarps, and damp cardboard boxes. The front part of the warehouse wasn't large, and Bear knew from Brandon's hasty explanation of the floor plans that the rest of the building was split up into half a dozen small rooms that had once held offices and meeting spaces. There was a back entrance. That was where Iris would be sneaking in. That's also where he had to draw everyone else away from. She was going in armed, but it'd be better for her if she had fewer people to deal with.

Bear ducked and rolled as another shot came barreling his way, barely missing his left shoulder. He popped up on his feet, took aim, and squeezed the trigger twice, catching his opponent first in the shoulder and then the neck. He walked up and ended the man with a third bullet.

He only had two left.

The crunch of footsteps on broken glass had him spinning around with his gun raised.

"Don't shoot!" the figure said, his arms raised.

It took Bear a moment to realize who he was looking at. Blue suit. Coiffed hair. A face that was absent of a wry grin. Bear didn't lower his weapon. "Thorne."

"Don't shoot," Thorne said. "Please."

"Never thought I'd hear you say *please*." Bear didn't move. "What are you up to?"

"Trying to help you," Thorne said, scowling. He kept his arms in the air, but he didn't look happy about it. "Mr. Reagan is—"

"I know who she is," Bear said. "Try again."

Thorne huffed. "The weapons. You only have a few minutes to dismantle them. She has Caldwell in the back."

"Really, Thorne. I'm not used to seeing you ten steps behind everyone else."

"I know," a woman's voice said from the shadows. "Isn't it pathetic?"

Thorne's eyes went wide, but before he could use that silver tongue of his, a shot rang out. Bear flinched, but it was Thorne who dropped to the ground with a cry. He held his hand over his knee, blood gushing between his fingers. Another shot hit him in the other knee. A third in the chest.

"Do you know how long I've waited to do that?" the woman said, and Bear didn't dare turn around and draw attention to himself. "It feels so good to be the one to kill you."

"Please—" Thorne begged.

"Like I said," the woman repeated. "Pathetic."

With a final shot, Thorne fell limp to the ground, blood seeping from between his eyes.

"You can turn around now, Bear," the woman said. "We have a lot to catch up on."

"Yes, we do." Bear raised his arms as he turned to face the gun pointing at his chest and the woman holding it. "It's nice to see you again, Maria."

57

Marcus sat next to his uncle, the sound of computer fans whirring and the smell of coffee pervaded his senses. More times than he could count, he'd wished he were a fly on the wall since finding out about his uncle's secret life as a genius computer hacker. And now he was here, doing exactly that.

But it wasn't quite what he'd imagined. Brandon had been right to be annoyed by the movies they'd watched. Real life was nothing like what was portrayed on film, and it was a hell of a lot more dangerous. Mandy's dad was out there, trying to take down Reagan, and so was Iris and the Director of the CIA. Who knew how many other people were involved? There was no guarantee the good guys would win. No guarantee any of them would come home at the end of the night.

Panic squeezed Marcus' chest. Tears pricked at his eyes. He did his best to remain still and silent. Brandon's fingers flew over his keyboard faster than Marcus had ever seen them go. The last thing he wanted to do was be a distraction. Not when it could get someone hurt. Or killed.

Brandon grabbed his mouse and clicked around a few times before static sounded through the speakers. "Iris? You there?"

"Here." Her voice was muffled as though she was holding the phone as close to her mouth as possible. "You ready?"

Brandon had always been an upbeat sort of guy, someone who joked around a lot—especially with his nephew—and his level of seriousness now startled Marcus. "Was going to ask you the same thing. We gotta do this hard and fast. No room for mistakes or a lot of people are going to die."

"Understood."

Marcus drew in a deep breath, clenching his hands by his side. He was shaking and couldn't decide if he was grateful there was nothing he could do in a situation like this, or if he hated the feeling of being so powerless. If something went wrong and lives were lost, the responsibility wouldn't be his. But their deaths would still haunt his nightmares.

Brandon brought up a map of the warehouse they were storming. "Give me a play by play of your movements. Tell me everything you see and hear."

"Right." Iris sounded uncertain. "Just slipped in through the back door. Bear's doing a helluva job being the distraction. Not seeing anyone—"

She made a startled sound, and then the phone crashed to the ground. There was a grunt, and it sounded lower than a noise Iris would've made. There was shuffling, another grunt, and then a thud. The sounds sent a jolt through Marcus and he sat up straighter in his chair.

After a rustling from the speakers, Iris' breaths came in heavy. "Really wish we'd been able to stop for earpieces. Holding this phone is gonna be the death of me."

Marcus sagged, and noticed that Brandon's shoulders dropped in relief, too.

"Slow and easy," his uncle said. "No point in rushing this if we can't make it to the finish line in one piece."

"What happened to hard and fast?"

"Maybe we can meet somewhere in the middle."

"The back room has boxes piled to the ceiling. A couple filing cabinets." The shrill scrape of metal against metal sounded through the speaker. "Empty."

"Is there a door on the opposite wall?"

"Yes."

"Go through that. You'll enter a hallway. There's three doors on each side. No idea what's in those rooms, so you'll have to clear them one at a time."

"Great," Iris said. "Putting you in my pocket. I'll let you know if I find anything."

"Sounds go—" Brandon froze for a second before clicking around on his screen a few times. Marcus wasn't sure he wanted to see what his uncle was looking at. What if he couldn't scrub it from his memory? "Raine, you there?"

"Here." She sounded as breathless as Iris, though it seemed to be in excitement. "We're ready."

"That's subjective," another woman said, her voice bored. "Considering you haven't told us what we're doing here yet."

"All in good time," Brandon said, his fingers flying over his keyboard once more. "Everyone else ready?"

A chorus of affirmatives sounded from the line, and Marcus was sure he heard four or five additional voices. His uncle hadn't told him the plan, just that they needed some extra help making sure the drones didn't cause widespread panic—or destruction.

"Just waiting on one more," Brandon said.

The line was silent for a moment before a man's deep voice reverberated around the room. "Ms. Bauer, it is in your best interest to—"

"Hey, Chuck." Brandon's voice was cheery, but his entire body had gone rigid. "Thanks for joining us today."

The man hesitated before he spoke again. "Ms. Bauer?"

Raine sighed into the phone like she hadn't signed off on these theatrics but had resigned herself to them, regardless. "Mr. Lancaster, I'd like you to meet a few of my friends. I'd introduce them by name, but something tells me they wouldn't appreciate it."

"Damn straight," the woman with the bored voice said.

"Lancaster?" This man's voice was high and nasally. "Charles Lancaster? As in the Deputy Director of the NSA?"

"Ms. Bauer, I highly recommend you tell me exactly what is going on here." Lancaster's voice left no room for argument.

"Right." Raine's voice shook a little before she cleared her throat. "Okay, so Mr. Reagan—"

"I'd be *very* careful what I say next, Ms. Bauer. There are a lot of people who say you're on the wrong side of this."

"No offense, *sir*, but they're wrong." Raine huffed out a breath, and even Marcus could tell she was doing everything in her power to remain calm. "We've tracked down Mr. Reagan and have assets in place to deal with the threat she's posing."

"She?"

There was clacking from Raine's end of the call, and Marcus imagined her fingers flying over her keyboard even faster than Brandon's had been. "Yes, *she*. I'll explain everything afterwards, but for now, we need your help."

"I'm listening."

Brandon sagged a little in his chair. Marcus did the same. Getting someone to help was imperative to save the lives of hundreds of thousands of people, and the first step was just getting them to listen.

"You've got about a hundred fully autonomous drones headed in your direction," Brandon said. "We're working at taking them down at the source, but we're not sure we can get to them in time."

"What's your name, son?"

"Can't tell you that."

Lancaster muttered something that sounded a lot like *damn hackers* and then said, "What can I call you, then?"

"Call me Prophet," Brandon said, turning in his chair enough to give Marcus a wink. "I'm here with my main associate, Shaman. We've got a team standing by to assist you."

"We would've noticed drones on radar," Lancaster said. "Ms. Bauer if this is some kind of prank—"

"Charles," Raine snapped. "For the love of everything you hold dear, *listen to us.*"

"You're not going to see these on your radar," Brandon said. "Not until it's too late. We've only got minutes—"

Iris' voice cut in. "Found the room. Caldwell is tied up in the corner. She's unconscious but breathing."

"Leave her," Brandon said, and Marcus was surprised by the curtness of his tone. "Tell me what else you see."

"Who is that?" Lancaster asked.

"Iris Duvall," she said.

"FBI?" Lancaster sounded startled.

"For now," Iris said. "We'll see where the chips land after all this is over."

"We don't have time for this," Brandon said. "What do you see?"

Iris let out a soft gasp. "Oh God, they've already been deployed."

Brandon swiveled in his chair and moved some windows around on his screen. "The weapons are active. We only have a few minutes. Jericho, did you get our own drones up in the air?"

"Done."

"All right, everyone. You've each been given access to one of our drones. They don't have weapons on them, but they are equipped with a short-range EMP burst. You need to fly your drone close to one of the enemy drones and deploy the burst. Take out as many as you can."

"Concerns about damage when they fall from the sky?" someone else asked.

"Can't worry about that right now. We'll have bigger problems if we don't stop them from hitting their targets."

"What are the targets?" Lancaster asked.

"White House. Capitol. Pentagon. We'll do what we can from the air. Move fast, everyone. We're sorely outmatched. Lancaster, you need to get your people in line. Take out as many as you can before they reach their targets. We don't know what kind of weaponry they're capable of, but these don't need a final command to execute. I have a feeling they'll be going for maximum damage and casualties. They're better than anything I've seen before."

"Whose are they?" Lancaster asked.

Brandon paused for a tense moment. "Ours."

There was silence on the line as everyone took that in, and even Marcus knew what was running through their minds because it was running through his too. Someone had turned their own weapons against them, and even worse, it was someone from the inside. Someone who had decided their own personal vendetta meant more than the lives of thousands of people.

"You gotta walk me through this," Iris said. "I don't know how to shut down the system without the password."

"We'll circumvent it," Brandon said. "It'll take a minute, but I've got some ideas. I just need you to—"

There was a cry of surprise, and the phone rattled as if it had dropped to the ground. Thuds that sounded like fists hitting flesh erupted from the speakers, and there was another cry of pain. Then a grunt and muffled words that certainly didn't belong to Iris.

Then everything went silent as the line cut off.

58

It had been over fifteen years, but Bear remembered the young girl he'd rescued from the basement of a house used to traffic women. Back then, Maria had been thin and pumped so full of drugs she could barely remain conscious. Her blonde hair had hung down in greasy curtains around her face, her stained white dress making her look even younger than she was.

He remembered being with her when she woke up, staying with her as she fought through the withdrawal, and then watching her face fall when her uncle Daniel Thorne told her she was collateral damage. It had all been a ruse. She had never gotten over that, no matter how loyal she'd remained to Thorne in the aftermath.

Bear looked over at Thorne's body, bloody and full of bullet holes. There was no love lost between the two of them. He couldn't bring himself to care that the man was no longer amongst the living. But Maria shouldn't have been the one to pull the trigger. Not in such a cold, calculating way. Had she hesitated at all? Had she even flinched when the first bullet struck its target?

He hadn't seen her face when she'd shot Thorne, but looking at her now, he doubted she felt any remorse. And she looked nothing like that young girl he'd met all those years ago.

It wasn't lost on him that she was dressed exactly like Caldwell in her tight black dress and strappy heels. Even her hair matched the Director's, dark where it had once been light, short where it had once been long. And all the innocence had been drained from her face, now all sharp angles covered in makeup and bitterness.

"Is it?" Maria asked, raising an eyebrow. "Nice to see me again, I mean."

"It's nice to finally put a face to the name of Mr. Reagan. You had us going there for a while."

"I'm glad to hear it." She glanced over at Thorne's corpse, then looked back up at Bear. "And I'm glad you were here to witness that. Though I'm sure you've thought about pulling the trigger on him yourself over the years."

Bear shrugged. "Once or twice."

Maria nodded. "Drop your weapon, Bear. Kick it over to me."

"Really? But we were having such a pleasant conversation."

"We still can. But I need you to drop your weapon."

"And what about yours?"

Maria tilted her head to the side. "What about it?"

"Are you going to hold me at gunpoint all night?"

"Not all night."

With no other choice, Bear did as he was told, taking as long as he dared to bend over, place his gun on the ground, and kick it over to her. It bounced off her shoe and came to a stop. Maria didn't bother bending down and picking it up. Her eyes never left Bear's.

"Where's Iris?" she asked.

"You know," Bear said, straightening. He didn't bother holding his hands up any longer, but he kept them where she could see them. "Around."

"Causing trouble, I'm sure." Maria's eyes grew wider, and he saw a hint of the girl she once was. "You know it's too late, right, Bear? You can't stop what I put into motion."

Bear feared she was telling the truth. "What happened to you, Maria?"

"It's Reagan now," she corrected with a click of her tongue. "Maria died fifteen years ago."

Bear nodded his head, drawing this out. "Reagan it is. But I still don't understand. When I last saw you—"

"When *was* the last time you saw me, Bear?" Maria narrowed her eyes, a flash of anger passing over her face before she smoothed it away. "Did you even look for me when I disappeared?"

He remained silent. He wouldn't lie to her. Not at a time like this.

"Exactly. You were so worried about locking my uncle up that you didn't even bother checking up on me. Did you think of me at all throughout the years?"

"Of course I did," Bear said, and it was the truth. "But I had no idea—"

Maria stepped forward. Her hand shook, not from fear but from fury. "Because you didn't want to know. You didn't care. No one cared."

"Is that why you're doing this?" Bear couldn't keep his own anger at bay. "As some twisted plea for attention?"

"You're so small-minded, Bear. I didn't see it before, but I do now. This is about more than you, more than Thorne. It's about everyone who ever turned their back on me."

"Caldwell?" Bear asked.

"The whole institution. I was homeless for a year, and no one cared a single iota about me. No one tried to help me. Despite all Thorne's training, it was if I didn't matter at all. I could've been an asset, but because of who I was related to, the CIA turned their back on me. Tried to have me killed, but it didn't take."

"I'm sorry—"

Maria took another step forward and threaded her finger through the trigger guard. "Don't you dare. Don't you dare pity me, Bear. I've gotten everything I've ever worked for and so much more. By the time I'm done, I'll have accomplished more than Thorne ever *dreamed* in his measly life."

"But he's not even here to see it."

Maria shrugged and glanced at his body. "I don't need his approval. I just wanted to be the one to put a bullet in him. Or several, for that matter."

"And me? Are you going to do the same to me?"

"Eventually. But I want you to feel helpless first. I want you to stand by, unable to do anything to save your precious country. I want you to watch while I burn it all down."

"I've got a daughter—"

"She'll be with us soon enough."

"Don't bet on it," Bear said. "She's smarter than I am. Smarter than Stonewall."

Reagan's eyes flared. "How did you—"

There was a noise from across the warehouse and Bear and Reagan turned to see Reid pushing Iris.

"Found this one in the back," he said. "Trying to stop the launch."

"Did she?" Reagan asked.

"No. " Reid puffed out his chest. "Everything is ready to go."

Iris caught Bear's gaze. Even though not a single muscle in her face twitched, Bear knew they'd been successful at getting Brandon inside. He just hoped they weren't too late to stop any major damage. How many people would be killed before Brandon shut it down? How long until they were killed once Reagan found out?

"Glad you could join us, Iris." Reagan kept her gun trained on Bear. "Why don't you join your colleague here?"

Reid shoved Iris in Bear's direction, and she stumbled over to his side, falling into him. She didn't look injured, but she gripped Bear's arm like he was the only thing keeping her on her feet. When he placed a hand on her back to steady her, he felt the outline of the weapon Reid foolishly hadn't thought to look for.

Without warning, Reagan turned to Reid and fired two shots, center mass. Reid stumbled backwards, his jaw going slack with shock as he looked down at the blood blossoming across his chest. His gun slipped from his hand, but he stayed up on his feet. When he looked up at Reagan, she shrugged in answer to his unspoken question.

Reid gurgled something Bear couldn't understand, then collapsed to the floor.

Iris gasped, but she wasn't looking at Reid. She'd taken a step closer to Maria, her eyes boring into the other woman's. With a shaky breath, she said, "Bridgette?"

"Took you long enough, Iris. You really had no idea, did you?"

"But you're supposed to be dead."

"I've heard that before."

"But you're—you're Mr. Reagan?"

"God, you're slow." Maria rolled her eyes, and she looked like a petulant child, shaking her head like she was disappointed. "All these years of chasing after me, and it never once crossed your mind? I thought you had ruined everything when you took down that drug ring, but I managed to get my hands on Agent Peake after all. It's a shame he's dead now too. I actually liked him."

"You seem to be losing a lot of allies, Maria," Bear said. "You'll have no one left in your corner."

"There's always someone to fill the void."

"What's your plan after this?" Iris asked. "There will be nowhere for you to hide, no one to cover for you."

"Anyone who knew my identity will be dead. And D.C. will be in ruins for years to come. No one will be able to find me."

"I don't remember you being so arrogant," Bear said. "Or delusional."

Maria opened her mouth to respond, but a ping had her pulling her phone out of her pocket. She looked down at it with her gun still pointed at them, her eyebrows furrowing. Then her face transformed into a mask of fury. When she looked up again, she only had eyes for Iris.

"What did you do?"

"Stopped you, just like—"

Her sentence was interrupted by a gunshot. Iris jerked and stumbled backwards into Bear's arms. Red blossomed from her chest, and she sputtered in disbelief at what had just happened. Bear sank to his knees, cradling her in his arms.

"Iris," he said, jostling her.

All Iris could do was sputter in disbelief.

"Iris, please—"

"She'll be dead in a minute." Maria's tone was ice cold. "You might as well say your goodbyes."

Bear wrapped his arms around Iris' body. "I'm sorry. I'm so sorry—"

"God, you got soft too, didn't you?" Maria scoffed. "Really, I expected—"

Another gunshot sounded, and this time it was Maria who stumbled back in shock. Her gaze went from the wound in her stomach, and then back to Bear, who held the gun from Iris' waistband in his hand.

Maria looked confused, like there was no scenario in which she saw this as a possible outcome. "Bear—"

He squeezed the trigger again. And again. And again.

By the time Maria hit the floor, she was no longer moving. But he didn't care. Iris' breaths were getting shallower by the second.

"Bear, I—"

"Shh," he said. "Save your energy."

"I'm so sorry." A cough wracked her whole body. He could hear her wheezing. "About Mandy. Please. Tell her I'm sorry."

"You can tell her yourself." Bear pulled out his phone. But his hands were too slick with blood and he couldn't get the screen to work for him. "You hang on."

"Tell her I'm sorry," Iris repeated, quieter this time.

Bear tried wiping his hand clean on his pants, but there was too much blood and not enough time. He looked back down at the woman who'd given her life to stop Mr. Reagan and had succeeded.

"I will," he promised. "I'll tell her."

Iris let out one more wheezing breath, then fell still.

59

BRANDON LEANED BACK IN HIS CHAIR AND TOOK HIS GLASSES OFF. THE lights looked like saucers. His monitor was a blur. His heart was still pounding from everything they'd just done, and he took in several slow breaths while he got his thoughts in order.

Iris had saved them all, and she'd paid the ultimate price for it. She'd ignored Brandon's command to leave Director Caldwell where she was, deciding to cut her free before turning to the computer to stop the drones from inside the system. A few minutes after Iris was taken, Caldwell had stirred and found the phone. It hadn't taken her long to shut the drones down with Brandon giving commands over the line.

There'd be plenty of cleanup, of course, injuries and casualties to consider. But considering what Reagan had planned, this was as close to the best outcome they could've hoped for. Lancaster had mobilized the right people quickly and efficiently, and between them and Jericho's drones, they'd taken out dozens of the enemy weapons before they'd been neutralized.

The media and public would have a field day with the averted disaster, especially if they found out who Reagan was and how she'd gotten her hands on the weapons, but that wasn't Brandon's concern. His top priority now was sitting in a chair behind him, shaking like a leaf.

Brandon muted himself before turning around and opening his arms up to his nephew. "Hey, come here."

Marcus didn't hesitate. He rose from his chair and stumbled into Brandon's arms, not bothering to hide the tears falling down his cheeks or the sobs wracking his body. Guilt twisted Brandon's stomach into knots. He'd never wanted his sister's kid to know what he got up to in his spare time. But Marcus was a helluva lot smarter than Brandon was at the kid's age. This would either turn him away from the lifestyle forever, or he'd double down on his interest in helping people once he got through the worst of the shock and grief.

Brandon was pretty sure he knew which direction Marcus would turn in.

"It's okay," Brandon said, rubbing Marcus' back and doing his best to soothe him. He'd always been the fun, goofy uncle. They'd had some deep discussions, but nothing like this. What Marcus had just witnessed was a tragedy.

"She's dead," Marcus whispered. "She's really dead."

"I know, buddy." Brandon pulled back so he could look Marcus in the eye, but he squeezed the kid's shoulders in what he hoped was a comforting gesture. "I'm sorry you had to go through that."

"Oh, God." Marcus' eyes widened. "Someone has to tell Mandy."

"Hey, that's not your responsibility, okay? Bear will do that. It'll be hard for a while, but Mandy will be okay. You both will be."

Marcus nodded and wiped his face free of the tears. "I'm sorry—"

"You have nothing to apologize for." Brandon waited until Marcus met his eyes again. "What just happened was hard on us all. You cry if you feel like crying. Don't keep it bottled up, okay?"

Marcus nodded. "I think I want to go lay down. Try to get some sleep."

Brandon searched Marcus' face, but it didn't feel like his nephew was running away to hide. In fact, he looked exhausted. Getting some sleep wouldn't change what had happened, but maybe he'd feel better in the morning.

"All right, you go do that. I'll be out in a few minutes, okay? And if you need anything, you wake me up Whether it's because you want to talk or you want me to kick your ass in *Mario Kart*."

Marcus rolled his eyes. "You wish."

Brandon hugged him one more time, then let him go. He watched as Marcus slipped through the door with his head held high but his eyes downcast. He waited until he heard his nephew's footsteps fade and the door to his room close before turning back to his computer and unmuting himself.

"I'm back."

"How's the kid?" Raine asked.

"Scared and grieving, but he'll be okay."

"You sure?"

Brandon's fingers tightened on the arms of his chair. "He has to be. If he wants to help people, then he'll have to figure out how to navigate this stuff far more often than any person should have to."

"You think he'll be back for more after all that?"

"Yeah, I do. He's too much like me to walk away."

"That makes three of us." Raine sighed, and Brandon could almost hear it come from the depths of her soul. "I'm gonna be in a world of hurt after all this. My choices are either desk duty for the rest of my life or resignation."

"You can't seriously believe they'll punish you after everything you did to save them all?"

Raine barked out a laugh. "No, but they would punish me for disobeying orders. They like free thinkers until your thoughts are a little too free, you know? They need to know you'll do what you're told when the time comes."

Brandon leaned his head on his hand and cupped his jaw. He hadn't known Raine for long, but he'd looked into her. Knew enough about her to trust she was who she said she was. And you got to know someone rather quickly when you worked alongside them. She was smart, gifted with the computer, and had her heart and mind in the right place. She'd be an asset to anyone she worked with, both inside and outside the NSA.

"I've been batting around this idea for a while," Brandon said.

"I'm listening."

"You ever thought of becoming an independent contractor?"

"All the time. Don't get me wrong, I love my job. Did a lot of good for a lot of people over the last few years. But after all this stuff with Reagan? I don't know if I can look at any of them the same way again."

"Nothing's official yet, but I've got an idea for a company. There's plenty of capital to get us started, and I've got a ton of contacts who'd be happy to use our services for whatever fee. Even got a couple employees lined up already."

"Sounds like you're all set. What's been holding you back?"

"Felt like we've been missing something." He leaned back in his chair, thinking back through all his meetings with Thomas and their discussions about finding someone else to round them out. "Or someone."

"I'm in. But only if I can have the code name Mystic."

"Just like that?"

He could practically hear the shrug in her words. "I don't want to go back to what I was doing. I've seen enough of your operation to know what you're capable of. Bear vouches for you, and I'd be an idiot not to trust his judgment. If you'll have me, I'd be happy to join you."

"I've got one more question before either of us makes any decisions," Brandon said, keeping his tone flat and serious.

"What's that?"

"Reagan might be dead, but she had plenty of co-conspirators. How do you feel about ruining some lives?"

Raine's chuckle was full of mirth. "I'd say I feel pretty damn good about that."

"Good. Let me patch Thomas in, and we can discuss specifics." For the first time in a long time, Brandon was hopeful. After all the destruction he'd witnessed today, having a gameplan for the foreseeable future kept him grounded. "And after we're done with that, if you really want to put your skills to the test, there's this puzzle I've been working on for a couple years. Could really use your thoughts on it."

"You've got yourself a deal, Prophet."

60

ONE WEEK LATER

Mandy bent down and placed the bouquet of irises against the marker, marveling in the brightness of the violet petals against the fresh mound of dirt. The inscription was a simple one, bearing only Iris' name and her dates of birth and death. It seemed wrong to Mandy that a stranger could walk past her final resting place and not know everything she'd done for the country.

She stood and stepped back, allowing Bear to pull her into his side. She relished in his warmth against her and the cool December air surrounding them. Her breath came out in white puffs that dissipated into the air. She knew without looking that her nose was cherry red. A tear leaked from the corner of her eye. Would it freeze to her skin?

Bear had told Mandy what Iris had said with her dying breath. The words brought a fresh wave of tears to her eyes. She was so angry at Iris for not telling her or her father about Reagan's connection to the academy. All she wanted to do was yell and scream at her friend, and instead, she had to stand here and say goodbye to her.

"Does it get easier?" Mandy choked out. "Losing people you care about?"

"No," Bear said, his own voice husky with emotion. "No, it doesn't."

Mandy looked up at him. "Sometimes I wished you'd lie to me."

He chuckled, and while it was weak, it made Mandy feel better. "I'll remember that next time."

They stood in silence for another moment, despite the cold whip of the wind around their shoulders. It felt like penance for not being there by Iris' side, for not finding a way to stop Reagan before it came to this. For being able to walk away when she didn't have that option.

Bear had pulled Mandy out of school as soon as he could and hugged her tighter than he ever had. She'd known, before he'd even said so, that Iris hadn't made it out alive. It'd been a week, and she was just starting to accept that this was her new reality. She hadn't known Iris for long, but the woman had had an impact on Mandy. She'd never forget her.

Better yet, everyone would know Iris Duvall's name and what she'd done for her country.

That had been Bear's stipulation to Caldwell. Bear had agreed to hand over all the evidence he and Mandy had found, along with an anonymous statement, as long as the CIA said it came from Iris and gave her credit for all they'd done. Mandy and Bear's name would stay out of it, and they'd be free to go, living their life without worrying about looking over their shoulders.

Caldwell had agreed, and it hadn't taken her long to gather a team to take down the rest of Reagan's network. Maria's reach had been far and wide, and Bear had already warned Mandy that someone out there could slip through the CIA's fingers and come after them sooner or later. But she wasn't worried about it. Not after everything they'd survived together.

She was more worried about her friends. Bear had assured her that they were perfectly safe. Now that Stonewall was in jail, she had bigger problems to deal with than a couple of fifteen-year-olds. But just in case, Coach Foley—who, it turned out, was a *retired* special agent and did work for the school—would keep an eye on them as well as Amy, who'd stopped talking to Mandy altogether.

Mandy was less concerned about Marcus now that she knew Brandon would keep watch over him. Somehow, they were keeping everything a secret from Marcus' mom, which was probably for the best. If she found out, he'd be grounded for life and he'd never get to see his uncle again.

Bear patted Mandy on the shoulder, and the pair turned away from Iris' grave, trudging back down the path and out into the parking lot. Mandy looked at all the gravestones on the way, wondering how many of the people buried in that cemetery got to live a full life and how many had their stories cut way too short.

The pair were silent as they climbed into Bear's truck. The first thing he did was crank up the heat, and they spent a couple minutes holding their hands up to the vents until they could feel all ten fingers again.

Instead of putting the truck into drive, Bear twisted in his seat and looked down at her. "You're gonna be sixteen soon."

"Oh, yeah." She'd honestly forgotten the date was creeping up.

"What do you want?"

Mandy thought for a moment. After everything, she didn't really care about her birthday, but she supposed Bear needed this as much as she did. Tapping her chin, she finally said, "Pizza."

Bear huffed out a laugh. "Out of everything in the whole world, you want *pizza* for your birthday?"

All she wanted was to spend time with him, but she couldn't bring herself to say that without crying. "What's wrong with pizza?"

"Nothing," Bear said. "I can do pizza."

She perked up a little in her seat. "Does that mean we're going back to New York?"

"Better."

"Better than New York pizza?" She gasped. "Are we going to Italy?"

"Why the hell not," Bear said, pulling out onto the main drag, small snowflakes falling against the windshield. "I think we could use a little vacation. Don't you?"

BEAR & MANDY'S story continues *Caught in the Web*, coming mid-2024. Click the link below to preorder now:

https://www.amazon.com/dp/B0CPTFN5SL

JOIN the LT Ryan reader family & receive a free copy of the Jack Noble prequel novel, *The First Deception, with bonus story The Recruit.* Click the link below to get started:
https://ltryan.com/jack-noble-newsletter-signup-1

LOVE BEAR? **Mandy? Noble? Hatch?** Get your very own L.T. Ryan merchandise today! Click the link below to find coffee mugs, t-shirts, and even signed copies of your favorite thrillers! https://ltryan.ink/EvG_

ALSO BY L.T. RYAN

Find All of L.T. Ryan's Books on Amazon Today!

The Jack Noble Series

The Recruit (free)

The First Deception (Prequel 1)

Noble Beginnings

A Deadly Distance

Ripple Effect (Bear Logan)

Thin Line

Noble Intentions

When Dead in Greece

Noble Retribution

Noble Betrayal

Never Go Home

Beyond Betrayal (Clarissa Abbot)

Noble Judgment

Never Cry Mercy

Deadline

End Game

Noble Ultimatum

Noble Legend

Noble Revenge

Never Look Back (Coming Soon)

Bear Logan Series

Ripple Effect

Blowback

Take Down

Deep State

Bear & Mandy Logan Series

Close to Home

Under the Surface

The Last Stop

Over the Edge

Between the Lies (Coming Soon)

Rachel Hatch Series

Drift

Downburst

Fever Burn

Smoke Signal

Firewalk

Whitewater

Aftershock

Whirlwind

Tsunami

Fastrope

Sidewinder (Coming Soon)

Mitch Tanner Series

The Depth of Darkness

Into The Darkness

Deliver Us From Darkness

Cassie Quinn Series

Path of Bones

Whisper of Bones

Symphony of Bones

Etched in Shadow

Concealed in Shadow

Betrayed in Shadow

Born from Ashes

Blake Brier Series

Unmasked

Unleashed

Uncharted

Drawpoint

Contrail

Detachment

Clear

Quarry (Coming Soon)

Dalton Savage Series

Savage Grounds

Scorched Earth

Cold Sky

The Frost Killer (Coming Soon)

Maddie Castle Series

The Handler

Tracking Justice

Hunting Grounds

Vanished Trails (Coming Soon)

Affliction Z Series

Affliction Z: Patient Zero

Affliction Z: Abandoned Hope

Affliction Z: Descended in Blood

Affliction Z : Fractured Part 1

Affliction Z: Fractured Part 2 (Fall 2021)

Love Bear? Mandy? Noble? Hatch? Get your very own L.T. Ryan merchandise today! Click the link below to find coffee mugs, t-shirts, and even signed copies of your favorite thrillers! https://ltryan.ink/EvG_

Receive a free copy of The Recruit. Visit:

https://ltryan.com/jack-noble-newsletter-signup-1

Made in the USA
Monee, IL
12 January 2024

51654711R00164